# WAR OF FLESH AND METAL

# WAR OF FLESH AND METAL

## ALICIA ELLIS

WAR OF FLESH AND METAL

This is a work of fiction. All characters, organizations, and events portrayed in this book are products of the imagination or are used fictitiously.



Cover design by J Caleb Design

Published by Figmented Ink in Atlanta
First Publication, July 2023
September 2023 Edition
Trade Paperback ISBN: 978-1-939452-57-3

Library of Congress Control Number: 2023911777

*To my readers.*

"I'M NEVER GOING BACK TO CYBERCORP TOWER." I stuck a forkful of cheesecake in my mouth and let them chew on my words.

My housekeeper Marcy and my best friend Olivia stopped eating to stare.

The kitchen went quiet except for the faint sound of a vid-screen playing news in the next room—a new reporter, but the same story from the last three days:

CyberCorp's Model One androids had malfunctioned. Hundreds of them had ignored a corporate-wide standby order and powered themselves on—something robots were *not* supposed to do. Still, it was the least of my issues with the company.

Marcy, Liv, my four-year-old sister Allie, and I sat at one end of our massive kitchen table. The dark-stained, solid-wood surface was designed for three times the number of people in my actual family.

Allie stuck her fork in her mouth and licked it clean. "What?" Cheesecake sprayed everywhere.

"Don't talk with your mouth full." Marcy grabbed Allie's napkin and dabbed her own cheek. "Or at least aim in the other direction."

"Now you." Marcy jabbed a finger at me. "Explain yourself." Her expression radiated sternness, but she couldn't hide the lines around her mouth and eyes from decades of smiling.

Liv aimed her fork at me like a sword.

"Simple. If something goes wrong with . . ." I waved my left arm in the air. Beneath the synthetic skin was a state-of-the-art, one-of-a-kind, artificially intelligent prosthetic made by none other than my parents' company and the bane of my existence. "I'll call Dr. Fisher, and she can show me how to troubleshoot issues on my own. There's no reason for me to set foot in that building anymore."

"How about the fact that you're the heir to the company?" Liv tossed the words at me casually, but I felt them like bricks.

"Allie can have it."

Across from me, Allie obliviously licked a piece of dessert from the edge of her lips. Even at her age, I'd learned everything I could about the company. She'd rather spend evenings watching cartoons.

Marcy and Liv stared at me, skepticism etched into the height of their brows.

"You can't be the only one managing your arm," Liv said. "It's not a micro-comm or a vid-screen. When something goes wrong, there's only one place to get it serviced." She crossed her arms over her chest and dared me to argue.

"It's working fine." I sliced my cake with a fork and raised the piece to my mouth. It hit my cheek instead.

Marcy offered a less-than-subtle grunt.

I set the fork down, drew in a long breath through my nose, and let it out through my mouth, loosening the tightness in my hands, neck, shoulders. My new therapist emphasized how important it was to keep my stress level in check—not just for my peace of mind, but also for my arm's artificial intelligence.

I didn't want the AI reacting to my tension.

She also urged me to make peace with the things I couldn't change. She probably hadn't meant for me to put space between myself and CyberCorp. If I had to guess, she'd probably meant the opposite. But we healed how we healed, right?

"I'll admit it's been a little stiff," I said.

"I guess you need to go back after all." Despite Marcy's soft tone, her smug look spoke volumes.

I stretched my arm in front of me and flexed the elbow. "Still works, still attached. Good enough."

"You can't hide from fate forever," Liv said.

"It's *my* fate, and I'll do what I want with it."

A familiar name caught my attention on the vid-screen in the next room. ". . . Claire Payne, who hijacked several Model One androids and even killed someone with them, is just now stepping out of an autocar in front of Cyber-Corp Tower."

Liv, Marcy, and I all shot from our seats and into the family room to see the report.

"What happened?" Allie caught up to us, her eyes huge.

Marcy covered her face with one hand but peeked through her fingers at the disaster playing out on screen. "What is she doing?"

I shushed her.

She shushed me back. These days, Marcy was technically Allie's nanny, but she could still put me in my place just as easily as she had when I was small. I muttered an apology.

"Claire! Claire, do you have a few seconds to speak to our audience?" The reporter shoved a microphone in her face.

Liv dropped onto the couch and leaned forward, rapt. As she watched, she mindlessly toyed with one of the two long cornrows plaited down her back. The braids were a chestnut color a couple shades darker than her skin tone, and a red streak threaded its way down the left one.

Claire batted the microphone away, and it hit the ground with a reverberating thunk. Her mouth moved in sharp words that could only be curses, but without the microphone, it was too quiet to make them out.

A hand reached out from off-screen, swept up the mic, and handed it back to the reporter. She didn't lose a step as she hustled after Claire and shoved the mic back at her. "What were you thinking when you sent a Model One to kill Paris Winter and two detectives?"

"I didn't kill those cops!"

Even if I weren't watching the display, I'd know that

voice anywhere. It used to belong to a friend—someone I trusted. Today, it turned my stomach. I retreated to the kitchen.

My cheesecake was gone, but I needed the comfort food. I slid Liv's dessert toward me and shoved half of it into my mouth in one bite. I closed my eyes and forced myself to concentrate on how the creamy dessert felt like heaven on my tongue.

"I'll talk when I'm inside and I get what I was promised," said Claire's voice from the vid-screen now out of my eyeline.

"Can you turn that down?" I shouted. When the volume was still blasting a few seconds later, I did it myself. "Vid, volume down to ten."

The volume plummeted so low that I could no longer hear it, and thankfully, my stress level went down with it.

"Now *I* can't hear it," Liv shouted back. "Vid, volume to thirty."

I groaned as the sound shot back up. Of all the people in the world, I was the only one wanting to escape Cyber-Corp. Everyone else was more engaged than ever, despite the recent tragedies.

The only reason reporters weren't on the lawn outside this house right now was because they knew my parents would ruin them if they bothered me anymore. For once, I appreciated the clout their reputation carried.

Everything else about CyberCorp could go to hell.

"Vid," I shouted, "volume to twenty-five." It dropped just a fraction.

Claire spoke again. "I'm not the devil. I came to share my side of the story, and I'll do that inside."

Yet another reason to stay as far away from that building as possible.

2

Liv stood in the doorway of Allie's room, arms crossed over her stomach. Her gaze tracked me across the room.

I tucked Allie's blankets in around her as her eyes fluttered. When I kissed her cheek, a smile played on her lips. I hoped her mind was far away from here and from the mess our parents' company had made of our lives.

"I know you hear me," Liv said. "We should go."

I knew exactly what she was talking about. "Where?" I asked in a tone as sweet and innocent as simple syrup.

It was after seven in the evening. Only a couple hours had passed since the vid-screen report, and Liv had tried in a hundred different ways to convince me.

"Don't tell me you're not dying to know what she's telling people."

Honestly, it was shredding my insides—and my resolve. Curiosity had plagued every second since I heard the report. It had teased me as I played a card game with her and Allie, taunted me as we raided the fridge one more time before Allie's bedtime, toyed with my emotions even now.

But no. Definitely not.

I was not going within a hundred yards of CyberCorp Tower. I was done, finished, checked out. I wouldn't give Claire the satisfaction of knowing she played any role in my life. She'd set herself on a path that killed someone—all because she was angry at me for actions that were out of my control. To hear her tell it, her choices were as much my fault as her own.

My conscience had taken enough beatings for three lifetimes, and now I had Claire's actions to add to my list of sins.

My hand-screen vibrated, clacking against the night-stand next to Allie's bed—a convenient distraction from this conversation. I snatched up the device before Liv could get in another word.

Jackson's name showed up on the caller ID. When I waved my palm over the display, the call connected on speaker.

"Hey. What's up?"

"Are you watching the news?" he asked.

I turned my back on Liv's self-satisfied face and beckoned for her to follow me out of Allie's room. "I'm not going."

"Your girl is a stubborn pain in my ass," Liv shouted as we stepped into my bedroom, and I closed the door behind us.

"No argument there," Jackson said.

"I'm not his girl. And do y'all want to talk to each other? Do I even need to be here for this conversation?"

"Ron just walked into the building," he said.

Ice splashed through my veins. "He's at CyberCorp Tower?"

"Turn on the vid."

Liv turned toward the wall across from my bed. "Vid on."

A large rectangle on the wall disintegrated since it was just a digital image hiding the screen.

"Switch channel to the news," Liv said.

An instant later, we were watching a replay of Ron Franklin arriving in front of CyberCorp in an autocar with a burly security guard at his side. He ignored all requests for interviews and marched to the front doors, back straight, chin up, soul severed.

My left hand balled into a fist. It was probably a good thing I wasn't there right now because, if I were, I would use the cybernetic arm he gave me to bash his face in. "What is he doing?"

"He didn't say," Jackson said.

"That can't be a coincidence," Liv said. "Both of them deciding within a few hours of each other that they need to be at the Tower."

Ron had used me to kill one of my best friends. His plan, but my hands. My nightmares.

Dr. Fisher had said there was no evidence Ron had pulled off that hack from inside CyberCorp, and he didn't have the resources anywhere else. That meant there was an accomplice—a backer with a supercomputer.

"You think he's ready to name names?" I asked.

"Maybe," Jackson said.

I swept Liv's jacket up from where she'd thrown it on the bed and shoved it at her. "We're going."

Three minutes later, we were in the car and on our way. Usually, when I had the misfortune of having to go to the Tower, I took the back streets. Any stoplight between me and there was a welcome delay. Today, I steered the car onto the highway and shifted into the fast lane.

"Hey, slow down," Liv said. She tapped the back of her ear to activate her micro-comm. Her eyes blanked as her attention shifted to her incoming call. "Hunter?" She paused as the response came in. "We're on our way. How far out are you?"

From the pocket of my jacket, my hand-screen buzzed. "Read message," I told my car, and a sugar-coated electronic voice came through the speakers.

"Message from Jackson," the voice said. "Had to do something for my mom. I'll be there in twenty."

A drone zipped past us overhead, and I ducked instinctively. Liv was still on her call and didn't seem to notice. Outside, dark had fallen, so the drone population had quadrupled. They raced from one side of town to the other, delivering packages and notes too sensitive for digital transmission.

Buildings stretched skyward on both sides of the highway, and electronic billboards flashed technicolor messages. We raced past one that showed an image of me brushing a hair product through my dark hair. In the image, my wild curls fell in tamed coils. In real life, I had them pulled back into a ponytail in desperate need of detangling.

The ads always picked me.

As we passed the billboard, the image shifted, and a white woman around her thirties replaced me, still combing the same product through her hair.

I laid my foot on the accelerator and zipped past cars going the speed limit. Most had their windows tinted to black, the passengers inside probably napping or watching vids on their EyeNet-enabled contact lenses as the vehicles self-navigated.

We inched past an autocar, a slim, bullet-shaped design with currently untinted windows. Plush seats lined the interior, without a single steering wheel or dashboard in sight. A red bulb on top of the vehicle blinked from green to yellow to indicate the car had been hired. The vehicle coasted into the slow lane and took an exit off the highway to pick up its fare.

Beside me, Liv shouted into her micro-comm, "Home-work? Are you serious? It'll still be there when you get home." She paused as Hunter said something on his end. "Just meet us there when you can." She tapped the back of her ear to disconnect. "He's on his way."

"Jackson too. We'll beat him there."

"Melody?"

I cringed. As the twin sister of Ron's first victim, Melody was one of the few people in the world who needed a resolution to all this more than I did. Before the end of the day, I would get it for us. Then I would put serious distance between me and my parents' company. "She's probably there already. Any updates on Ron?"

"Nope."

I gave her a pointed look.

With an eyeroll, Liv tapped her micro-comm and instructed it, "Search news updates on Ronald Franklin." Her eyes went blank as she listened to the reply from the tiny device stuck behind her ear. She tapped her micro again. "He still hasn't talked."

My fingers tightened around the steering wheel, and even the synthetic skin on my left hand whitened with tension. "He'd better."

She rubbed my shoulder.

"He's going to spill his guts today, whether he likes it or not. If he's lucky, that will only be figurative, and I won't actually rip his intestines out through his stomach."

"You can't gut people, Lena."

"Can't I?" I raised my left arm from the steering wheel. "This metal arm begs to differ."

"Okay, then you *shouldn't* gut people." Her lips pursed. "Ron might be an exception."

I slammed one hand against the steering wheel, and the car swerved before I straightened up. Next to us, a vehicle blared its horn and shifted one lane over.

"Maybe you should concentrate on driving."

"What about Claire? Any news there?"

"I have alerts set up on the newsfeeds. There's nothing."

"Then what is the point of this?" I gestured toward the

road. "Why torture us if they're not going to give full confessions?"

"I can't say I blame them."

"Excuse me?"

"I mean, yeah, I blame them for killing people, obviously. But if I'm Claire, there is no way I'm admitting to killing two cops unless there's a serious deal on the table. And in Ron's case, as far as I know, they haven't offered him anything for the name of his financial backer."

"If he tells, I offer not to bash his face in."

Liv kept her gaze on the road and her face stony.

"You're not still into him?"

"Would you please slow down?"

The other cars fell behind us as we raced forward. I eased my foot off the accelerator until our speed matched the other traffic. A minute later, I shifted into the far-right lane and exited the highway.

Liv squeezed my shoulder. "It's going to be okay."

Weeks ago, I might have asked her when our lives would get back to normal, but now I knew better. Normal was just the space between tragedies.

There was no *okay*. There was only that moment of peace in the morning upon waking. That minute when cold water hit me in the shower when shock removed all thought. That second when I closed my eyes at night before the dreams brought it all back.

It wasn't my fault—I knew that.

It didn't help me sleep better.

I took a long inhale through my nose, exhaled through

my mouth, and repeated Liv's words of okay-ness in my head. They rang false. "It's not," I whispered.

"What's not what?"

"It's not okay. Why do people say that? Like, if we ring the *okay* bell and press the *I'm fine* button, suddenly the world is no longer a giant rock spinning at a thousand miles an hour while hurtling through a freezing vacuum to orbit a giant ball of fire."

"Wow. That was . . . descriptive."

"We can't control any of it. Five people are dead because of their connection to me." I took my left hand off the wheel and wiggled all five fingers at her before slamming it back down. "Seven, if you count those two detectives. Melody is devastated. *I'm* devastated. Ron was my friend, and Claire . . . How can I trust my judgment about anything? How can we—"

"Breathe, honey." She glanced toward the road. "Stop!"

"What—" I slammed my foot on the brake, but my reaction time was too slow. My cherry-red, limited-edition classic car slammed into the bumper in front of us. Metal crunched, and my head spun back to that day when I'd been on my way home from the club.

Harmony was there, and Melody, and Jackson, and I'd drunk a little too much. And my head was spinning with frustration and alcohol, and I was pissed at my mom about things that didn't matter anymore. The silver car left its lane and shot toward me, and I reacted too slowly, and the pain in my left arm eclipsed everything else.

That was the beginning.

"Lena, it's okay."

There was that word again.

"Lena, it's just a fender bender."

I sucked in breaths, but my chest was full of holes, and the air whistled through. The vehicle tilted around me, so I laid my head against the steering wheel. This was a furnace, and my lungs were on fire.

I fumbled for the door switch but couldn't find it.

My hand-screen vibrated in my pocket, and an upbeat tune filled the car's interior. I kept my head down. Only a second after the sound stopped, the hand-screen vibrated again.

"Answer the call," Liv shouted at my car. "Answer it!"

Thankfully, the music stopped, and a familiar female voice filled the interior. "Lena?"

It took me a few more seconds to catch my breath. "Bri?"

Liv pulled my face off the steering wheel and turned my head toward hers. She mouthed the name like a question: *Briana?*

I nodded.

"You know you hit me, right?" she asked through the car speakers.

I squinted out the windshield, and sure enough, Claire's girlfriend waved at me from the car I'd just hit. As usual, her long dark hair fell in a braid down her back. No small amount of irritation painted her olive-toned features. Or maybe it was *ex*-girlfriend now? Personally, I'd break up with anyone who cheated on me and then killed the person she cheated with, but to each her own.

I waved back. "I'm so sorry."

"Did you not see me stopped here?"

"Why *were* you stopped here?" Liv asked. "It's not an intersection."

The line went silent for so long that I thought we lost the connection. "Second thoughts about going in."

To our right, CyberCorp Tower loomed over us. Rose-colored stone and tinted windows covered the exterior, but inside, it was over seventy stories of metal and circuits and no heart.

I was having second thoughts too.

"I'll take care of any damage, Bri."

"I'm sure you're good for it." Another pause. "I guess we should get inside."

"Yeah."

We sat on the connection for almost a minute in complete silence until Briana disconnected, and her car jumped forward. I followed.

I was back at CyberCorp Tower, and as usual, nothing was okay.

3

AT EIGHT O'CLOCK ON A FRIDAY, THE WEEK'S ACTIVITIES were spinning down in the lobby of CyberCorp Tower. Automated lighting had dimmed from the usual bright white to amber for the evening. The darker tone warmed up even the silver-white tiles of the floor as we stepped out of the elevator bay that led up from the guest parking garage.

Despite the hour, two receptionists sat behind the desk, their backs straight, eyes bright, and faces fixed in polite masks. A sleek black desk stretched across a wall of windows, beyond which several reporters and their crews had taken up posts.

The ceiling soared sixty floors above the atrium-style lobby. Sweeping glass walls marked each level, shimmering in the refracted light of illuminated globes hanging from the ceiling far above. The interior vibrated like a tuning fork, hummed with the electronic sounds of work that would shape the future—for better or worse.

An annoyingly familiar voice hit me as soon as we entered.

Dark haired and dark eyed, Philip Pollock stood in front of the desk in a tailored charcoal suit buttoned over a red-and-gray vest. Cherry shoes were polished to perfection, and the silver watch on his wrist glinted in the artificial light. His angular face wore arrogance like a second skin.

"I'm ten-percent owner of this castle." Pollock stood in front of a female receptionist named Vanessa and gestured at his surroundings. His hands came within inches of her face. "If I want to go up and talk to the Hayeses, you can't stop me!"

Pollock was CyberCorp's only investor, to the tune of ten percent of the company's value. But my parents drew a stark line between investor and owner. As far as they were concerned, they sent Pollock his money and detailed reports, and that was the extent of their relationship.

I stopped walking to stay out of his line of sight. The other receptionist, a man who appeared to be in his twenties with a plaque in front of him that introduced him as Raul, beckoned us forward.

Bri charged past me. "We need to see Claire Payne."

"Um . . ." The man dutifully ignored her fists clenched on top of the desk. He kept his expression pleasant and his voice bright. "That's restricted information."

Another man's shoulder rammed into mine as he barreled past without a glance. He gestured wildly, too focused on his conversation with someone in the virtual world to pay attention to reality. Liv glared at him until a pair of elevator doors shut him away and ferried him off to the employee parking garage.

"They can't be serious." Pollock rattled a sheaf of papers in Vanessa's face. "I have every right to say whatever I want in my audio program. *Freedom of speech.*" His hands slapped the desk three times to emphasize each word.

Vanessa was barely out of college, with nutmeg-colored hair tucked into a skull-pulling bun on the back of her head. Here at CyberCorp, the receptionists could be just as robotic as the products, but Vanessa and I had a rapport. I waved at her, and her business face slipped for a moment as she rolled her eyes toward Pollock before waving back.

Then her attention snapped back to him, and the polite mask returned to place.

"They can't cease-and-desist me," Pollock shouted as spittle sprayed from his mouth. "I can say what I want!"

"I'm not qualified to speak on that, sir, but I'm pretty sure the First Amendment doesn't protect you from fraud claims." Her false smile still locked and loaded, Vanessa rolled her chair back a foot to escape the spray. She extracted a single tissue from the desk and mopped up the spittle. "I have been told specifically not to let *you* upstairs, Mr. Pollock."

A security guard slid in place behind Pollock. The guard's broad shoulders were almost twice as wide, and Pollock shot a couple wary glances his way.

Briana finished her conversation with Raul, the other

receptionist, and stomped back to me. "He won't tell me anything."

Pollock took one step toward the main elevators leading to the higher floors of the Tower before the security guard blocked his path.

"I'm sorry, Mr. Pollock," Vanessa said, her tone all sugar and barely a hint of spice. "No one goes up without authorization."

"I authorize myself."

He sidestepped the security guard, but the big man was quicker. He gripped Pollock from behind by the shoulders and steered him toward the front doors.

"You don't understand," Pollock said as the other man ushered him away. He shook the papers in his right hand. "These accusations have gone public. People are lined up to accuse me of theft, fraud, and who knows what else."

"Sounds about right." The words popped out of my mouth before I could stop them.

Until now, Pollock hadn't seen me. Now, he spun and scowled so deeply that the crevices in his face rivaled the Grand Canyon. "You did this." He rattled the papers in my direction.

I raised both hands in mock surrender. The guard squeezed Pollock's shoulder. Pollock winced and obediently moved toward the door.

"Dude, what did you do?" Briana whispered, her gaze locked on Pollock.

"I might have mentioned to my parents that Pollock was taking donations from people while promising to put that money toward taking CyberCorp down," I said, "all while cashing his quarterly checks from the company he claims to hate. Now they're threatening to foot the bill for a class-action lawsuit against him."

"Serves him right," Liv said. "The man is a leech."

Once upon a time, I'd considered myself a part of the anti-tech movement and had religiously followed Pollock's audio program. In it, he ranted about the evils of technology—how each invention of CyberCorp pushed humanity further apart, leading to some abstract future where people no longer interacted with one another and computers ruled their lives.

I had believed every word, but I saw things differently now.

Bad people could use technology for evil, but the technology itself wasn't at fault. Humans were the real monsters. Humans like Ron and Claire and leeches like Pollock, who preyed on people who saw the holes in their lives and needed something or someone to blame.

As soon as Pollock exited through the front doors, Vanessa let out a long, exaggerated breath and shifted her attention to me. "Let me guess. You're here for Ron."

Most people outside these doors knew half the story. They knew Ron hacked my arm's AI and forced me to strangle three of my classmates in my sleep. The part that hadn't made the news was that Ron and I were friends.

I trusted him, and he turned me into a killer.

"I hate to ask," I said.

"And I hate to turn you down."

"Please." Liv stood shoulder to shoulder with me, facing Vanessa. "We're begging."

He betrayed her too. Ron and Liv had been dating, and he used her to keep me in line.

"They've kept his location inside the building on a strictly need-to-know basis." Vanessa gestured at the giant black reception desk and the vid-screen in front of her. "I'm not exactly top tier."

"Then what's the point of his being here?" Liv asked.

"I'm not sure, to be honest."

We stood there staring at her. I'd spent all evening debating whether to come here, and suddenly, all my plans were shot.

"What about Claire?" Bri asked.

"I know where she is, but that information is restricted to certain personnel only."

Liv jerked her head toward the receptionist.

I pasted my best business smile on my face, the one that looked just like my mother's and got her everything she demanded around here. "I'm going to need Claire's location." For good measure, I added, "Please."

"Nice try, but your parents already asked me not to tell you." She cast me an apologetic look. "They think you're too close to this."

I leaned closer. "Come on. Isn't there anything you can do? You know I need closure on this."

Vanessa's delicate features pursed.

I put both hands on the desk in front of her. "I'm begging."

Vanessa typed something on her keyboard and then swiped her fingers across her vid-screen display. "Doesn't your ID chip have full access to everything in the building?

You don't need to be given additional authorizations, right?"

I nodded.

She straightened her back and spoke each word deliberately, her gaze never leaving my eyes. "I hear they've renovated the conference rooms. The ones on the fifty-seventh floor in particular are nice. Padded walls for soundproofing, smart lighting and ventilation, virtual vids that cover all four walls. The works, you know?"

Bri leaned over the desk and embraced Vanessa. "Bless you." She was halfway to the elevators before Liv and I caught up with her.

The elevator bay had six elevators on each side. Briana waved her wrist at a black panel on the wall. The panel spit out a sharp buzz. The ID chip embedded in her wrist wasn't authorized, so she beckoned me over with sharp hand waves.

When I waved my left wrist, the scanner let out a high-pitched beep. A few seconds later, a pair of doors opened, and we stepped inside.

The elevator slid closed with a whisper, and Briana gave it our floor. "Fifty-seven."

"Ron may be on the same floor, right?" Liv asked as the cab rose upward. Digital numbers tracked our progress in person-sized digits on the walls to our left and right.

"I hope so," I said. I was glad Bri was going to get her closure with Claire, but I came here for Ron.

The giant numbers hit fifty-seven, and we stepped out onto a carpeted hallway. CyberCorp Tower had more floors than I cared to visit, and this one was new to me.

The walls on both sides were vid-screens. Since the business day was long over, each screen featured a dull gray background with the block-lettered CyberCorp logo. The logos on both sides followed as we walked, staying at our flanks and casting an eerie red glow.

Briana took the lead. Liv and I followed. Something about the air in this building made my heart kick into high gear.

Open doorways were spaced along the vid-screen walls. As we walked, digital room numbers lit up next to the doorways and faded away as we passed—as if the numbers followed us down the hall along with the red logos.

57A, 57C, 57E . . .

As we passed one room, I peeked at the three padded walls, the charcoal-gray carpet, and the twenty-foot-long conference table. Beyond the table, a lone glass wall revealed the brightly lit atrium that opened all the way to the lobby below. I stuck my head inside, and the corner of the room by the doorway illuminated as the automated lighting activated.

When I turned my head, the other side of the room still lay in darkness. I moved inside, and more lights came on toward the room's center. A faint hum and a blast of heat from overhead told me the heating system had activated.

"Not bad," I said under my breath as I stepped back into the hallway. CyberCorp Tower might not be my favorite place in the world, but even I wasn't immune to useful, resource-efficient features.

Ahead of me, Bri peeked through each doorway. She

reached the end of the hall and turned the corner. Liv followed, and I trailed behind them.

Finally, Briana stopped. The next door was the only one closed. A black metal surface blocked our view of the conference room that lay beyond. She waved her wrist at a small black square on the wall beside the doorway, and the scanner buzzed.

She stomped her foot and shot me a pointed look. Liv and I hurried to catch up. As if to make a point, Bri scanned her ID chip a second time at the sensor for 57J, and again, it emitted a sharp buzz.

When I scanned mine, it issued a high-pitched ding. The pocket door whooshed open and disappeared into the wall.

A security guard stood in the doorway. Like the guard downstairs, he wore a dark suit but no tie. He was shorter, with a blond buzz cut, but his face wore just as little emotion.

He opened his mouth, but then his gaze swept over my face, and he clamped it shut and stepped aside.

Bri offered me an impressed nod.

This room was like the other. Padding covered the walls and ceiling, except for a couple vents, and a large wooden table stretched across the dark-carpeted floor. Claire sat on the opposite side of the room at the foot of the table, in front of the lone glass wall.

She jumped up. "Bri." Claire hurried over to us but stopped in the face of Briana's curled lip and pinched nose.

Bri took a gigantic step backward toward the door, which slid open automatically.

Claire inched backward, as if Briana was a startled deer that she didn't want to spook. "Hey," she said more quietly.

"Hey, yourself," Liv said loudly. She and Claire had never meshed, even before we knew Claire was a killer. If she hadn't dated Ron, I might have said Liv had better instincts than me.

Claire's attention flicked to Liv, and a scowl creased her model-sharp features.

"You good?" I whispered to Bri.

She stepped out of the doorway, and the automatic door slammed shut again. "I didn't come here because you asked me," she told Claire. "I came for answers."

The security guard slid in front of Briana and squared his shoulders.

"It's fine," Claire said.

The guard retreated to the corner of the room.

When Briana cast him a wary glance, Claire added, "He's here to protect me in case anyone here feels the need to retaliate. I'm not under arrest or anything."

"Again," Liv muttered.

We all looked at her.

"You're not under arrest *again*, but you still have to stand trial."

I stabbed my elbow into Liv's side until she yelped. This was supposed to be about Briana, not about Liv's smugness for having pegged Claire correctly after all.

"Was all of it a lie?" Bri whispered.

I had to strain to hear her, and the room went silent except for the soft hum of the heater overhead.

Seconds passed before Bri spoke again. "You said you

loved me, but were you telling Paris the same thing before you killed her?"

Liv raised her hand. "Let's not forget the two police detectives."

I gave her another elbow.

Claire's gaze cut toward Liv for only a split second before landing back on Bri. "I didn't do that."

Briana stuck out her chest, and this time her voice boomed. "That's not what I asked you. How many lies did you tell me about where you were or what you were doing when you were really with Paris? How much of a coward do you have to be to kill a girl to hide your cheating, instead of telling me the truth?"

"I'm sorry."

Briana stared at Claire through slitted eyelids. When no better answer came, she cast a last withering look and stomped from the room. The metal door whooshed open and slammed close behind her.

Claire dropped back into her chair. Boredom painted her features, masking the pain. "Now what?"

Liv headed for the door, which shot open as she approached. "I'll catch up to Bri." It slammed shut behind her.

I hadn't planned on talking to Claire, but if I couldn't get to Ron, this would do for now. I claimed a chair and propped my elbows on the table with my chin on my fists. "You tell me."

She spread her hands wide. "I don't know what you want from me. Everything I've said is true. Paris's death was a stupid, reckless accident. At first, all I wanted was to get back at you for letting Ron use you to kill my friend, and—"

"We all miss Harmony."

"—I had nothing to do with those cops."

I rolled my eyes so hard it hurt. "It's just a coincidence that two Model Ones attacked and killed them the same way one killed Paris?"

"The program I used to control the androids was sitting right there on Mr. Miller's company client cube. Other employees probably have it too. Anyone with access to a CyberCorp client could have done it."

"What about the Model One server? How did you get it to attack us so you could escape after we figured out what you'd done? It almost killed us."

"There was a pop-up on Mr. Miller's client cube after the second time I used the program. It asked me if I wanted to connect my micro-comm to the server. I thought it would make things easier if I needed to use the Model Ones again."

"In case you wanted to kill someone else?"

"Paris was an accident, and I didn't—"

"So you've said." I kicked my chair back and stood. It rolled backward until it bounced off the padded wall. "Do you know where Ron is?"

Her eyes slitted. "If I did, I would have killed him already, and not by accident."

4

By the time Liv and I reached the lobby, my mood had plummeted from *kind of bad* to a hundred miles south of that. My entire purpose for coming to CyberCorp Tower—wringing Ron's neck—metaphorically of course—was a failure.

"Where do you think Bri took off to?" Liv asked as we exited the elevator on the main floor.

"Maybe home. Maybe somewhere to cool off." I extracted my hand-screen from my pocket and quick-dialed my mother. It rang on speaker.

Liv shot me a questioning look.

"I'm hoping she'll tell me where Ron is."

Liv's lips twitched. "You think your overprotective mother is going to tell you where to find the guy who used you to kill three people, thus traumatizing you for life?"

I disconnected and tried my dad instead.

He picked up after the third ring. "Hey, baby girl. You okay?"

"It would really help with my closure if I could—"

"Stop."

I clipped off the rest of my plea.

"No one is going to tell you where to find Ron."

I blew out air and scowled at the hand-screen.

"Anything else?"

"I'll see you at home." I disconnected.

Vanessa was nowhere in sight, but Raul, the male receptionist, still sat behind the desk. I was ninety-nine percent sure this guy knew the same information as her and no more. But at this point, our options for finding Ron were limited.

As we approached reception, Jackson shot out of one of the parking-lot elevators and barreled toward us at top speed. I flinched, expecting a collision, but he halted only a foot away as if someone had hit a pause button. His Cyber-Corp-rebuilt legs worked differently than most. Sometimes, his movements were still unreal to me.

He grinned, and his blue eyes shone. He offered Liv a quick hug and then held out his arms to me. I fell into him.

He stood over half a foot taller than me, and his collar hinted of cinnamon and vanilla with a touch of spice. We'd broken up months ago, but he still smelled like *normal*.

I could really use a dose of normal right now. I breathed it in before taking a step backward.

"Did you find Ron?" he asked.

Liv scowled. "Just Claire."

"What is it with you two?" I asked. "You haven't liked each other since day one."

"And I was right."

Hard to argue with that. "They're keeping Ron's location top secret."

"Even from you?" Jackson asked.

"Especially from me. And Claire isn't talking. Same story. Paris was an accident and—"

"*I didn't kill those cops*," Liv broke in, standing on tiptoes and jutting her lower lip out in an exaggerated impression of Claire.

Jackson rolled his eyes. "You want me to follow you home? We could watch a movie. I'll let you talk over it the whole time about how shit your life is." He flashed me a Cheshire Cat smile. "Like last time."

Liv raised her hand. "I need a ride back to my car at your place."

"I didn't talk over the *whole* movie." I tried to fix a scowl on my face. When I failed, I settled for punching him in the arm instead.

He flinched. I'd used my left hand, and it was stronger than I realized sometimes.

"I'm so sorry!"

"Kidding." He grinned. "I'm indestructible."

I punched him in the arm again, harder this time.

Jackson had been in the same car accident that left me with this arm, but he'd taken the brunt of the impact. CyberCorp had replaced a significant portion of his bones and skin. Fortunately for him, he hadn't had Ron on his medical team.

Maybe that was fortunate for all of us. I'd made a formidable weapon when Ron had controlled me. Jackson would have been unstoppable.

"I'm dying!" He bent over and clutched his arm.

I kicked him in the shin.

He flinched for real this time and hopped on one foot. "That's my actual shin. They didn't replace that one."

When he put the foot down, I kicked again but he dodged it.

"If you two are done playing footsie, I'm going to give reception one more shot." Liv straightened her shoulders and stomped toward Raul at the reception desk, her head bent forward like a bull on the charge.

A tall woman in a charcoal pantsuit clacked ahead of Liv on her high heels. Liv stopped abruptly and glared at her back, but the woman didn't seem to notice.

"Annabelle Walker. Access please." The woman swept her wrist over the scanner in front of Raul. When nothing happened, she huffed impatiently.

"Give me a second, please." His eyes had a droop that they hadn't had earlier in the evening, but he keyed in a command that made the scanner light up blue.

This time when she waved her wrist, the scanner beeped as it recognized her and gave building access to her ID chip.

"You can go on up." Before he finished the sentence, she'd already turned and headed for the elevators.

Liv marched up to Raul and started her plea. "Can you tell us where . . ."

I missed the rest of it as my attention locked on the

woman in the suit. I grabbed Jackson's wrist and hauled him toward the elevators after her.

"Hey, I thought we were—" Jackson started.

I shushed him and stopped ten feet from the woman in gray.

She wore a briefcase-style handbag over one shoulder and looked comfortable and confident in her sky-high heels. Not many people carried briefcases. When they did, it meant they protected something extra confidential. Otherwise, it would be digital. Hard copies couldn't be hacked.

Ms. Walker waved her wrist at the scanner in the elevator bay. It buzzed. The woman swiped her wrist a second time and issued a low growl when it buzzed again.

"Sir," she called across the room, although the man was engaged in a conversation with a desperate-looking Liv. "It's not working. It should be working." She kept her words crisp.

Between the briefcase and the tailored attire, I pegged her as a lawyer. Why would a lawyer be here at nine in the evening?

"Do you think that's Ron's attorney?" I asked Jackson, my voice low for only him.

"She could work for your parents."

I shook my head. "Trust me. I know all our lawyers, and none of them is Annabelle Walker. They might as well be my siblings as much as they're around."

Plus, my parents' lawyers would already have the authorizations they needed to access the building. This woman had to ask for hers. She wasn't a regular here, but her presence was expected tonight.

"I'm here with Lena Hayes," Liv was saying to Raul. "She has to be authorized."

"I know and I'm sorry. If I knew where he was, I would tell you, but I don't."

Ms. Walker squeezed next to Liv, making liberal use of her elbows to take the space right in front of Raul. "It's not working." She jabbed her wrist out to his scanner.

"It's my turn," Liv snapped.

"I told you I can't help you." Raul blinked and shifted his attention to the woman. "Let me check on that." He pressed a button, and the scanner lit up and beeped as it scanned her chip again.

The lawyer made a show of shifting her gaze upward hard. EyeNet-enabled contact lenses displayed the time at the extreme top of the field of view, and she wanted Raul to know she was on a schedule.

"I—I'm so sorry. It looks like I gave you access to the conference room but not the elevator. Give me one more moment." He typed furiously on his keyboard, muttered something, and then pounded the backspace key before typing another string of data. The scanner lit up blue.

"Is it right now?" the woman snapped.

"Yes, ma'am."

She offered a curt nod, swiped her wrist, and spun back toward Jackson, me, and the elevator bay.

Liv immediately resumed her whisper-shouting match with Raul.

"You're staring," Jackson whispered. His breath tickled my forehead, and I looked up into stunning blue eyes.

He pulled me closer and brushed his lips against mine. They were soft, sweet, familiar. I turned my face upward to meet him. He held me tighter.

I froze. "What do you think you're doing?"

His mouth stayed millimeters from mine. "I feel like the answer to that would be obvious if I were doing it right."

"We don't do this anymore." I pointed back and forth between us. We stood so close I could feel his breath on my lips, sending my chest into a flutter.

He didn't move. "I thought we were past that."

"Believe it or not, I have priorities other than you at the moment." Again, I pointed between us. "I don't have time to think about this right now."

"Very well." He shoved my shoulder to make me step backward and took two long-legged steps back as well. "I promise not to kiss you again until you ask me." Despite the rejection, his lips turned upward.

A pair of elevator doors slid open, and Ms. Walker's pencil-sharp heels clacked against the tile as she entered. I grabbed Jackson's wrist and dragged him in after her.

"Liv," I shouted toward the reception desk. "Move it or lose it!" I held my hand between the doors to keep them from closing, ignoring the other woman's glare.

"Fifty-eight," she said to the elevator. She glanced briefly at Jackson and me, giving us a chance to tell the elevator where we wanted to go.

Liv skidded in beside us.

I released the doors. "Seventy."

"Why are we going to seventy?" Liv asked. "He's not—"

"Trust me," I said.

The giant numbers floating on the elevator walls increased as we rose into the sky. On the fifty-eighth floor, the doors whispered open, and Ms. Walker stepped out. Jackson started after her. I grabbed his wrist and locked him in place.

The doors closed, and the elevator continued upward.

"Elevator," I said, "cancel floor seventy."

The numbers on the walls froze at sixty-six.

"Fifty-eight."

The numbers rolled downward. The elevator moved so smoothly that those digits were the only hint that we were moving at all. When the doors opened, the hallway was empty.

I didn't often say good things about CyberCorp Tower, but one thing I could say was that it was consistent. This floor looked much like the one I'd left fifteen minutes ago, with vid-screen walls in power-saving sleep mode because of the late hour. As on floor fifty-seven, the CyberCorp logo floated beside us on the walls.

Liv stomped forward with Jackson and me close behind. She led us down the hallway and around the corner to the only door that was closed. Conference room 58J, exactly one floor above Claire.

I swiped my wrist at the scanner, and the door whooshed open. Liv shot through the doorway, and Jackson slid in front of me before I could follow. The door shut with Liv on the other side.

"We should give her a minute, huh?" I said as Jackson still blocked the doorway.

He grunted in answer.

When he moved, I pressed my ear against the door, but Vanessa was right—these rooms were seriously sound-proofed. After a minute, I widened my eyes at Jackson in a silent question, and he nodded.

I scanned my wrist and stormed into the room.

Liv had Ron in a standoff.

She leaned toward him, her jaw set and eyes furious. The lawyer from the elevator stood behind Ron on one side. One hand rested on his shoulder. On his other side stood a security guard who looked very much like the one in Claire's room. Black shirt, black slacks, blank expression.

Ms. Walker's gaze found me and Jackson and then slipped back to Liv. "So you're all together." Her tone prickled with icicles as she nodded toward security.

The guard stepped toward us.

"It's okay," Ron said.

The guard slid back into place.

"You can't escape your fate," Liv told Ron before spin-ning on her heel. "I'm going to find Hunter." She brushed past Jackson and me, and the door banged shut behind her.

Ron flashed us a lazy grin. "How have you been?"

He wasn't wearing his glasses.

When I'd met him, he was wearing black plastic ones that lived at the cross street of cool and nerdy. I'd liked that about him—the imperfection in a world where everyone else had their eyes fixed. It made me feel almost comfortable right after I'd lost my arm.

But here he was, amber eyes no longer behind black plastic frames. Even that was a lie.

I settled on the edge of the chair closest to the door, a good twenty feet from him. "We're not friends."

"Aren't we?" He showed all his teeth.

Jackson dropped into the seat beside me, between me and Ron. He probably thought he needed to block the direct route between the two of us in case I decided to wrap my cybernetic hand around his lying, betraying neck.

Months ago, Ron had pretended to be my friend. Then he'd modified my code so he could use me as a weapon to murder my classmates in my sleep, all because of a grudge he held against CyberCorp.

"I assume you're here to name your financial backer." I made my voice as sweet and smooth as honey—and just as sticky.

"Is that going to get me what I want?"

Jackson might be faster than me on his rebuilt legs, but I moved before he could anticipate it. I grabbed Jackson's chair from the bottom and tipped it on its side, spilling him to the floor. Before he could get up, I was past him.

Ron screamed for security. I yanked him off his chair and slammed him against the glass wall. My left hand wrapped around his neck and held.

"Who backed you?" I screamed in his face. "I swear I will put you through this glass."

"Let go of him," Ms. Walker shrieked into my ear. She yanked my arm, but it didn't budge.

Jackson recovered and caught up with me. But instead of pulling me off, he hid a grin. "Put him down, babe."

The security guard must have recognized me because, instead of fighting, he tapped his ear to activate his micro-comm. "Get me Marissa Hayes," he said into his device, each syllable short with urgency.

I returned my attention to Ron's face, which was reddening. His lips gaped open. I wasn't squeezing him that tightly. Not tight enough to kill him—maybe.

"Do you think I can put you through this window on my first try?" I made a show of looking over Ron's shoulder to the atrium and the lobby far below. "Fifty-eight floors. Fifteen feet per floor. How many feet is that?"

"Miss Hayes." The security guard hurried to my side, his eyes wild, but still lacked the nerve to touch the daughter of his employer. "Please release him."

Ron's gaze shifted upward for a split second, and when it returned to me, his eyes were twice as wide. I guessed he'd done the math on how far a fall that would be. He was a prodigy at engineering, after all.

"Next question, and it's another easy one." I bared my teeth. "How much force can this safety glass take, and how much can I apply?" I increased the pressure behind my cybernetic arm, pushing him harder into the glass and raising my hand until his tiptoes barely scraped the carpet.

He whined.

"Miss Hayes." Panic seeped into the guard's voice.

"Liv should be coming to rescue you, right?"

Ron looked past my shoulder at the door, but Liv was long gone.

I lowered my voice. "Do you know the story of Frankenstein's monster? It eventually turned on its creator." My hand squeezed tighter.

The red in Ron's face deepened.

I didn't want to kill him—at least I didn't think I did.

My hand tightened. I stared at it and willed it to obey, to loosen.

Ron's lips moved, but no sound came out. Not that I'd hear it over the sound of blood rushing to my head. My whole body trembled as I strained against my own arm.

No. This wasn't who I was.

"Lena?" Jackson's voice was a quiet rumble.

Despite the tension pulling at every muscle in my body, I fought for my composure. I breathed like my therapist taught me—deep inhales through the nose and out through the mouth.

Ron's breath hitched, and I felt the vibration in my synthetic fingertips. Soft and flimsy, his skin made a weak package for the vital body parts underneath.

"He's trying to talk!" Jackson grabbed my wrist and tugged, but my left arm was just as strong as his.

My grip held. And tightened.

His neck was so frail, just muscle and bone. Crushing it would be so easy. Inhale. Exhale.

My hand twitched, and my fingers loosened.

Ron gasped as air came flooding back into his lungs. I lowered him until his feet were firmly back on the floor. Between more gasps, he coughed out a name—a name I knew very well.

Suddenly, my body was too heavy. The world was spinning too fast. Jackson shoved a chair under me as I dropped.

"I don't believe you," I said.

Ron grinned even through his coughing fit. "Thomas Hayes gave me the equipment I needed to hack the EyeNet and send malicious data to manipulate your arm's artificial intelligence."

The room went so quiet that I could hear everyone breathing like it was a thunderstorm. "What?"

"Your dad. All of this is his fault."

5

After all he'd put me through, Ron Franklin still wasn't done torturing me. I hated that stupid, smug grin on his face.

I lunged, reeling my left hand back, and drove my fist toward his face.

Ron screamed.

Ms. Walker screamed.

The security guard looked away.

My fist slammed into the glass wall behind him. Glass crunched. When I pulled back my hand, it left a circle of cracks with spiderwebbing lines crawling outward. But the window held.

Ron doubled over. His breaths came in long, jagged draws.

"He's having a panic attack." Ms. Walker shoved me aside and glared at the guard, who looked utterly helpless.

I grabbed for Ron again, but a split second later, my

feet dangled in the air as Jackson carried me and set me on my feet farther away. He kept one arm gripped around my waist.

"He can't get away with this," I shouted at Jackson. "He's lying!"

"This is harassment!" Ms. Walker screamed from across the room. Her finger jabbed in my direction.

"Let's not go overboard," the guard said. His words sputtered. He swiveled his head back and forth between Ron and me. Panic lit his eyes. "See, he's fine."

I lunged again, but Jackson's arm stopped me. "For now," I said. "But he can't hold me forever."

Ron finally caught his breath. "I'm not lying."

Jackson released me. Before I could attack Ron myself, Jackson grabbed him by the shoulders, swung him around, and slammed him against the side wall. Ron's head bounced against the padding.

"Seriously?" Jackson growled.

Now that he was dealing with a threat that wasn't his bosses' kid, the security guard jumped into motion. He grasped Jackson's forearm and yanked, but he was nothing compared to CyberCorp's top-of-the-line metal composite that made up both of Jackson's arms.

Ron slapped wildly at Jackson's grip.

I slid into the nearest chair and admired the view.

Jackson pushed his face next to Ron's, his eyes sharp. "Hasn't she been through enough?"

"I'm not lying!" Ron stopped struggling and caught my eye. "I have never lied to you."

"You deceived me from the moment we met." To Jackson, I added, "Let him go."

He raised an eyebrow.

"It's okay."

He released Ron, whose butt hit the floor with a thud. His face pinched in pain. Instead of standing, he pulled his knees into his chest and sat there in a ball. He was probably safer that way.

"I'm calling for more security." The security guard tapped the back of his ear to activate his micro-comm. "I need help in 58J."

"It's fine." I flashed my best innocent face at him. "See. Ron is fine."

He stared at me, fingertips still hovering around his micro.

"Really." I turned toward Jackson. "Right?"

Ms. Walker finally stopped gaping at us and slid into the small space between Ron and Jackson. "I should have you two arrested for assault. If you touch my client again, that's exactly what I'll do."

Ron pushed himself off the floor and slumped into the nearest chair. "Can't say I didn't have it coming."

"That's hardly the point." She straightened up to her full height of about five-feet-ten in her heels. "You have rights, and your visitors will respect them." She cast a sharp glance at me. "No matter what their last names are."

I raised both hands in the air. "That depends on what other lies your client is going to tell me."

"Cancel that," the guard said into his micro.

Ron rubbed the back of his head. "Mr. Hayes and I

have been communicating for months. Everything I did, he helped me. I wouldn't have been able to do it without him." To his lawyer, he added, "You can go."

"Excuse me?"

I cringed at her shrill tone.

"You can go. I didn't call you here. If I wanted representation, I would have called you myself."

Ms. Walker sputtered. "You can't just show up here and expect me to—"

"I've made an arrangement, and I don't require your services tonight. I'll call you in the morning to discuss the plea deal."

She stomped one pencil-thin stiletto. "I really must object."

"Then you're fired."

Her mouth opened and closed. Then she spun on her sky-high heels and stomped out.

Ron's gaze followed her until the automatic door slammed closed. "I never liked her anyway. Always telling me what to do."

"I think that's her job," Jackson said. He leaned over Ron, and the other boy shrank deeper into his chair. "You don't expect us to believe that Mr. Hayes wanted you to use his daughter to commit murder. Why would he hurt Lena? Why would he hurt his company?"

The security guard maneuvered his way between the two boys, and Jackson backed off. Still, he kept his glare fixed on Ron.

Ron scrubbed a hand over his face. "I can't tell you his motives. I can only tell you what happened."

I leaned forward in my chair, and it took every ounce of my will not to jump up and slam Ron's head into the table. Of all the lies he could come up with, why this one? It wasn't enough to destroy my life—he had to come after my entire family.

"I was angry about everything that happened with my parents . . ." He gestured at everything. "You know the story. Anyway, I was using my micro during my lunch one day to search for security flaws in the Model One androids. I wasn't assigned to the Model Ones anymore." He gestured toward me.

"My parents had pulled you off the androids to work on my arm."

"Right. You were in a coma, and Dr. Fisher and I were told to focus on you. Still, I didn't think my searches would throw any red flags since we worked on the androids in the past."

"Can we move this along?" Jackson was pacing while shooting murderous looks in Ron's direction.

Ron sat up straighter, as if feeding on the tension. "The message was anonymous. It said I would receive all the hardware I needed to fix my problems. A day later, two top-of-the-line machines arrived at my house. And when I say top-of-the-line, I mean the type of power that's not yet available to the public."

"So you removed my patch for the EyeNet loophole," I said, "and used the computers to hack the EyeNet to send my arm the data it needed to weaponize me. How do you know the computers came from my dad?"

"I didn't remove the patch right away. The first thing I

did when I turned them on was trace the source of the messages to my micro-comm. They originated from Thomas Hayes."

I slammed both fists on the table, and the wood under my left cracked. "Stop lying."

Jackson circled the table and dropped into the seat beside me. "Even if what you say is true, how do you know what Mr. Hayes intended you to do?"

"The next day, Lena woke up from her coma. I received a message on my micro-comm. It was an image of the program code for the patch that kept the Model Ones from receiving malicious code over the EyeNet. I didn't know what it meant, but I kept receiving the message, every day, minutes before I saw Lena each morning. So I removed that code from her software."

"And you stopped receiving the messages?" Jackson asked.

"I kept receiving them for a few more days, which makes sense. There would have been no way for Mr. Hayes to know the job was done because Lena's arm isn't connected to our network. I realized I was being told to use Lena to take my revenge on CyberCorp."

My chest felt cold and empty.

"Lena?" Jackson was staring at me with compassion etched into his brow. I could see him out of the corner of my vision, but I couldn't look at him. If I met those blue eyes, the dam inside me would break.

"It's a lie," I whispered.

"What proof do you have?" Jackson said, his attention back on Ron.

"Nothing except the process of elimination."

"You want to explain that?" Jackson's tone held a threat.

"My mysterious partner has a lot of money. He knew when I interacted with Lena, so he could make sure I received the messages when I was with her."

"Circumstantial," I said.

"If this is true—" Jackson started.

"It's not!"

He held up a hand, and I let him finish. "*If* it's true, why are you telling us this now? It's been weeks."

"The prosecutor and my lawyer struck a deal days ago for a reduced charge if I give a full confession. I was thinking about it when I got your message." Ron nodded at me. "Knowing you'd forgive me and talk to Liv on my behalf is what pushed me here."

"My message?" I asked.

He squinted at me. "You asked me to come here."

6

"WHAT ARE YOU TALKING ABOUT?" I WAS OUT OF MY seat again and, before I knew it, leaning over Ron.

The door whooshed open, and all of us turned.

Ms. Walker stormed into the room with another security guard at her side. I recognized this one as the guard who'd been in Claire's room half an hour ago. Jackson and I both stumbled backward from Ron, innocent expressions painted on our faces—as if we weren't just trying to intimidate him with our enhanced potential for physical harm.

"My client is done talking." She flashed Ron a pointed look. "I'm your attorney until the judge approves my withdrawal, and as long as I am, *this*"—she jabbed a finger back and forth between Jackson and me—"isn't happening."

The new security guard gripped Jackson's upper arm and tugged. Jackson stared at him but stayed put as the guard yanked.

"Say nothing else," Ms. Walker added. "You've already hurt your case."

Ron squinted at her. "I thought we had a deal with the prosecution."

She groaned. "That deal was on the table for twenty-four hours, and it's been almost a week. If you're going to blabber all over the building, at least let me see what I can do for you first." She returned her attention to Jackson and me and pulled herself up to her full height. "Out."

The new guard pulled Jackson's arm again, and Jackson's mouth twitched with suppressed laughter.

"Let's just go." I stomped toward the door. "He doesn't know how to tell the truth anyway."

Jackson brushed the guard off and followed.

"I'm not ly—" Ron called as the door slammed shut behind us.

I leaned against the wall in the hallway and sighed until my chest deflated. The space was empty except for me and Jackson. Liv had taken off to who-knew-where.

Jackson leaned beside me. "What happened back there with your arm?"

Instead of answering, I slid my hand-screen out of my jacket pocket. "Call Dad." When it didn't ring after a few seconds, I checked the display. A circle kept rotating on the screen as the device attempted to connect my call. "Call Dad," I said again.

Jackson peered over my shoulder, where the circle kept spinning, but the call wasn't connecting. "Is it busted?"

"It's been slow this evening." I slid the device back into my jacket.

"Are we going to talk about what just happened?"

I tapped my pocket. "That's what I was trying to do." On second thought, I removed the hand-screen again and, this time, tried to call to Melody. Again, no connection, so I dropped the device back into my pocket. "Can you call Melody?"

Jackson tapped his micro-comm. "Call Melody on speaker."

I stepped closer to Jackson since the sound bubble on a micro-comm's speaker was small. Warmth emanated from him, and I leaned in to catch another whiff of the spicy-sweet scent that was so distinctly Jackson. Melody picked up on the second ring.

"Hey, Jackson." Her voice sounded over-the-top cheerful, a deep contrast to what I was. "What's up?"

"You okay?" I asked before he could answer.

"Lena, hey. Yeah, I'm great."

I narrowed my eyes at Jackson's micro. Melody was typically perky, but lately—understandably—not so much. "We're at the Tower. Are you here yet?"

The pause extended for so long that I thought we might have been disconnected. "I'm not going." Her tone was still about two degrees north of cheerful.

"Really?" Jackson asked.

Another pause and then, "Really."

"A week ago, all you could talk about was how much Ron needed to pay," Jackson said, "and now you don't want to confront him?"

"My dad thinks it's best if we try to make internal peace, and confronting Ron will just upset me."

"In that case," I asked, "do you want me to punch him in the face for you?"

"With your left hand?" There was a low voice in the background that sounded vaguely like Mr. Miller, and Melody cleared her throat. "Thanks for checking on me. I have to go."

She disconnected.

"Weird," he said, "but probably the healthy choice. If you're done stalling, can we talk about your arm?"

I tried my own hand-screen again. "Call Dad," I told it, but again it refused to connect.

Jackson grabbed the hand-screen and tugged.

My grip tightened, and the device's edges crunched under my fingertips. My fingers wouldn't give until he peeled each one off one by one. He pushed it back into my pocket.

I lowered my gaze to the floor so I wouldn't have to see the concerned look on his face.

"You need to see Dr. Fisher," he said quietly.

"I am so done with being poked and prodded."

"I get that. I've had more parts replaced than you, and somehow I have fewer appointments."

I shook my head hard and stomped toward the elevator. "It's fine. I'm fine. Let's just get out of here."

He followed and didn't object while I waved my wrist at the scanner. "There have been a lot of bugs that Ron should have handled if he was actually doing his job, instead of pretending to do it while turning you into a weapon."

The elevator doors opened, and I stepped in.

Jackson followed. "None of that changes the fact that you need to get the arm working perfectly if you really want to escape this place."

I opened my mouth to tell the elevator to take us to the lobby, but Jackson grabbed my hands and turned me to face him.

"You're a good person, Lena. You care about people. Neither of us wants you to have to live with what might happen if something else goes wrong."

We never spoke of it, but he knew how those three lives I'd ended grated on my soul. I blinked, and tears stuck on the ends of my lashes. My voice caught in my throat, so I gestured for Jackson to instruct the elevator.

"Fifty-four," he said.

We found the six-foot, stocky blonde doctor tilted back in her chair, gesturing at the space above her with her eyes narrowed toward the ceiling. Her shoulder-length hair hung in a straight cut around her shoulders. We stood in her doorway for almost an entire minute as her hands twisted and swiped through the empty air.

It was after hours now, but Dr. Fisher was one of the most dedicated people I knew. *Obsessed* was really a better word for it.

She had a massive window as one of her office walls, but she always kept it tinted white. If she wasn't using it as a virtual whiteboard at any given time, she didn't like the distraction of the outside world.

"What's she doing?" I whispered to Jackson.

"Lena!" Dr. Fisher finally noticed us and swiped in the air to shove aside whatever had her attention. "I was just rearranging some program code for the Model Two."

"I don't want to disturb you." I stepped backward and ran into Jackson, who shoved me fully into the room.

"Nice try. We're staying."

Dr. Fisher jumped to her feet and offered us a wide, welcoming grin. "Please come in. Always a pleasure."

Once upon a time, I'd been the last person she wanted to see. After my car accident, my parents had temporarily yanked her off the Model One project right before the androids hit the market. They had demanded she focus on my arm and my recovery, and she'd resented it.

After I saved her life, though, she was suddenly my biggest fan. And I was slowly becoming one of hers.

She waved toward the two chairs opposite her desk. "Was there something else?" I'd had an appointment with her earlier that day, but admittedly, I'd rushed the process to get home faster.

Jackson flopped into one of the seats. "Her arm doesn't respond sometimes."

Fisher nodded and raised an eyebrow at me. "You didn't mention that."

"I figured it was psychological, not physical. It's like it gets stuck when I get emotional."

"Which is always," Jackson added.

I shoved his arm.

"You can be a little dramatic sometimes." Dr. Fisher's lips twitched, but she kept her expression neutral. "Tell me specifically what happened."

"When she slammed Ron—"

I cut Jackson off. "A minute ago, I was upset because I couldn't reach my dad, and I couldn't let go of my hand-screen. And earlier this evening, I was upset about having to run CyberCorp someday, and my hand-eye coordination went wonky."

"Let's see what's going on." Dr. Fisher reached into her desk and came out with a cable and a scalpel.

We'd been through the process many times, but still, I turned my face away as she sliced into my synthetic skin just above the elbow. I felt the pinch of the scalpel and the tug of my skin as she slid the cable through the opening and into the outlet in my arm.

I turned back and then closed my eyes for two seconds to activate my EyeNet view. Lines of code filled the far wall, which now acted as a virtual whiteboard.

Dr. Fisher made a collection of *mm-hmm*s and *uh-huh*s as she examined my program, swiping through the air to scroll the display. After ten minutes, she sat up straighter and made a grand swipe from left to right. A virtual keyboard zoomed out of nowhere from her left and stopped in front of her. It hovered, translucent and ghostly.

She typed, and several lines of the code on the wall disappeared, replaced by new instructions. "This should do it."

"What's the problem?" Jackson asked. He leaned back in the chair, but despite the casual posture, worry etched a crevice in his forehead.

Dr. Fisher typed for a few more seconds and then

gestured to swipe the virtual keyboard aside. It zoomed into the wall and disappeared. "How does it feel now?"

"Good." I flexed my arm at the elbow, and it moved just like natural—as if it was the arm I was born with. "Is it fixed? Because, no offense, but I never want to see you again."

She chuckled. "Just a minor issue that came over from the Model Two. Since your accident was unexpected, we had to adapt the code that we were developing for our next androids. But unlike you, the Model Two is a robot."

I raised a brow at her as I waited for her to get to the point.

"Just a slight calibration to account for your internal body temperature being higher than our androids run."

"What about Jackson? Doesn't he need the same adjustment?"

"Your temperature is a little above the average—still within a healthy range though." Dr. Fisher shifted toward Jackson. "If you have any hiccups, let us know, but it's very possible that your current calibration is fine for your particular body temp."

"It helps that the interns working on me were actually doing their jobs," Jackson said.

"Yes, there is that." Dr. Fisher waved her palm at the text on the wall, and it blanked. She pulled the cable, and it popped loose from my arm.

The synthetic skin sealed up as if zipped closed. No scar. Nothing to suggest she'd stabbed me with a scalpel a dozen minutes ago. I stretched the arm out in front of me, and even the color was a perfect match of light brown. As much as I detested this company, they made some quality products.

I would trust those products more if murderers didn't keep using them to kill people.

"So you fixed it?" I asked.

"I did my part. Remember, the arm is connected to your nervous system. You've been under a lot of stress. Stress can raise your body temperature, and your AI will make dynamic adjustments based on how it expects you to behave. If you want your arm to adjust properly to the new calibration over the next twenty-four hours, you have to do something about your anxiety."

I jumped to my feet so quickly that I toppled my chair.

"Did you hear what I just said?"

I took three deep breaths before righting my chair. "I just want to get out of here."

Dr. Fisher gestured toward my arm. "This is a lifetime commitment."

"We can do this remotely in the future."

"There's no remote access," Jackson said.

"I know." My words came out sharpened to an edge by irritation at still being in this building.

Dr. Fisher leaned back in her chair, her expression doubtful. "You're going to cut into your own arm? You still turn your face away sometimes when *I* do it."

That had definitely occurred to me, but eventually I'd get used to that part. Right? I pressed my lips together.

"Or," Dr. Fisher continued, "you could simply go without the skin."

"Just walk around with this metal arm?"

Her face went serious. "You have to choose—keep coming back to CyberCorp or wear your arm in its full glory."

There had to be other options—options that didn't have my life intertwined with this company indefinitely. I turned to go and made it halfway to the door before I stopped. "Thanks for everything. As much as I like you, I don't plan to see much more of you."

"We'll see."

Jackson followed me out the door and down the hall. We stood in silence as we waited for the elevator, with him sneaking not-so-subtle concerned glances at me.

"You're not rid of me yet." Dr. Fisher hurried down the hall and joined us. "I'm needed up on seventy." She scanned her wrist to call another elevator as a smile played across her face. She *lived* to work on CyberCorp's androids, and the seventieth floor was where a lot of that happened.

The elevator doors opened, and Jackson stepped inside.

Despite my better judgment, though, my curiosity won out. "Is everything okay with the Model Ones?"

"I'm not sure *okay* is the right word. We're still trying to figure out what went wrong with the mass exodus. We rounded up all the androids." She pointed straight upward. "They're up there getting the full quality-control treat-ment. As far as we can tell, they're receiving instructions from the Model One server like they're supposed to. Those instructions must be getting misinterpreted."

I stepped into the elevator with Jackson. "I'm sure you'll figure it out."

She nodded. "We will. But apparently, there's something going on with the Model Twos as well. Sophie wants me to take a look while I'm up there."

My body went rigid. The elevator started to close, and I jumped back into the hallway.

Jackson moved into the doorway to block the doors from closing. "Are we going?"

"Shouldn't we see what's going on?"

He flashed his famous grin—the one that won over every female within a three-mile radius and a sizable percentage of the males too. "You know I'm always game for an adventure. I just thought you were in a hurry to get out of here."

"The EyeNet loophole that gave Ron unauthorized access to my AI started as a Model One issue too. Our hardware and software are even closer to the Model Two. If they're both having problems . . ." Plus, although I didn't say it aloud, this would give me the opportunity to talk to my dad about Ron's accusation.

Another elevator opened, and Dr. Fisher slid into the doorway to hold the cab. "It's probably nothing that pertains to you. This isn't going to be like Ron."

"Or Claire," Jackson added.

Dr. Fisher sighed and rolled her eyes skyward. "It's nothing like that."

"Then what is it like?" I asked.

"I'll find out when I get up there."

I couldn't afford any more security loopholes—I was still recovering from the last one. I made my decision and joined Dr. Fisher in her elevator. Jackson shrugged and tagged along.

"Seventy," Dr. Fisher said.

The elevator rose upward. A thick, sticky feeling swelled in my gut as we traveled deeper into CyberCorp Tower.

7

The seventieth floor of CyberCorp Tower was a disaster.

Jackson, Dr. Fisher, and I stepped off the elevator to find over a hundred Model One androids scattered around the room in various states of intactness. Most stood in neat lines in front of a huge vid-screen occupying one wall. The rest lay crumpled on the floor, separated into pieces, or spread across tables in the middle of the space.

The highest several stories of the Tower narrowed as they reached the top. This floor had only one vast room with a glass-enclosed office in the back corner. Both my parents stood in the office, their heads bent close together and lips moving.

"Excuse me for a minute." Dr. Fisher hurried by me toward them.

She stepped around Dr. Sophie Kim, a petite engineer with blunt-cut black hair who sat cross-legged on the floor with a partially disassembled android across her lap. Her back was to me, and she didn't move as Fisher brushed past.

I squatted beside Dr. Sophie to inspect her work. "What's wrong with them?"

Without turning, she half-stood and leaned forward, gripped both sides of the android's head, and yanked. "If I knew the answer to that, we wouldn't be here." She grunted as the back of the android's skull popped loose, and she fell back onto her butt.

Although she usually worked on this floor alone or with only a few others at a time, today dozens of people had invaded her space—including me.

"Can you just talk to me for a second?"

Jackson reached out to touch the android skull, and Dr. Sophie slapped his hand.

"I am." She set the part to one side to reveal three circuit boards and a small rectangular hard drive in the Model One's head. "How are you?"

"Dr. Sophie?"

She finally looked up. Tension drained from her face, leaving it looking tired. Red rimmed her eyelids. "I'm sorry, Lena. I enjoy your curiosity on most days, but today is unfortunately not like most."

"All of this affects me too."

Jackson raised his hand. "And me."

"I don't mean to seem uncaring. I promise you that I'll be more likely to discover what's going on if you're not hovering."

I took two large steps back and continued to watch her

as she worked. Jackson wrapped an arm around my waist, and I leaned into him.

My parents stepped out of the corner office and strode toward us, with two engineers in tow, prompting Dr. Sophie to hop to her feet and stand at attention. Like her, my parents hadn't slept much in the past week, and it showed in their droopy eyelids and downturned lips.

Mom wore the same navy pencil slacks and pink shirt she'd worn yesterday. I remembered the shirt because the color perfectly accented her dark skin. She'd traded yesterday's navy jacket for the camel-colored one that usually hung in her office as a backup. Dad's dark hair fell over his forehead rather than being perfectly placed off his face as usual.

Dr. Sophie opened her mouth, but I beat her to it.

"What do we know?"

"Don't you have homework?" My mother's tone was sharp, its edge filed to a point by caffeine. She clutched a paper cup in both hands. As she spoke, her assistant slipped it from her grasp and replaced it with a fresh one. She sipped, and her expression softened. "Jackson, how are you?"

He dropped his arm from around me and stood up straighter. "I'm good, ma'am."

She shifted her attention to me. "How was school?"

"It was fine. It's school. Please tell me what's going on." I threw up my hands. "You promised me more responsibility and transparency." I pointed back and forth between the two of us.

She offered a quick nod. "We were successful in

rounding up all the androids, and we're inspecting every single one."

"And?"

"It's not clear why they ignored the standby instruction after poor Paris's death. How is your friend Claire, by the way?" Her brow pinched.

"Claire is a killer, and I don't take her calls. They're all on standby *now* though, right? Do you think they'll stay that way?"

"That's really the question. Isn't it?" She gulped her coffee and swallowed hard.

Dad filled up the space. "We can't guarantee anything until we know why they behaved how they did to begin with. Luckily, they didn't hurt anyone else."

"Androids don't just wake up and take off though. Where did they go? Shouldn't that give you a clue about what caused this?"

"As far as we can tell, nowhere in particular. We rounded them up across a mile radius from here."

"They just went for a stroll to enjoy the evening? Maybe get an oil change?"

"The sarcasm isn't helping," my mom said.

And that was really a shame because sarcasm was one of my best attributes.

"We'll sort this out—I promise. It's only been a week, and this is over a decade's worth of work we need to sort through. We're reevaluating every line of code and every piece of hardware." She yawned as if to make her point.

My father dropped a hand on my shoulder. "This is our

responsibility, and we'll handle it. Please go home. Eat dinner. Do your homework."

"Can I talk to you about something first?"

"Of course." He offered me a weak smile, too flat around the edges.

I jerked my head toward an empty corner of the room. My parents had a lot on their plates, and the last thing my dad needed was for me to publicly announce that Ron was now accusing him of sabotaging his own company—and murder.

His gaze flicked straight upward, where his EyeNet-enabled lenses would display the time. Eyes upward meant he was checking it.

"Forget it. It can wait." It was a bullshit accusation anyway. No need to waste his time with it.

"Great. We'll chat when I get home." He kissed me on the forehead and rotated my shoulders until I faced the elevators. Then he cast a pointed look at Jackson.

Obediently, Jackson grabbed my wrist and tugged me in that direction.

"Kiss your sister for us," my dad called. "As soon as we have an answer, you'll be the first to know."

Before I could wave my wrist at the scanner for the elevators, one opened.

A young man stepped out. "Mr. Hayes!" His voice boomed through the space, freezing every movement in the room.

My dad pushed my mom behind him and pulled himself up to his full six feet. "You can't be here." The tiredness was suddenly gone from his face, replaced by the competence and confidence we all knew him for.

The newcomer was taller but lean as a knife, his gaze sharp as it scanned the room and landed on my father. His dark-blond hair was cut close to his temples, and dark circles put his hollow eyes on center stage.

"This is a restricted area," Dr. Sophie called. She took a step toward the man, but my mother's pointed look pinned her in place.

Jackson slid into his path and squared up. The two of them stood eye to eye.

"Get out of the way." The man's voice rumbled like an earthquake, low and dangerous. "This program needs to shut down."

"We'll do whatever is necessary to make these androids safe." Mom kept her tone soft and soothing as she edged toward the newcomer, both palms up. "Disabling them forever *is* an option on the table."

The man's chest deflated, and his fury seeped away. Beneath the angry mask, sadness cut into every line of his face.

"Let's all stay calm," my mom continued. "This is Kyle Winter. He's a technician who worked on the Model One release."

It took a second for the significance of the name to sink in. *Winter*, as in Paris Winter, the girl Claire killed.

"He works here?" I whispered to Dr. Sophie.

"He's been placed on paid leave," she whispered back. "With good reason."

"Kyle, I'm going to have to pause your access to high-sensitivity areas for the time being." My mother tapped her ear to activate her micro. "CyberCorp control—"

"Wait!" He reached for my mom, thought better of it, and lowered his hand. "Will I still be able to stop at tech support on my way out?"

"Make it quick." She tapped her micro again. "Cyber-Corp control, withdraw Tier Three access for Kyle Winter."

Two security guards appeared out of nowhere and clamped hands around Kyle's upper arms.

"You're on paid leave effective last week," Mom continued. "Take your time, and you can come back whenever you like. If you'd rather not come back, we would be happy to provide a reference."

He yanked his arms free from the guards. "I don't want anything from you."

"The young lady who caused your sister's death will stand trial."

"And Ron Franklin? If it weren't for his actions, Claire Payne would never have accessed the Model Ones to begin with. And what about all of you?" His gaze searched the room, landing on each of us in turn.

I shuddered as his eyes met mine, and the pain in them twisted my insides.

"You're supposed to be creating these machines to help us—not hurt us."

Silence hung over us until my mother cleared her throat. "Ron will also stand trial. You'll have your justice." My mother nodded to the two security guards, who ushered Kyle toward the elevator. "You can head to your office and grab your things before you leave."

Kyle planted his feet but offered no other resistance. He let the two guards drag him to the elevator as he watched us over his shoulder.

"Nothing to see here," my dad shouted to the entire room. "Crisis averted."

His employees jumped back into motion, conversations restarted, and engineers returned to their work of disassembling and analyzing androids.

As the elevator doors slid closed, the look in Kyle's eyes was pure murder.

8

Dr. Sophie sidled up to my father. "Could we pick up that other conversation where we left off?" Her voice was an intimate whisper that made me feel like I shouldn't have been there.

He nodded and, with one hand on my mother's back, guided her with Sophie to the glass-walled office at the back of the floor.

I trailed after them, positioning myself on the periphery while they leaned their heads close and spoke in hushes. What secret conversation was important enough to make both my parents step away from the Model Ones?

Despite the glass wall that would make it easy to spot me, they stayed engrossed and oblivious to my presence.

Dr. Sophie's voice grew louder, more urgent. "Do you understand what I'm saying?" she hissed at my dad.

My dad gestured downward with both hands and his lips made two words that I read clearly on his lips—as if anyone in the history of the world had ever calmed down by being told to *calm down.*

"Just tell me if we're shutting down the Model One server," she said. "Are we starting from scratch and instituting a full reprogram, as per policy, if we can't identify the problem?"

My mom rubbed her temples. "The last thing we need is more injuries and deaths related to these things." She glanced at my dad for support.

He rocked from foot to foot. "We've come too far to give up now. This is a breakthrough. An incredible leap into a new age of technology that took a decade of work. We're not flushing all that down the nearest toilet."

The air tensed around them as my mother leaned away. Her top lip curled upward.

"But we're considering all options," my dad added with less enthusiasm, taking her hint.

"Certainly," my mom said. "Given the expense of starting from scratch, it's a last resort."

"To be clear," Dr. Sophie said, "I'm not suggesting we shut down the server. I'm merely asking for enough warning to disconnect the Model Two androids from it first. Doing so would be several days' worth of work, so I won't be able to execute it on demand."

Mom patted her shoulder. "The Model Twos are the least of our worries. They're still in prototype and not even in the public eye yet. Let's concentrate on the crisis at hand."

My parents turned to walk away, but Dr. Sophie stopped them.

"The Model Twos are mostly autonomous now, but their original programming makes them reliant on the Model One server. If it goes down, the Model Twos may experience irreparable harm."

"Again," my mother said, this time in a too-soothing voice that sounded artificial, "we'll keep it in mind as a secondary matter."

"Just wait." Dr. Sophie pointed to a collection of Model Two androids huddled in a cluster in the main space outside the glass office. Unlike the Model Ones scattered throughout the room in various states of disassembly, these eight androids stood tall and intact.

I was right in the line of Dr. Sophie's pointing finger, so I darted to the side to avoid being spotted.

"Lena." My mother gestured at me, never missing a beat.

"Sorry." I waved and started to slink away.

"Come in here. You can be a part of any conversation here that you like. I was serious when I said we'd be transparent with each other."

"Next time without the spying though," my dad added.

I slipped into the room, head bent, as my father's stern eyes lectured me. Unblemished white framed the minimalist office, with stark angles and lines accentuating the space. Two large panes of glass met at a corner, affording a sweeping view of the hectic work on the Model One androids.

Now that I was in here, the tension in the room vibrated through my bones. I shot a glance back at the doorway but stayed put. At least I'd get to hear the rest of this conversation, to know whether I should add it to my list of worries.

Dr. Sophie cleared her throat and picked up where she left off. "The Model Twos weren't programmed to huddle together like that," she continued, her tone trembling with restrained excitement. "But here they are, exhibiting empathetic behavior. A desire to be near one another."

I stepped out of the room and approached the Model Twos. Their limbs were slimmer than those of the Model Ones. Also unlike the Model Ones, their silver bodies lacked a slightly gold tint, and their eyes glowed a darker red.

I squeezed behind one of them and shoved it forward, away from the others. After I gave it the initial momentum, it completed the step on its own. Now, I stood between it and its buddies.

As soon as I moved, the android's head turned toward the group, and it stepped back to join them.

I returned to the office to find Dr. Sophie beaming.

"They're not programmed to do that?" I asked.

She rushed past me toward the androids, grabbed one of their arms, and yanked it to one side until it stepped forward. She pushed another one backward until it followed suit, speaking animatedly as she repositioned each android.

"I just want you to appreciate what an evolution this is. Humans cluster in cities. They're uncomfortable at restaurants alone. They feel awkward with no one to talk to at parties."

She shifted the last of the Model Two androids, leaving the group of them in an asymmetrical octagon.

"No, they weren't programmed to do this." Once done tinkering, Dr. Sophie stepped back.

The androids stepped and slid and sidled until they reformed their perfect formation. They cast glances among themselves as if confirming that they were indeed together and satisfied.

"We must preserve them at all costs," Dr. Sophie concluded, out of breath as she rejoined us in the glass room.

An engineer on the main floor waved frantically toward us, pointing at a partially disassembled Model One next to him.

My dad nodded to him before returning his attention to Dr. Sophie. "It's certainly worth exploring, but this company is in crisis. If you must, you can find a safe way to sever the Model Twos from the server on your own time." Without another word, he left the office and strode to the engineer.

My mom gave Dr. Sophie's shoulder a squeeze. "We will do everything in our power to save all of our inventions . . . when we have the time." She followed my dad, leaving Dr. Sophie with a shocked look on her face.

I stopped Dr. Sophie before she could go after them and press the issue. "Are you sure this huddling thing isn't a bug? I'm sorry to ask because I can see you're excited about it, but I'm running almost the same software as the Model Twos. What happens to them impacts me even more than what happens to the Model Ones. Is this something I should worry about?"

She continued to stare after my parents. "It's more than huddling. It's mimicry, which is a symptom of the desire to learn and evolve. This is the first step toward true AI sentience."

I tried to catch her eye, to make sure she was truly hearing and understanding my concerns.

A flicker of determination glinted in Dr. Sophie's brown eyes before she finally turned them toward me. "If you insist on worrying, worry about the Model Ones. They're unpredictable."

9

"LOBBY," THE ELEVATOR REPEATED BACK TO ME AFTER Jackson and I were inside.

"No, wait," he said. "Take us to tech support—whatever floor that's on."

"Twenty-sixth floor," the elevator said in its too-smooth computerized voice.

I glared at Jackson. "I thought we were leaving."

"I'm trying to help you leave this building permanently, like you want." He pointed at my jacket pocket. "If that hand-screen stays on the fritz, you'll be back here tomorrow. We might as well get it looked at while you're here."

I crossed my arms over my chest. "Fine."

The elevator doors opened on twenty-six, and we stepped out onto a floor that was decidedly less welcoming than other floors in the Tower. The hallway lacked the vid-screens that filled each wall of most of the building's spaces. Instead, gray-painted surfaces lined the space. We followed the carpeted hall to a wall of glass on one side. Beyond the glass, a fishbowl of a room held the IT office.

CyberCorp's information technology department could support a small city. Its twenty desks in rows of fours held twenty people at a time. Professionals staffed the place twenty-four hours per day in three shifts. Part of the glass wall slid to the side automatically, creating a doorway, as a cluster of techs inside rushed toward it.

I flattened myself against the wall as a stream of people rushed from the room, some carrying work bags or purses, several with their fingertips to their ears as they instructed their micro-comms.

The graveyard shift was just starting, and only four people remained in the overnight skeleton crew.

In the desk closest to the door, a man with slicked-back, sandy-colored hair who appeared to be in his thirties slumped forward in his chair, his nose only inches from a desktop vid-screen. His mouth sagged open as the text on the screen scrolled up and down with every slight movement of his head.

Jackson waved me toward him. I stepped through the door and took a spot in the man's peripheral field of view.

Thirty seconds later, when he was still staring at the screen instead of at me, I cleared my throat.

"Can I help you?" The man's mouth closed, as if he'd just noticed it hanging open, but his nose stayed pointed at the vid.

"I'm having a problem with my hand-screen."

"That's because it's an obsolete device, and no one uses them anymore."

I gritted my teeth. "Can you take a look anyway please?"

He puffed out a long, exaggerated sigh and finally glanced my way. "Miss Hayes, I didn't realize . . ." He hopped to his feet and smoothed his polo shirt and slacks. "How can I help you?"

I held the hand-screen out.

He snatched it from my palm and used a cable to connect it to his vid-screen. "Let's see what's going on."

When he settled back into his chair, this time, he kept his back straight and his mouth shut. He navigated through various menus of my hand-screen by gesturing in front of the vid, which zoomed through the menus and submenus too quickly for me to register what he was checking.

"Can you see what's wrong?"

"As far as I can tell, it's behaving normally . . ." He tapped the display and scrunched his eyes at it before tapping again. "It's a little slow accessing anything over the network."

"I can't even connect a call."

"I don't work on hand-screens often since everyone has a micro-comm. It's odd that two of you in a row would bring them in."

My dialer appeared on the vid-screen, and he typed in a string of digits I didn't recognize—his own ID code, I assumed. The word *CONNECTING* took over the screen, and we waited for almost half a minute.

The bright-white lights overhead flicked off, the vid-screen went black, and darkness swallowed us. My breath caught in my throat. Two seconds later, duller amber lights came on. The vid-screen flickered before coming back on several shades dimmer than before.

"Crap." The man pushed back his chair and spun his head to meet the gazes of the other three techs.

One of the others gripped the desk in front of her. "Oh no."

"What just happened?" I asked.

"I think . . . we may have had a power outage." Our tech tilted back his head to examine the now-amber pot lights in the ceiling. "Yeah, it looks like my client cube's running on the building's backup power too."

Just as quickly, the lights overhead bloomed alive again, and the vid-screen brightened.

"Problem solved?" I asked.

The wall to my left suddenly lit up like a Christmas tree. Individual blinking white, yellow, and red lights appeared on the wall, which now I could see was a communication panel.

Behind our tech, the other three in the room talked animatedly. They swiped and gestured in the air and on their vid-screens as they addressed new emergencies presented to them in both real life and virtual.

Two of the techs leaped from their seats, and one of their chairs toppled backward. They hurried from the room and ran toward the elevator bay.

"Francis," the last other tech called in a panic. "A little help."

"Sorry," our guy—Francis apparently—said. "I need to get back to work. If that unplanned outage hit the entire building, lots of people are going to need assistance with test projects that weren't wired to the backup system."

"The hand-screen issue isn't a big deal." I pointed at my device on his desk. "I'm sure it will work itself out after a couple restarts."

"If you let me hold on to it for a day or two, I can do a full diagnostic. You can use your micro until I finish. Even if the problem is connected to the profile associated with your global ID chip, micro-comms handle data differently, so that will probably solve the problem for now."

"I don't have one."

One eyebrow shot upward for only a second before settling back into place. "I'll issue you a loaner." Before I could object, he was on his feet and reaching for a drawer in the far wall. He extracted a brand-new micro-comm still in its small plastic casing.

I waved it away. "Even if I used that, I still need the screen for display."

His brow scrunched into a question as he pointed at his eyes.

I didn't have EyeNet-enabled lenses like most people. Despite that, I could access the EyeNet using the connection CyberCorp had established between my eyes and the chip at the base of my skull. That meant I could see any displays from a micro-comm.

Still, I preferred to keep my EyeNet connection off. I found the whole idea of seeing virtual objects a little creepy—as if the real world wasn't complicated enough.

"Never mind. I'm good." I held out my palm, and he

returned the hand-screen to it. "I'll deal with it. Maybe it's time to just buy a new one."

Jackson followed me back into the hallway.

"Can we go now?" I stomped toward the elevator bay.

"As you wish." He scanned his wrist to call an elevator. Although access to floors above the lobby was restricted, anyone could call an elevator headed back to the main floor.

The scanner dinged, and a pair of doors opened.

I stomped inside. "The sooner I'm out of here, the sooner I never have to see this place again."

When the elevator doors opened into the lobby, Jackson and I stepped onto the silvery white tile floors. Directly across from us, another elevator opened, and Kyle Winter appeared.

Jackson and I froze. So did Kyle.

He stood as tall as Jackson, but leaner. His veins stood out on the wiry muscle of his arms and neck. Unlike most CyberCorp employees, he was casual in a T-shirt and jeans, and I couldn't fault him for it. If my little sister had just died, I wouldn't have bothered to put on outside clothes at all.

"You're Lena Hayes, right?" Kyle's voice came out low and hoarse. Upstairs, I'd read that as a threat, but he could just be hoarse from crying.

"I'm sorry about your sister."

"I'll bet."

"I can't imagine . . ."

He flinched, and I clamped my mouth shut.

Jackson's hand on my lower back urged me toward the exit.

Kyle's voice got louder. "You and your parents pretend to care, but here they are, right upstairs getting ready to re-release their androids. If they cared, the project would be scrapped."

"I'm not a part of that." Despite the pressure of Jackson's hand on my back, I locked my legs in place.

"You're the CyberCorp Princess. Of course you're a part of it."

"I've been against the AI projects since day one."

Jackson stepped between the two of us, but I held out an arm to keep him back. Kyle didn't need anyone intimidating him. He needed compassion.

But Kyle was a snowball rolling downhill, growing and sharpening as he picked up speed. He met Jackson and me in the middle of the elevator bay and straightened up. His voice boomed across the lobby. "You think you can tuck your head and disappear?" Spittle sprayed from his mouth and smacked me on the cheek. "This isn't over just because you say it is."

I shuffled backward out of spraying range, but Jackson stayed put with his gaze steady on the other boy's face.

Kyle took another step forward, and Jackson did the same, bringing the two face-to-face. Jackson didn't say a word.

I grabbed Jackson's clenched hand and pulled him backward. "Jacks, he's grieving."

"It's funny." Kyle laughed in a way that made it clear

nothing here was funny. "My entire life is destroyed, and the world keeps spinning. CyberCorp is making more money than ever. The Model Ones are the top story in the news, and it's just bringing in more customers. And you are still friends with the girl who made that robot attack my sister."

"We're not friends." The rest I couldn't deny.

"She didn't mean to," Jackson said at the same time.

"Well, if she didn't mean it . . ." Kyle's voice was heavy with sarcasm.

Another elevator opened, and two Model One androids clomped out. Their metal feet clanked against the tile floor.

My parents had made them humanoid. The after-hours amber lighting brought out the hint of gold tone in their silver limbs. Their eyelids clicked closed in an unnerving approximation of a human blink.

One pair of glowing red eyes target-locked on me, and a whimper built in my chest. The world went cold as fear gripped my heart and squeezed.

It was fine though—only two androids. Jackson and I could take them down if they were out of control.

No need to panic.

"What's happening?" Jackson whispered.

Across the elevator bay, another pair of doors opened, and my muscles tensed for a fight. Liv and Hunter stepped out, and relief blossomed in my chest.

"There you are," Liv called. She pointed at Hunter. "Look who finally showed up."

"We've been looking for you." Hunter smiled his usual charming, crooked grin that reached all the way to his brown eyes circled in green. As often, his brown hair hung a bit too long over his forehead, and he wore a graphic T-shirt just snug enough to show off the lean muscle of his biceps.

With a ding, more doors opened, revealing five more pairs of glowing red eyes encased in humanoid metal bodies. The five androids marched out of the elevator. Their metal feet clanged like a rhythmic gong.

Clank. Clank. Clank.

Kyle cursed and flung himself back toward the wall.

"Get out of here!" I shouted at Liv. She pulled Hunter back into their elevator cab, and the doors shut them inside.

Yet another elevator opened, and my parents shot out with Dr. Sophie and two engineers in tow.

"Stop them!" Dr. Sophie screamed.

All seven pairs of android eyes found the front doors, and their metal feet stomped toward the exit.

10

ANOTHER ELEVATOR OPENED, AND THREE MORE MODEL One androids stomped out. That made ten in total.

Jackson shifted backward until his body shielded mine. He reached behind himself until his fingertips found my body.

His anger forgotten, Kyle pressed himself against the wall, eyes wide and shoulders tense—a mirror of everyone else in the lobby.

Behind reception, Raul ducked under the desk. A man and a woman on their way to the parking garage elevators broke into a run. Several others in the lobby area froze. Their gazes darted to the exits.

"Stop them!" Dr. Sophie screamed again.

In shining metal, the Model Ones clomped toward the front doors, their postures erect, their red eyes staring straight ahead. We all knew about the programming loop-holes that had made them dangerous—about how they'd attacked people over the past weeks, and how the cause of their exodus hadn't yet been identified.

A robot on the fritz was not something any of us wanted to confront.

Two women stood directly in their path. One woman grabbed the other and yanked her out of the way. Both went tumbling to the floor. On their hands and knees, they scrambled to clear a wide berth around the androids.

Jackson shifted to the far side of the elevator bay, opposite the main entrance and opposite the direction the androids were stomping. He pushed me with him. His hand never left contact with me.

"We can't let them leave," I said.

Jackson tensed. He swiveled toward the exit and back toward me. He wanted to protect me, but I wasn't defenseless. It was everyone else who needed help. We ran at the androids.

I followed a step behind him. We skidded past the Model Ones and spun to face them. Now, the robots had to get through us to leave this building.

The nearest ones stopped, squared up, and the others kept marching until they fell in line. Ten androids versus two humans. We might have a few upgrades on our side, but I didn't love our odds.

"Are you sure about this?" Jackson said under his breath.

"You got a better plan?" Nothing good ever happened at CyberCorp Tower.

My father showed up at my side a second later. He squeezed my hand and straightened his shoulders to face the androids. "Marissa," he called to my mom, "what's your status?"

Mom stood on the other side of the robots with Dr. Sophie and two engineers I didn't know. All four of them gestured frantically in the air, typing and swiping at virtual controls that would be visible through the EyeNet.

"They're not obeying instructions!" my mom shouted back.

"No shit," Jackson mumbled at my side.

Dad shot a glare his way, and Jackson clammed up.

Taking the cue, the two women who had dodged out of the way now scrambled to their feet and stood in line with Jackson and me. Their terror was plain in their wide eyes and trembling hands, but they stood their ground.

Three other men stood beside Jackson. Now, we were up to eight.

Eight humans. Ten androids. Extremely shitty odds.

Tension pulled every muscle in my body tight to the edge of snapping as the androids stared at us with eerie red eyes.

I tapped my dad's leg with the back of my hand, keeping my attention straight forward. "Why aren't they moving?"

"Marissa!" he shouted again.

"We're doing the best we can," she called back. "Do not let them out."

Dr. Sophie propelled herself past the Model Ones and skidded into line with the resistance.

The androids moved.

They marched straight at us. Their metal feet clanged

in unison against the tile floor. Jackson lunged forward and grabbed the nearest robot by the arm, spun a circle, and hurled it to the side. It hit the tile floor with a clank, and metal cracked under its weight. The android skidded and bounced across the alley between the androids and humans.

The others kept coming. Jackson circled back and grabbed another android from behind before tossing it over his head. It landed on top of the other one in a crunch of metal on metal.

I followed his lead and grabbed one above the elbow with my left hand. I spun in a circle and used the momentum to toss the android back the way it came. It hit the floor with a satisfying crunch.

The CyberCorp employees in line with us inched forward. Between them, two women grabbed both arms of a Model One and hauled it away from the front doors. It shook them off and sent them tumbling to the floor. Each woman clutched a robot leg, and it dragged them toward the door with each step.

When the androids reached the line of humans, they tossed them aside like rag dolls. One shoved an older man out of the way, and he landed on his butt. Pain pinched his features. The elevator doors opened again, and two security guards rushed out.

"Don't let them leave," one shouted. "They're dangerous."

"What does he think we're doing?" Jackson said as he brought both hands down in a clasped fist on a metal skull. It crunched inward. The android slumped and lay still.

The one Jackson had tossed earlier clanked to its feet. With one hand, it grabbed its other arm and straightened the bent metal, which crunched into place. Its red eyes clicked toward Dr. Sophie, and it marched forward.

Dr. Sophie straightened to her full height of five-feet-nothing. She ran forward and hit the ground in a slide, feet forward. She hit the android's legs and rolled to the side as it toppled over and slammed into the tile. Its face crunched on contact.

I punched through the chest of the nearest robot and ripped out its battery cell. It slumped to the floor. I rotated and grabbed another robot before wrenching its arm from the socket.

More androids clanked off the elevators and marched toward the front doors. I lost count of how many. Thankfully, they were more interested in getting out of here than in hurting people.

"Lock this place down!" my mom shouted.

"If you plan to leave this building . . ." My father's voice boomed across the lobby. "Do it now. We are closing the safety doors."

"Safety doors?" Jackson asked. He used both arms to shove two androids to the ground and hurried past me to help other people struggling to slow the robots.

I didn't answer him because I didn't know what that meant.

Most of the robots we knocked down got right back up. A few had made it out the doors, and I shuddered to think what they'd do out there. Out of control. Unsupervised.

"I said *out*," my dad bellowed.

Except for Dr. Sophie and one man I didn't know, the other employees helping us left their posts and ran toward the doors. The man beside me stood his ground, but his gaze trailed after the others disappearing through the doors.

"Go," I shouted.

He hesitated only a second more before turning and darting to the exit. Jackson and I grabbed the androids nearest to him, and he made it through the door with long, quick strides.

A series of loud beeps filled the room, and red lighting emanated around the doorway. A metal barricade emerged from the ceiling above the glass front doors and rolled downward. The beeping continued as the safety door inched downward.

It clanked to the tile floor, sealing us inside.

11

Everyone froze—both androids and humans. Most people on this building level had made it out in time. The only ones remaining were my parents, a few security guards, me, Jackson, Dr. Sophie, and an engineer who was now staring at the sealed exit as if he regretted all his choices.

I did too.

After two seconds of silence, metal screamed as Jackson ripped an android's arm from its socket. He tossed it aside with a satisfied smirk on his face.

The androids leapt back into motion. They scattered.

Two darted into an open elevator that would lead down to the VIP garage. Several more hurried back toward the main elevators. The rest bolted for the two fire exits around the lobby.

Since I was one of the few people here with access to the VIP garage, I darted after the two who went that way.

The elevator doors slammed before I got there. I scanned my wrist at the black panel between the two sets of doors, and the scanner beeped its approval. The other pair of doors opened, and I stepped inside.

As the doors closed, Jackson raced toward me, waving at me to wait.

"Help the others," I shouted as the elevator closed me inside.

Inside the cab, the letter *L* displayed on each wall to indicate I was at the lobby level. As the cab moved, the letter blinked out, replaced by the letters *VP* for the VIP parking garage. I leaned forward, anticipating the doors opening so I could shoot out and stop the Model Ones.

Instead, the light blanked out. The elevator went inky black. My chest constricted and went icy cold.

"This is the security office." Inside the cab, a male voice sounded loud and clear through hidden speakers connected to the announcement system. "We've cut the main power to shut down the Model One server, but that also powers most of the building. Backup power should go on in a few seconds and will carry most building operations."

*Most?* I crept to the back of the elevator and leaned against the wall. Its smooth metal gave little comfort to my pounding heart and trembling fingertips in the face of potentially being trapped in a dark elevator.

Hardly anyone used the VIP garage, especially after hours. I could be stuck here overnight if it wasn't part of that *most*.

Deep inhale through the nose. I was fine. If the backup

power didn't feed the elevator, I could just wrench the doors open. Out through the mouth.

"Without the server," the voice continued, "we understand the androids will keep running on their own for only three minutes. Your safety is our number-one concern, so please stay clear of them until they shut down."

Dim lights came on overhead, and the letters *VP* reappeared on the wall. My breath popped out in relieved laughter as the elevator slid open. I stepped into the VIP parking garage.

This exclusive space could house only fifty cars at a time. Right now, only four vehicles filled the slots. None of them were mine since I had accompanied Briana to the guest lot after our little fender bender.

Normally, the garage was brightly lit with pot lights set into a white ceiling lined by white walls. For anywhere else, white would be an odd choice for a garage, but CyberCorp always kept the surfaces sparkling clean.

I slowed as I stepped into the space. The dim lighting resulting from the use of backup power cast my shadow long against the floor, and no one bustled through the space in a hurry to get to work or home.

The gong of metal against the concrete floor drew my attention toward the vehicle exit. Two Model Ones faced away from me and toward the large metal door that blocked the exit, just like in the lobby.

One of the two raised both fists and pounded against the safety door.

Bang. Bang, bang.

When it pulled back its fists, the dents were barely noticeable. That safety door was no joke.

"Hey!" I shouted.

One android stopped long enough to cut its red glare at me.

"Hey!"

I ran at them, grabbed one around the waist, and yanked it away from the door. As it skidded backward, its feet slid against concrete in a metal scream that pinched my eardrums.

The android spun to face me, and the one examining the bottom of the safety door straightened and turned my way. Two pairs of red eyes bored into me from both sides.

Maybe I didn't think this through.

My hand-screen vibrated, and an upbeat tune spilled out of my jacket. *Now* the thing wanted to work, when I was otherwise occupied. I inched backward. Neither Model One moved, and my hand-screen continued its party in my pocket. After thirty seconds, the ringing stopped.

Their red eyes clicked closed and open again.

I never understood why my parents felt the need to give them eyelids that blinked. It didn't make them look more human. Completely the opposite, in fact.

My hand-screen started vibrating again, emitting inappropriately cheerful music. Both androids flicked their gazes down to my pocket.

"Answer call," I said, my voice low and steady, my knees bent and ready to move. "I'm kind of busy. Whoever this is, can I call you back?"

"What are the androids doing?" It was Jackson's voice.

"Trying to escape."

"Are you sure?"

In my peripheral vision, the android to my right took two steps closer. I mirrored it with two steps backward to keep both Model Ones in my field of view. "What else would they be doing?"

"I followed a few to one of the fire exits. They seem more interested in playing with me than leaving." In the background, metal crunched, and Jackson grunted. "Just watch them."

I stood still as one android returned to banging its fists against the door. They didn't try to raise it. They didn't claw at it or even work together. That one just continued its rhythmic pounding, which did nothing more than dent the reinforced metal, while the other watched me from the opposite side.

On Jackson's end of the line, I heard the same steady banging.

They were top-of-line artificial intelligence. Couldn't they see they needed to try something else?

The android opposite the door lunged at me. I flung my left arm out like a clothesline and nailed it in the chest before flinging it back the way it came. The android flew backward and landed on its back. Its metal skull slammed against the floor.

It lay there for only a second and then sprang back to its feet.

The other one continued banging on the door.

"I'll admit it's not their best effort," I said to Jackson,

who was still on the line. "They've got me two on one, but they're not taking advantage. Maybe they're just not as smart as humans."

He grunted.

The android came at me again. I swung my left arm at its center of mass, aiming to yank out its power cell. It threw itself to the floor under my blow, skidded across the concrete floor, and bounded to its feet with the grace of an animal. When I followed and threw another punch, my opponent ducked away.

We continued our dance of punching and dodging while the other android pounded against the safety door.

Bang. Bang. Bang.

"I see your point," I said, out of breath from chasing the robot around the garage.

At once, the lights dimmed in both of my androids' eyes, and they crashed to the floor. Through my hand-screen speaker, I heard the crash of the robots going down near Jackson too. Their three minutes were up.

"That was a little anti-climactic," I said.

He didn't answer, and fear tightened my chest.

"Jackson?" My voice trembled. He was fine. He was always fine. Right? "Jackson!"

"I'm here. That was over three minutes. More like six."

"They only operate for three minutes after losing connection with the server. That's a hard-wired safeguard —remember?"

"Maybe they *didn't* lose connection with the server. Wouldn't CyberCorp's most valuable machine be connected to backup power?"

"Good point. So what, then? They shut down because they got bored?"

"How should I know? All I know is that was longer than three—"

The voice of my mother's assistant, Missy, filled the garage through the announcement system. "The crisis has been handled for now. We expect the building to be locked down for at least an hour while we ensure there will be no repeats of what just happened. There is no need for alarm. Thank you so much for your cooperation." The announcement ended.

I slipped my hand-screen from my pocket and spoke directly into it. "I'm heading back up to the lobby."

"See you there." Jackson disconnected.

A minute later, I was back on the first floor. Androids littered the tile near the exits and elevators—mostly intact but crumpled to the ground in heaps.

Jackson ran toward me and wrapped me in his arms. "You okay?"

I nodded against his chest and then pulled him toward my father, who stood near the reception desk. He'd shed his suit jacket and now wore his pale-blue shirt open at the collar. As we approached, another man joined him. He held what looked like a solid metal briefcase with a handle but no way to open it. The two of them knelt over a fallen android.

Dad pointed at the android while speaking to the other man, who knelt and unspooled a cable from the side of his briefcase device. He plugged the other end into a socket in the android's side.

As we approached, Dad straightened and held out an arm to me.

I ducked under it and accepted a squeeze around the shoulders. "What's going on?"

He cast me a tired smile. "Just a scare. Nothing to worry about."

"When are the doors opening?"

He released me and gestured toward the engineer he'd just been speaking to, who now had the cable hooked up between his briefcase device and the Model One and was monitoring a display on the side of the briefcase. "It may be a couple hours. As a precaution, we're draining the power from them just to make sure they don't go psycho again. Then we'll turn the main power back on and open the doors."

"Why leave the power off?" Jackson asked. When my dad looked at him, he added, "They kept going for six minutes, sir. The server must be on backup power."

"They did indeed," my dad said. "Security cut the power without consulting me, but the server is *obviously*"— he shot an irritated look in the direction of the security office—"connected to our backup generators. The androids kept going until I got down to the server room and instructed the server to stop them."

I nudged the nearest android with my toe. "I was kind of too busy to count the time."

Jackson stood straighter. "Can we do anything to help?"

"You've done a lot already." Dad patted him on the shoulder. "Just sit tight until we've drained all their power. Then it will be safe to retract the safety doors, and we can all go home. If it keeps our security team and everybody else calm to leave the power off for another couple of hours in the meantime, then so be it."

"Dad, there's something I want to talk to you about." I gestured with my head to an empty corner where the technician wouldn't overhear. Ron's accusation was probably total nonsense, and the last thing my dad needed was gossip among his employees.

He raised his brows, his eyelids drooping underneath them. "Can it wait?" Three more people with briefcase-style battery packs stepped out of the elevator bay, and my dad raised a hand to get their attention.

"Sure," I said.

He rubbed my shoulder and then started toward the technicians.

Soon enough, we'd be out of here, and my father and I could have a long chat about Ron. For now, all of that could wait—I hoped.

12

LIV AND HUNTER HAD LAID LOW THROUGH THE MODEL One escape attempt, and I'd lost track of Briana too. I couldn't blame them. Unlike Jackson and me, they didn't have upgrades that allowed for head-to-head standoffs with androids.

Jackson and I found comfortable chairs in the lobby, out of the way of the engineers draining power from the Model Ones all over the main level of CyberCorp Tower.

Like the rest of the lobby, the sitting area was sleek and cold, with club chairs made of plush black leather and feet in ebony-stained wood. The three chairs faced a coffee table that looked like a long sheet of glass folded in thirds, with one third resting on the floor and the opposite third forming the top surface. More artistic than functional. Across the table stood a bench with the same dark wood accents as the chairs.

I slipped my hand-screen from my pocket. "Could you call Bri?" I asked Jackson. "I'm going to try Liv."

He stood and tapped his micro-comm before moving several feet away so we could make our calls in peace.

"Call Liv," I told my device. The display went white except for a circle rotating in the center with the word *CONNECTING* under it. I raised my left fist, as if that would scare it into working again.

The circle was still rotating when Jackson popped back into my view. "Bri is fine. She wants to be left alone, and she doesn't want to see Claire again." He peeked over my shoulder. "No luck?"

I bared my teeth at it.

He tapped his micro-comm. "Call Olivia." I couldn't hear the line ring, but his gaze shifted into space as he waited for her to pick up. After a moment, he tapped his micro again. "No answer. Give her some time. She and Bri are kind of in the same deal."

True. If I'd been dating a killer, I would probably need some alone time after facing them too. I sat in one of the chairs, which was just as uncomfortable as it looked.

Jackson perched on the armrest, slinging one long arm behind me. "How are *you*?"

Instinctively, I leaned my head against his shoulder. As usual, he smelled of his spicy vanilla cologne. Once upon a time, I found it obnoxious, but now it was just Jackson. "I'm good. You?"

He offered me an overly wide grin. "I'm invincible, remember?" His eyes glazed over as his attention shifted to a voice in his ear. "Hold on. Claire is calling." He tapped his micro. "Everything okay up there?"

He flinched away from the side of his head where he wore the micro, and his eyes clenched.

"Please don't shout." He sat up straighter. "When? Why?"

More shouting—I assumed—from Claire's end because Jackson continued to cringe.

I kept a bored expression. Under no circumstances was I allowed to care about Claire. We'd been friends all of high school, but that ended when she killed someone. I'd taken the first exit on the fast track from our friendship, and I was determined to stay that way.

Jackson bolted to his feet.

I tensed but stayed seated.

"Ron is in Claire's room—something about needing to consolidate security."

"And that's our problem?" I pushed all the boredom I could manage into my tone.

"Claire is our friend."

I scrunched my face.

"So that's what you do? You just turn off feelings when the people you love make mistakes? Is that what you did with me?"

I jumped to my feet. "*Mistakes?* Jacks, she killed someone. A teenager like us with an actual life and an actual family and friends—Paris is in the ground somewhere."

"You think Claire did that on purpose?"

"I think Claire was angry, and she *chose* to reprogram a

bunch of Model Ones to attack people to make her problems go away."

"This isn't who you are. You're not someone who hates people for their mistakes."

"Maybe it is."

"It isn't. You're hard-headed and a little naive about your own privilege, but—"

"I'm—"

He held up a hand. "I know you're working on that. Let me finish."

I clamped my mouth shut.

"You care about people. You're empathetic, and that's why you're so mad at Claire. She hurt someone, and you hate for people to be hurt. But remember when you first got this arm, and everyone was weird about it in school *except* Claire—and Liv?"

Hunter too, but Jackson wasn't about to give Hunter credit for anything since Hunter and I had spurred a little romance right after Jackson and I broke up.

Jackson continued. "You accidentally hurt Harmony in the cafeteria, and Melody was furious. Claire was the one trying to convince her that you were still *you* and hadn't meant to hurt anyone."

I grumbled something that was more of a sound than actual words.

"You don't let people hurt on purpose. It's one thing I love about you. Right now, Claire needs your help. You have authority in this building. You can use it to give Claire some peace by getting her separated from Ron, or else *she* is the one who'll be hurt."

"Maybe she doesn't deserve peace."

I could see the calculations running behind his eyes. When he blew out, his next words tumbled over one another in a jumbled rush. "You made a choice to turn off your auto-drive months ago instead of just letting your car take you home. If you hadn't done that, we wouldn't have been in the car accident . . ."

"Harmony wouldn't have died." My breath stuck in my throat. "Claire wouldn't have been angry with me, so she never would have reprogrammed the Model Ones. Paris wouldn't have died either."

He knelt on the floor in front of me. "We make choices without knowing the future. We *have* to—that's life. You struggled with whether this was all your fault and decided, correctly, that it wasn't. All I'm asking is that you offer Claire that same grace. Years of friendship didn't suddenly disappear because she made an awful choice that led to an even more awful consequence."

My resolve was breaking down. "*Really* awful."

"Absolutely, but who can she count on right now?"

I pushed myself out of the chair.

"Good girl." Jackson got up from the floor and shot me his megawatt grin. "Do I get that kiss now?"

"Don't push it." I rolled my eyes and marched toward the elevators. My conscience was full to the brim with guilt that I hadn't earned. Maybe helping Claire could lighten the load.

When we reached conference room 57J, I waved my wrist at the scanner, and the metal door slid open. Claire's security guard took a step forward when we walked in, recognized us, and retreated back against the wall.

The room was over twenty feet long, with a table that extended across most of it. Ron sat on one end, his elbows propped on the surface and his chin in his hands. He stared across the room at Claire with a smirk on his smug face. Claire sat on the other end, closer to us and the door. She had her chair rotated away from him and arms folded across her stomach.

She jumped to her feet as we came in. "They can't keep me with him."

Ron's smirk got deeper, but other than that, he didn't move. Jackson took two steps in that direction, and the smirk washed away. Ron rolled his chair backward until it hit the wall—the farthest point he could get from Jackson.

I pulled myself to my full height of five-feet-five and faced the guard. "Where's Ron's security? Why was he brought here?"

"I'm just following instructions, ma'am." The guard's face remained impassive. "We're short-staffed because it's after hours, and Stan was called away to deal with some scuffles. Tensions are high, and we don't have the personnel to assign one guard for each of them."

I pointed at Claire. "She accidentally caused someone's death because he"—I pointed at Ron—"killed her best friend. Do you think these two have any business being in the room together? Do you want to be responsible for what happens when they're stuck together?"

The man's gaze flicked between Claire and Ron. "Like I

said, I'm just following instructions. We're all doing the best we can."

Claire bounded the few steps toward us. The security guard tensed.

"You can't leave me in here with him." Claire pulled to an abrupt stop. She glanced from the security guard to me. "He's a murderer. Your job is to protect me."

The man's mouth twitched as he glanced back and forth between Claire and Ron. As far as he was concerned, they were both murderers.

I stepped between them. "How about this? Most doors in this building can be locked from the inside or the outside. How about you keep protecting Claire, and we find a room for Ron that he can lock from the inside and we can lock from the outside? That way, everyone feels safe. When the safety doors open, we can all go home."

"Maybe I don't want to be imprisoned," Ron said, his tone bored.

"Maybe you prefer to be uncooperative," I snapped without even looking at him.

"Perhaps," he said.

I stormed to his side of the room and bent over his chair. "Do you know how many people in this building would love to make you pay?"

He shrugged.

I jabbed a finger toward Claire. "Who do you think would be first in line to take you out if given the opportunity?"

Claire raised her hand. "She's not wrong."

Jackson raised his hand too. "Second."

Ron looked Jackson up and down and sank deeper into his chair.

I returned to the guard. "It doesn't matter what Ron wants anyway. Your job is to keep them safe. You can't protect them from each other when they're in the same room."

The guard nodded. "Claire, you'll come with me to another room. We'll lock this one from the outside." To Ron, he added, "Lock it from the inside too if you feel safer that way."

Claire let out a stream of breath, and her shoulders dropped as she released that tension.

The security guard grabbed Claire's elbow and led her to the door. The steel door opened as they approached, but she dug in her heels and turned back to me.

"Did Bri make it out?"

"I'm not sure."

"If not and if you hear from her, can you ask her to come see me?"

"You're asking a lot of me," I said, "and of her."

"I know, but if you see her . . ."

The guard led her from the room. The steel door lingered open since Jackson and I were close behind them. Ron had already proven I couldn't squeeze the truth out of him. Maybe it would come out when he went to trial.

Jackson stepped into the hallway first, and I followed.

"We didn't finish our conversation," Ron called after me.

I let the door slam closed. As far as I was concerned, Ron Franklin could rot.

13

"Lobby," I told the elevator as Jackson and I stepped onto it after leaving Claire and Ron. "Let's ask my dad for an update."

"Attention." Missy, my mother's assistant, spoke through the speakers inside the elevator cab. "We're all eager to get out of here. Unfortunately, it's going to be a little longer." She paused, and then, "Most of the catering staff has gone home, but we placed food for all of you at the reception desk. It's not much, but it's something."

"So we're stuck here for—" I started.

"We've granted authorization to access floor sixty to everyone in the building with an ID chip," the announcement continued. "There, you'll find chairs, couches, and blankets. Get comfortable."

Jackson and I stared at the ceiling, waiting for more—as in an actual timeline on when we could leave. It didn't come.

I cursed.

Jackson wrapped an arm around my waist and squeezed.

The elevator doors opened, and we stepped onto the tile floor of the lobby. Immediately, the smell of roasted meat and baked bread filled my nose, and my stomach growled.

As promised, an array of food sat on the reception desk. It wasn't the meager portions Missy had promised in her announcement. Two white-coated chefs stood on either side. Between them, ceramic trays of food filled the desk, loaded high with roast chicken, smoked salmon, rolls, salad, and a tiered display of desserts.

"Hungry?" Jackson asked.

"Pretty sure it's meant to appease the masses because we're not going anywhere anytime soon."

"Yeah, but are you hungry?"

I yanked my hand-screen from my pocket and checked the display. No new calls or messages. But it was possible someone had tried to reach me, and no messages were coming through.

"Any word from Bri, Liv, or Hunter?" I asked Jackson.

"Nope."

"Are you having any trouble with your micro? I think my hand-screen is still acting up."

Jackson tapped the back of his ear. "Status?" His eyes glazed over for a few seconds as the device responded at a volume too low for me to hear. "Operating within normal parameters. Maybe we should head back to tech support. We've got nothing better to do."

We did an about-face and got back onto the elevator. A moment later, it spat us out on the twenty-sixth floor.

Like the other floors, this one was on backup power. Strip lights lining the ceiling and floor illuminated our path. The pot lights overhead stayed dark.

When we reached tech support, Francis once again had his feet on the desk. He swiped his hand across the air in front of him, his gaze glued to something I couldn't see—probably data in the virtual world.

I strode into the office and waved so he'd notice us.

His attention lingered on his work and finally flicked toward me. "What can I do for you, Miss Hayes?" He stood and pointed at the hand-screen clutched in my grasp.

I slapped the device into his outstretched palm. "Same as before."

"Still acting up?"

I nodded.

"What about you?" he asked Jackson. "Any problems?"

"My micro is fine."

"Of course it is. The building's internal network is built for micro-comms." He turned the hand-screen over in his grip. "They send all communications through the EyeNet, so we don't have the same security guidelines as we do for old hand-screens to enforce our closed network."

I huffed at the word *old*.

"Closed network?" Jackson asked.

"Corporate devices can only connect to other corporate devices and can't transmit data from inside the Tower to off-premises." He gestured at my hand-screen. "Certain external devices can transmit whatever they want—we can't stop that—but we prohibit our internal corporate devices from connecting to them wirelessly. With micro-comms, it's easy to enforce because they have to transmit data over the EyeNet, which strips out anything suspicious anyway."

"So the security policy is stricter when I connect to this network," I added for Jackson's benefit, "as opposed to someone using a micro-comm."

"That may or may not be the problem, though." Francis tilted his head and peered at me down his nose. "It usually works fine?"

"Until today. Can you fix it?"

"I can fix anything." He connected the device to his vid-screen. His fingers danced through the air as he navigated to menus I'd never seen. He squinted at scrolling text on his vid and touched his way through a series of commands too fast for me to follow. "A file transfer is monopolizing your processor and memory. Did you try to download something? It looks like a large file—perhaps a virus."

"I know better than to download data from unknown sources."

"Right, of course. Unfortunately, I'm slammed right now. You can imagine all the things that go wrong in this building now that we're suddenly running on insufficient power." Francis reached for the small plastic box on the other end of his desk and slid it in my direction.

Inside, a tiny micro-comm sat nestled on a felt pillow.

"Take the loaner. I'll try to get your hand-screen managed before the doors open."

I swiped it up, unboxed it, and pressed it behind my ear. It beeped to let me know it had detected my ID chip and synced. "Only in case I get desperate before I get out of here. My hand-screen works fine when I'm not in this building." I gestured for him to pass the hand-screen back.

He shrugged but did so.

We left Francis to his work.

"Any word from Briana?" I ask Jackson as we waited for our elevator. "She probably can't reach me even if she's trying."

Jackson tapped the back of his ear to activate his micro. "Call Briana." Seconds later, he tapped again to disconnect and shook his head.

The elevator doors slid open, and we stepped inside.

"Lobby." I chewed my lower lip as the doors shut. "Maybe she got out."

"I'm sure that's it. She probably cut out of here and as far away from Claire as possible."

"Good point." My mood brightened. "So what do we do until we're released from this hellhole?"

In the lobby, low murmurs of chatter met us on the right, where people had grabbed food and made themselves comfortable on the floor or in seating areas.

Jackson pointed to the other side of the main floor, which held doors to the facilities offices, security, and the giant underground room for the Model One server, hidden in plain sight behind a door labeled *Supplies*.

My dad and a man in brown coveralls exited the server room. My father gestured wildly at the man. His arm repeatedly jerked toward the room they'd just left. The other man nodded, eyes wide as if caught in a crosshair.

Jackson approached them with his best-behavior face on. "Everything all right, sir?" He straightened up to his full height, taller than both the other men.

"Just a little misunderstanding. Everything's good, son." My dad sidestepped us as if to move past. "Nothing security can't handle."

The electrician followed right behind him, his toes catching the heel of my dad's shoe. "I was hired to be here. I can send you the paperwork." He tapped his micro-comm. "Send—"

"That won't be necessary." Dad spun to glare at him before ducking to swipe at a brand-new scuff on his heel.

The man tapped his micro again and then raised both hands in the air.

My dad straightened up. "As I said, we don't hire outside electricians. Don't you think we have the manpower? We have PhDs doing our electrical work." He gestured upward to the building and its atrium ceiling sixty floors above it.

The other man's eyes narrowed. "Please accept my apologies for the confusion. I'll make sure any future work orders from CyberCorp are ignored, and I'll be on my way as soon as I'm able."

"There won't be any future work orders—certainly not any instructions to increase the power outage to . . ." He closed his eyes, and when he opened them, his tone was more level. "I suggest you check your system to ensure it's operating properly because we never sent you a work order."

"Yes, sir, and I suggest you check *your* system because I wouldn't have made it through that door without authorization via the work order." The two men glared at each other.

"Hey." I slid between them before they started pummeling each other. "Why don't you get some food since you're here?" I faced the electrician and gestured toward the huge spread on the opposite side of the floor.

He tore his glare from my father, and it morphed into wide-eyed delight as he spotted the food. With a final nod, he took off in that direction.

"Can you give us a minute?" I asked Jackson with a pointed look. Now that I finally had my dad alone, we could talk.

Jackson squeezed my shoulder and strolled after the electrician.

I grabbed my dad's arm and urged him a few steps in the other direction. "We're all a little tense."

He breathed out, and his chest seemed to deflate as his shoulders slumped.

Jackson waggled his brows at me as a reminder—as if I could forget Ron's accusation.

"Can I ask you something?" I said.

His gaze followed the electrician to the massive stacks of food. His stomach rumbled so loudly that he tried to use his hand to cover it. He had too much on his mind already.

"Have you eaten?"

"No time." He tapped his ear, and his attention shifted

to blank space over my head. "Message security: double-check access to the server room and other secure areas." He tapped his micro again.

My father scrubbed a hand through his hair, leaving the front sticking straight up. "What was it you needed? Oh, hold on." He tapped his ear again. "Message financial: make sure that outside electrician is paid for his time." Another tap, and then his attention was back on me. His gaze was expectant but tired.

Ron was a liar, and this conversation was bullshit. "It can wait."

He kissed me on the forehead and hurried away. As usual, when he strode away, his back was straight and his gait confident. He was the same dad I'd always known, hardworking and full of integrity.

But I couldn't get rid of the nervousness churning in my gut.

14

Jackson tapped his micro. "Call Briana." His eyes glassed over. After half a minute, he tapped his ear again and shook his head. "It's going straight to messaging."

He and I had found a sitting area in the lobby to regroup, and *regrouping* literally meant locating all members of the group. I hadn't set eyes on Liv, Hunter, or Briana since the Model Ones went crazy, and I hoped hearing from them would slow the churning in my gut.

My conscience was stacked full of bodies, and I couldn't handle any more.

"Should we be worried?" I asked.

"Not yet. Bri might have made it out of the building before the craziness, and maybe Vanessa has seen Liv and Hunter."

Behind the reception desk, both receptionists sat slumped in their seats. Vanessa's head tilted downward. It was late at night now, and usually, the reception desk would have been long since abandoned. Between the Model One crisis and this lockdown, though, it didn't look like any of us were going anywhere.

"How are you holding up?" I asked Vanessa as we approached.

She straightened up so quickly that she almost toppled her chair, grabbing the armrests to steady it. Her gaze darted around the space as if taking stock of her surroundings before settling on me. "As well as expected, I guess."

"Have you seen Briana? She came in with me earlier—short, white, with long brown hair in a braid." I gestured to show the length of her hair.

"I can't say I've been my best. I'm usually in bed with a book by now. Even if she came past here, I'm not sure I would have noticed." Her eyes drooped as she spoke, and her words slowed toward the end of the sentence.

"Then I don't suppose you've seen my other friend Olivia either, or a guy who might have been with her?"

She shook her head.

"Can I get you a coffee or something?"

"That's kind, but no. God willing, they'll be opening the doors any minute." She sat up straighter and looked toward the front door. "The last thing I want is to be hyped up on caffeine when I finally get to bed. I'm calling in sick on Monday." She lowered her voice. "Don't tell your parents I said that. Okay?"

"Your secret's safe with me." I started to walk away, but Jackson stepped around me.

"You don't have access to the internal security cameras or chip scanners from here, do you?" he asked Vanessa. "Could you check on our friends?"

"Only for the lobby." She tapped the vid-screen in front of her. "No one named Briana, Olivia, or Hunter is on this floor. All the chips on this level are linked with known identities"—she pointed at me—"including you. Your friend Jackson is registered from previous visits . . . and as a medical test subject." She peered up at him, as if trying to guess which of his body parts CyberCorp had replaced.

"Can you put out a call for them over the announcement system?" he asked, ignoring her obvious curiosity.

"I *can*, in theory, but I'm only allowed to do that in an emergency." She shifted her attention to me. "Is this an emergency?"

Jackson shrugged and glanced at me too.

"Maybe not yet. I'll let you know."

We turned away from Vanessa.

"So now what?" I asked Jackson.

"We could look for them on our own."

"Across seventy-two stories? It would be easier to ask my parents to locate their ID chips."

"I think your mom and dad have higher priorities right now."

As far as I could tell by the state of personnel still carrying around their battery briefcases, the engineers weren't even close to finishing their chore of draining power from the Model Ones. The first engineer I'd seen with a case had moved to a different spot on the floor. The plug from his oversized battery was inserted into another android, and he knelt over the prone metal body.

Around the massive lobby, one other engineer had a battery connected to a robot, draining its power. There were maybe twenty Model Ones on this floor, but up on the seventieth, there must have been a hundred—all needing their batteries drained.

"In that case, we should get comfortable. I—" My hand-screen buzzed, and I ripped it from its pocket. "Finally, some decent reception."

I had a new message from Claire: *Where are you? I need you!* I tilted the hand-screen toward Jackson to show him.

Without waiting for debate, Jackson tugged my arm and hurried toward the elevators that led up the Tower.

I scanned my wrist at the panel. "We're really just going to jump because she said so?"

The scanner beeped in recognition. A few seconds later, a pair of elevator doors opened.

"She's our friend," Jackson said. "Fifty-seven," he told the elevator. "She didn't stop being our friend when she made a mistake." He pressed a finger to my lips to keep me from rehashing our debate of earlier.

I swept his finger away but stayed silent. We both knew where we stood on the Claire issue.

When the doors opened on the fifty-seventh floor, I was the first to step out and led the way to conference room 57J. But when we reached it, the door didn't slide open for my ID chip. Instead, it issued a sharp buzz.

I waved my wrist again, and again the scanner buzzed.

"Right," I said more to myself than to Jackson. "Ron is secured in there now, so Claire must be in his old room."

"Lead the way."

We took the stairs up one floor. When we reach the room that had originally been Ron's, I waved my wrist in front of the small access panel. The door beeped happily and slid open.

Shouts greeted us.

Kyle Winter, Paris's brother, had Claire pressed against the wall. His sunken eyes glared at her, the whites completely hidden under slitted lids. Dampness pasted his dark-blond hair to his forehead, giving him a wild look.

Several feet away, the security guard who was supposed to be watching Claire held both hands in the air. His wide eyes stared, but he made no move to intervene.

Kyle had one forearm pushed against Claire's neck while the other hand held a small metal pistol pointed at the guard. It looked like a child's toy, but that little electromagnetic pulse gun could take down anything with electric parts.

That meant *me*, and Jackson.

The guard's eyes bulged at the innocent-looking weapon.

My heart hammered. "Leave Claire out of this."

"She killed my sister!" He swung the weapon toward me.

"Kyle, hey." Jackson pointed at his own chest. "Eyes on me."

Kyle's attention snapped to Jackson, and he lowered the weapon a fraction of an inch. I dove toward him and raised my left arm to smack the pistol from his hand. My arm twitched and stuttered for a single second on the down-strike. It was enough time for Kyle to see me coming.

Jackson lunged toward the pistol. Kyle squeezed the trigger just as Jackson wrenched it out of his hand.

A spray of blue light snapped out from the pistol's barrel like a flash of lightning.

15

The guard slumped over.

I ran toward him, but relief painted his features. He wasn't hit. "I thought you were protecting her!" I shouted.

Claire crumpled into a ball. Tears streamed down her reddened face. "What the hell kind of protection is this?"

"I didn't sign on to risk my life for some teenage killer." The guard clutched his chest. "I have a pacemaker."

"Everybody, calm down," Jackson said. He grabbed the guard's shirt collar and hauled him to his feet. The guard patted Jackson's arm and nodded his appreciation. Jackson's wide eyes scanned my body until they locked on my face. "Are you okay?"

"What? Yeah, I'm fine." I sucked in a long breath. "I just need to find my calm. Fisher said I may see some hiccups for the next day, especially if I'm stressed."

Still holding the EMP gun in one hand, Jackson grabbed one of the other boy's arms and wrenched it behind his back, where it could do no more harm. "That blast didn't hit you?" Alarm crept into his voice. "Your primary chip?" He tapped the back of his own head.

I tried to reach behind my head to check on it, but my arm didn't move. It felt numb, heavy. I tried again, this time with my right. The chip felt the same as always, a hard device embedded under the skin at the base of my skull. "I think it's fine. He didn't hit me."

"Can you move your arm?"

I gritted my teeth and strained, but my left arm remained an inanimate chunk of metal attached to my shoulder.

In one smooth motion, Jackson shoved Kyle toward the guard and swept me into his arms. "Let's find Dr. Fisher."

"I can walk. My legs work fine." I tried to push free of him, but with my stronger arm useless, nothing happened.

"Maybe I want to carry you."

I glared at him until he obediently set my feet on the floor.

"I'm fine too. Thanks for asking." Claire brushed imaginary dirt off her clothing. "Get that psycho out of here." She jabbed a finger at Kyle.

"*I'm* the psycho?" he shouted.

The guard finally inserted himself between them.

"You kill my sister and call *me* a psycho. What are you even doing here?"

Claire glared at me. "Great question. What the hell am I doing here?" She stared at me and waited.

Three other pairs of eyes stared at me. "Seriously, how

should I know?" I waited for the guard to compose himself. "Can you secure him somewhere?"

Jackson shoved Kyle again, and Kyle stumbled into the guard's chest.

The guard clamped strong hands on Kyle's arms. "I could secure him in another room like I did for Ron Franklin, but this isn't jail. We don't have the right to hold someone just because we want to."

"Call it a citizen's arrest," I said. "He assaulted both of you." With my right, I pointed at the EMP gun in Jackson's hand. "That's a deadly weapon. Speaking of which, can you do something with it?" I grabbed the gun from Jackson and slipped it into the guard's pocket.

"That's my property," Kyle said. "It's company issue, and I'm authorized to use it."

The guard turned Kyle toward the door. "I'll return it when we're far away from these people." To me, he added, "I'll take him down to security to talk this out."

The two of them exited the room, and the metal door clanked shut behind them.

Claire abruptly turned toward me. "Get me out of this building."

"Now's not the time," Jackson said. "I need to get Lena to Dr. Fisher, but are you going to be okay?" While a few months ago, Jackson might have wrapped an arm around Claire's shoulders to comfort her, now he hung back, leaving a radius of space around her. Despite his words that we should offer her some empathy, even he hadn't made peace with her actions.

"I'm definitely *not*. Any word from Briana?"

"None," I said. "Maybe not hearing from her is a good sign, and she made it out before the lockdown."

"Or she's hiding from me. How long are we stuck here?"

"Who knows? A few minutes. Hours. Overnight. Your guess is as good as mine."

She groaned. "Can I at least get some food?"

"We're not your servers," Jackson said before I could say exactly the same thing. "We'll keep you safe"—he pointed at himself and then at me—"but we're not here to make you comfortable."

He stepped toward the door, which opened to make room for him.

Claire grasped my wrist before I could follow. "Get me out of here. You think Kyle is the only one in this building who wants to hurt me?" She leaned so close to me that I could smell a candy scent. "You're the reason I'm here. You owe me that."

I shook her off and stepped through the doorway. Steel slammed shut behind me.

---

"I promise you this isn't necessary," I said as Jackson carried me all the way to Fisher's office. "I said I'd go."

"You are literally the most difficult person I know." He deposited me in the open doorway, but his fingertips lingered on my waist, warm even through my shirt fabric.

Dr. Fisher rotated her chair toward us as he stepped to the door and set me on my feet. "Lena and friend." She offered us a wide grin. "I hate to seem so thrilled that you're stuck here, but I must admit that your company is better than what I'm doing." She nodded upward at the space over her head.

"You're not working on something in virtual?"

"It's been a long day, and I thought a little meditation couldn't hurt . . ."

I closed my eyes for a few seconds, willed the EyeNet forward, and then opened them just like she taught me. Although I didn't have EyeNet enabled contact lenses, the chip in my head could access its data and display any visuals straight to my eyeballs. Most of the time, I kept the feature disabled, but I could always enable it with a mental summons.

Usually, when I stepped into Dr. Fisher's room, she was using her white wall as a virtual vid-screen. Today, instead, a three-dimensional puzzle floated over her desk with the telltale shimmer indicating it was an EyeNet display.

"This is meditation?" I closed my eyes again. When I opened them, the puzzle was gone.

"It helps me relax." She gestured toward the two seats on the opposite side of her desk, and Jackson and I sat down. "Boring as anything, though. What can I do for you?"

"I'm fine, but—"

"She was shot with an EMP," Jackson said at the same time. "She is stubborn but not fine."

Dr. Fisher held up one hand. "Lena?"

"I'm fine!" I said again. When Fisher peered at me, one eyebrow raised, I sighed and added, "My arm is dead."

"Sit." She hurried to my side of her desk and knelt by my side.

She poked and prodded the synthetic skin. It was designed with pain receptors, so I felt her pokes, but I couldn't move my arm away. It was this odd, surreal feeling of being totally aware of what was happening but unable to react to it.

"You can't move it at all?"

I shook my head.

Jackson got right in her face. "She's going to be okay. Right?"

She ignored him. "You can't move it, but can you feel my touch?"

"Yes."

"That's great news. The primary chip in your head is operational, so this won't require major surgery. That's the one that connects your hardware and software to your nervous system and includes most of the interface programming."

"The problem is the secondary chip?"

"Luckily, the blast hit your arm—not your head. Also luckily, while the chip in your head is precisely customized to interface *you* with the system AI, the chip in your arm is the same hardware we use in the Model Two prototypes."

"Great! So we just—"

She held up a finger on her left and used her right hand to tap the micro-comm behind her ear. "Call the Model Two team." After a pause, she added, "Yes, hi, it's Athena. I'm going to need to steal an android's hardware for a Lena Hayes repair." She stood, circled the desk, and dropped into her chair. Then she nodded, even though the person on the other end of the line couldn't see her. "Send one down, please." She disconnected.

"While you're at it," Jackson said, shooting a glance at me, "Lena also had a bit of a stutter right before she got hit."

Dr. Fisher let out a long-suffering sigh. "As I told her earlier, it's important to stay calm as the AI calibrates."

"It's not my fault Kyle Winter went on a rampage," I muttered.

She huffed. "Even so."

An android's metal feet clomped into the room. The Model Two android was based on the Model One, except improved in every way. The curves looked more natural, more human, yet somehow more feline. The composite of metal and plastic was less rigid and more flexible, so it would hold up under greater pressure.

Most importantly, the range of the things it could learn was unbounded, just like me. My arm was based on the hardware and software of the Model Two, which was still in prototype.

Dr. Fisher jumped to her feet and met the android on my side of the desk. "Model Two," she said, "identify yourself."

"I am android M2B5." Its electronic voice came out in a monotone.

"Power down, B5."

The android's deep-red eyes went dull. Its head dropped forward, unconscious, although the body remained standing.

Dr. Fisher pointed at her desk. "Grab me an ejector key from the top drawer, would you?"

Jackson popped to his feet, hurried behind the desk, and opened the top drawer. He extracted a silver piece of metal with a circle on one end and a needle-thin cylinder on the other. When he held it up, Dr. Fisher nodded, and he placed it in her hand.

She circled to the Model Two and inserted the key behind its shoulder. When she tugged, the arm came off in her hand. "We don't weld the parts completely together during prototyping, because we do as much disassembling as assembling." She inserted the key just below the now-separated shoulder and tugged to remove the shoulder from the rest of the arm.

After a few more insertions and part-separations, she extracted a small chip about a centimeter on each side. Despite its nondescript, smooth black appearance, it was the brain behind the arm.

"Other than this chip, your arm is largely mechanical. Most of the intelligence is in your head, but we needed something in the arm itself for the chip in your head to communicate with."

"That's what the EMP fried," I concluded.

Dr. Fisher waved toward Jackson. "Grab me the scalpel in there."

Jackson fished in the desk's top drawer and came up with the scalpel. He slid it across the surface toward her.

Without flair, Dr. Fisher jammed the scalpel into my skin just under the elbow. Usually, to insert a cable, she made a small slit. This time, she dragged the scalpel around my entire arm, cutting a clean circle into it. I gritted my teeth the whole time.

Jackson settled into the other chair, stone-faced.

Fisher drew the blade up my arm to the shoulder. I wouldn't call it pain exactly, but I felt it. More than that, the sight of a blade stuck into my skin set me on edge. My muscles tensed.

"Try to relax," Fisher said.

When she pulled the scalpel away, the skin was already healing. She gripped an edge and pulled the synthetic skin down toward my forearm, leaving my shiny metal elbow revealed. It made a sucking sound as it pulled loose from the metal, leaving a sticky red goo behind.

Dr. Fisher raised the tiny pinhead of the ejector key. The last time I'd seen my arm without the skin, I could barely stand to look at it. Now I noticed the eight miniature holes circling the upper part just above the elbow. She inserted the end of the key into one hole and pressed.

She worked the ejector all the way around until my arm separated at the elbow. I'd wanted this arm removed since the moment I woke up with it attached. Now, half of it dropped away, and my body felt lighter.

Instead of relief, I felt only panic.

16

DR. FISHER CAUGHT MY DISCONNECTED LOWER ARM IN one hand.

My stomach turned. I felt nothing as she rooted around inside the device that used to be my arm. Jackson's warm fingers gripped my right hand, and I twisted to face him so I wouldn't have to look. I wouldn't have to see my disembodied arm in Dr. Fisher's grasp as if it was nothing more than another CyberCorp part.

I squeezed my eyes shut to hide the tears building. That inanimate metal device had saved me multiple times. Not just me—Dr. Fisher and some of my friends might not be alive if I didn't have this one-of-kind CyberCorp invention that I'd hated since the first instant.

I pulled in long inhales and willed myself to calm. This was temporary. The doc could fix it like she always did. Right?

"Your personal ID chip looks fine too, so I'm only

replacing the secondary chip for your arm." She snapped the arm back together, and the weight of it brought gravity slamming back where it belonged.

My eyes popped open.

"How's that?"

It felt amazing. It felt whole.

When I stretched and flexed it, the arm reacted like I'd been born with it. "Better." A long breath slithered out of me, drawing my stress and panic out with it. I hadn't realized how losing the function of my arm would terrify me, even for that brief span.

"Now let's deal with that other problem." Dr. Fisher yanked a cable from her desk and popped the end into the socket above my elbow. She inserted the other end of the cable into a small cube, an inch on each side, sitting on top of her desk.

She and Jackson turned their attention to the wall on the opposite side of the room. I knew from experience that the code executing inside my arm was scrolling across the screen in the virtual world.

I leaned back in my chair and let Dr. Fisher do her job.

She *mm*ed and *ah*ed as she watched the virtual display. She swiped her hand downward several times, which I knew made the code scroll faster. Occasionally, she would face her palm straight at the wall to make it stop moving.

"What's up?" I asked.

"Everything looks fine here." She popped the cable loose and rolled the skin back into place. "Still calibrating. We should talk more about your plans."

As the parts of my flesh came back into contact, the

edges melded together and sewed themselves shut. Just like that, I was as good as new.

"My plan is to never come back here."

"Your arm isn't connected to any of CyberCorp's servers. I can't access it unless you're here."

"We're done with our scheduled appointments."

She gestured toward the cable still hanging loose from her client cube. "As you can see, things arise, and occasional tinkering is necessary. That's the case with every piece of technology, and it's always going to be the case."

"I promise not to get hit by an EMP blast again."

She waved the scalpel in my face, and my stomach recoiled.

"I'll make it work."

"You just went paler than I am." In a singsong tone, she added, "It would be easier to stay away if you got rid of the synthetic skin."

"I'm not going to just walk around with a robotic arm."

"Technically," Jackson said, "it's robotic whether it's sheathed in skin or not."

"That's easy for you to say since you love being a bionic man."

"Bionic man." He grinned, showing all his teeth. "I like that."

I rolled my eyes. "The whole point of the skin is to blend in and not be the subject of attention—not be a poster girl for CyberCorp."

"Maybe," Dr. Fisher said, "you're giving CyberCorp too much power over you."

"That's the whole point!" I slammed both my palms on

the desk. "I'm trying to take away their power." When I moved my left hand, a hairline fracture remained in her desk. "I'm sorry about that."

"It's just property. I'm more concerned about you. You say you don't want to come back here, but you don't want to do what's necessary to make that happen. The question is, do you want control of your life or not?"

It was a good question. I was tired of my life dragging me along for the ride.

---

Above me, the smooth metal ceiling blurred into view, obstructed by my mother's face. She'd pulled her afro back into a coily puff, and even her expert makeup couldn't hide the tired red rimming her eyes.

"Wake up, honey."

I was still in Dr. Fisher's large office. I lay curled up next to Jackson, his arm limp underneath my neck and the world smelling like cinnamon-vanilla this close to him. The display on my hand-screen glowed digits of an indecent hour on Saturday morning.

"Everything okay?" I asked. "Are the doors open?"

Jackson groaned. His eyes fluttered, spotted my mom, and he retracted his arm from under me.

Around the room, Liv, Hunter, and Dr. Fisher shook themselves awake. After my arm repair, Liv and Hunter had found me in Fisher's office. We located some large, overstuffed chairs from the various offices, dragged them in here, and made ourselves semi-comfortable on the floor.

Dr. Fisher groaned and stumbled to her feet. "I'm too old for this."

My mom laughed. "We successfully drained all the Model Ones of power and turned the building's primary power back on. The androids are staying put, so it's safe to open the doors."

Fisher smoothed her clothes. "You should have woken me earlier. I could've helped."

"There is nothing else you could have done." She cast Dr. Fisher a grateful look. "Besides, I trust you. I preferred you here, taking care of my most prized possession."

"I'm a possession now?" I asked.

She kissed me on the forehead. "It's time to go home."

"What about you? Are you coming?"

"Might as well. I'm running on fumes. Let's all go home, get some rest, and reboot after the sun makes an appearance."

The six of us collected our things and stepped out into the hallway. The lights had returned to evening mode, as opposed to backup-power mode. The strip lights edging the floor and the ceiling were off once again, and the pot lights overhead cast an amber glow.

Mom scanned her wrist at the elevator.

The doors opened, and we stepped inside. Glowing numbers on both side walls counted down as the elevator descended.

At the lobby, we stepped into a small crowd, probably half of the hundred or so people who'd been stuck here overnight. People surged and bobbed, parting like the sea as my mom appeared behind me. Varied gazes darted back and forth between her and the barricaded door.

The faces around me stung with fatigue, eyes reddened and glazed, hair matted, clothes wrinkled. Restless murmuring filled the space like a hive of bees.

Jackson's face suddenly went blank as he tapped his micro-comm.

"Someone's calling you this early in the morning?"

"It's Claire." Into his micro, he added, "What's"—he flinched—"I can't understand you. Could you slow down and stop shouting?"

I froze.

"I need you to slow down. What?"

"What's going on?" Liv asked leaning toward him as if she could hear his micro—which she couldn't.

"We're coming up!" Jackson tapped to end the call and propelled himself back into the elevator cab.

"Lena?" my mother called after me as I dashed in after him. "Is everything all right?"

"I'm not sure. Nothing for you to worry about, ma'am," Jackson told her, but the way he hopped from foot to foot as he held the elevator open said otherwise.

Liv hesitated with Hunter's hand on her arm, until Jackson jammed the close-door button, and it slid shut in her face.

"What's going on?" I asked.

"Fifty-seven," Jackson told the elevator.

"Fifty-seven," the elevator repeated in its steady, electronic voice.

"I may have misunderstood. Let's just . . ." He licked his lips. "Let's just see what's going on and try not to panic."

Dread grew like a lead weight in my gut. "Why would I panic?"

The elevator doors opened on the fifty-seventh floor. Jackson bolted down the hallway, using every bit of his enhanced legs for speed. I followed.

17

We raced down the hall, our shoes pounding against the floor and my pulse pounding in my ears. On his rebuilt legs, Jackson beat me to the door.

Conference room 57J had originally been Claire's room, but last I checked, Ron had been locked in here. Jackson beckoned me forward and waved at the ID scanner.

"What's going on?" I scanned my wrist. I expected it to reject me as it had late last night. This time, though, it dinged agreeably, and the steel door shot open.

Inside, Claire screamed her head off.

She stood on the other side of the conference table, staring toward her feet. Jackson and I circled the table. I stopped abruptly as if a brick wall had grown from the floor.

Ron Franklin lay there, his dead eyes gazing upward. They bulged almost comically, red veins standing out all around the white. One arm lay to the side while the other sat on top of his stomach. Blood covered the knuckles.

Behind him, more blood smeared the window out to the atrium. A metal chair lay on the floor right under it.

"What happened?" My voice was so soft I could barely hear myself. I cleared my throat and tried again. "What happened to—"

"I didn't . . ." Claire shook her head. "I swear I didn't do this." Her voice trailed off to whimpering. Her attention drifted to Ron's body, and she squeezed her eyes shut.

"You didn't do this," Jackson said. His tone was more pleading than anything else. "Tell us you didn't do this."

Her eyes popped wide. "I didn't . . . I didn't . . ."

I slipped my hand-screen from my pocket and placed a call to security. Instead of connecting, my hand-screen spun its loading sign on the display. "I still can't place calls. Someone call security."

Claire stood there vibrating like a plucked guitar string while Jackson scanned the room with intense, unblinking eyes.

He straightened his back. "First things first." He steered Claire to a chair, which he kicked out and pushed her into. "What happened?"

"I don't know. I came in and he was  . . ." She gestured toward the floor without looking.

Against my will, my gaze drifted to Ron's body. His face had frozen in a contorted mask. Bloodshot eyes bulged, contrasting taut blue skin.

I squeezed my eyes shut and counted backward from five in my head, taking a long inhale before each number, before opening them. "What happened?" I snapped, despite the effort to stay calm.

Claire swallowed. "I was looking for Briana. My security guard had to step out. They're short-staffed since the building is . . ."

She paused to lick her lips.

"He asked me if it was okay, if I felt safe enough, and I said he should go—I figured it would give me a chance to find Bri. If she was looking for me, she'd come back here." She gestured around the conference room. "She wouldn't know I moved." Claire twisted her fingers together as she spoke.

"The door was locked," Jackson said. He kept his voice even, devoid of the suspicion he had to feel right now. The girl had already killed *at least* one person, excluding the two detectives for which she claimed innocence.

"It wasn't. It opened when I scanned my wrist."

"Why did you even try the door in the first place though?" Unlike Jackson, I did a poor job of masking my doubt. It coated every word.

"I panicked. Bri could have come back here and ended up stuck in this room with Ron."

"Why should we believe you?" I asked.

"Because I'm telling the truth!" Claire's face was red and splotchy, and her gaze pleaded with Jackson, who'd been her defender so far.

This time, he stayed quiet.

"You want us to believe," I said, "that someone unlocked this door, came in, murdered Ron, and you just coincidentally found the body despite your strong motive to want him dead?"

"I'm not the only one in this building with a motive."

It was a fair point.

Ron had killed four people. Three of them had parents who worked here, and the fourth worked here himself. Certainly, there were people in this building who wanted revenge. Add to that the fact that Ron had used Cyber-Corp technology—specifically my arm—to commit those murders, and that meant pretty much everyone who had a stake in the company had a motive to hurt him.

But only one of them had been found over his dead body.

"He could have killed himself for all we know," Claire said.

Over the past month, Ron had asked for my forgiveness at least three times. Maybe he'd been having trouble forgiving himself as well.

I dragged my gaze over to the body. The blue lips and bulging eyes mirrored the image etched into my brain of Debbie Carlyle's body. I'd strangled her in my sleep, thanks to Ron's programming.

"This doesn't look like a suicide."

"You're a medical examiner now?" Claire asked.

"He didn't kill himself." Jackson pointed toward the blood-splotched window that led out to the atrium over the lobby, and to the chair still toppled underneath it. "There was a fight. Someone attacked someone else with that chair."

"Or"—I pointed at the body's bloody knuckles—"Ron

used the chair to try to escape through the window after he couldn't get through with just his fists."

When I pressed my face to the glass and looked down, I could see a small ledge about a foot wide just beyond the glass. It circled around the entire atrium. Maybe Ron had been trying to get to it.

He was so desperate that he punched safety glass. When that didn't work, he threw a chair because he thought that teetering over fifty-seven stories was a better option than staying in this room.

"Definitely not suicide," I mumbled more to myself than anyone else. But Ron couldn't have been that desperate to escape *Claire*, who didn't have a single cybernetic enhancement.

The metal sliding door shot open, and Liv rushed into the room. It took only a few seconds for her gaze to sweep the scene. Her eyes widened for only an instant when they landed on Ron, and her expression went dead.

"I guess that's that." She raised her brows at Claire. "You?"

Claire balled her fists and stormed across the room.

Jackson slid into her path and steered her back into her seat. "We have a building full of suspects."

I nodded at Liv. "Can you call security?"

She stepped aside and glared at Claire as she tapped her micro. "CyberCorp security." A few seconds later, she added, "Ron Franklin is dead." She opened her mouth to say more but then nodded as a person on the other end of the connection spoke. "I don't think I'm qualified to say.

We're in conference room 57J." She nodded. "We're not going anywhere." She disconnected.

The metal door slid open, revealing Hunter in the doorway.

"Hey, people, what's . . ." He took in our somber expressions before his gaze found the body. He plopped into the nearest chair. "What is it with you people?"

"It couldn't have been me." Claire pointed at the blood-splotched window. "Ron wouldn't have been scared enough to try to get through that window and risk a sixty-story drop. I'm not that much of a threat. I don't even have cybernetic parts."

Every gaze in the room skated toward me.

"I get it." I rolled my eyes. "I have a bionic arm and motive. But I was with Jackson the whole time."

"It wasn't you or me, but he was scared for his life." Jackson waved a hand toward the cracked window. "And whoever attacked him is still in this building."

18

Thirty minutes later, security had relocated Jackson, Liv, Claire, Hunter, and me to a conference room on the fifty-ninth floor.

The room was laid out the same—padded walls, conference table, and a window that dangled over the lobby far below. Unlike the conference room two floors down, though, this one didn't feature a dead body.

Despite that, I couldn't help my attention from sliding back to that spot on the floor.

Claire sat at the opposite end of the table, both forearms tense against the armrests of her chair. Two guards separated her from the rest of us, one on each side of the table, their arms crossed and faces stuck in neutral. Liv, Jackson, Hunter, and I clustered on the other end near the door.

Overhead, the automated ventilation issued a steady hum, the only sound in the tense room.

The sliding door whooshed open, and my parents rushed in.

My mother ran toward me, grabbed my face in her hands, and planted one kiss on my forehead and one on my cheek. "Are you okay?"

"Define *okay*." I let heavy sarcasm fill my tone.

Claire raised her hand and cleared her throat. "I didn't do it."

One guard placed a hand on the back of Claire's chair. "Should we secure her?"

"Why would she be a suspect?" my mother asked.

For once, it was Liv who came to Claire's defense. "Ron wasn't scared of her. He wouldn't have considered going through that window if the only thing he was up against was Claire." She flicked her hand toward the other girl.

"You could have said that without the implied insult," Claire muttered.

"Whatever happens to you," Liv shot back, "you deserve it."

Hunter set a hand on her arm, and her shoulders loosened.

"I'm not defending you because you're a good person— we both know you're not. I'm defending you because it's the truth."

The guard glanced at my father, who waved him off. He released Claire's chair.

"We examined the scene," Dad said, "and it's clear to us that Claire is in the clear . . . for *this* crime."

Claire mumbled something I couldn't hear.

"Agreed," my mother added. "She has more to answer

for, but that's for a different time and place." Her face softened as she looked at Claire. "I've known you for years, and I refuse to believe you're capable of purposeful murder."

Liv grunted.

My mother cut her with a stare that made Liv sit at attention. "I've known you for even longer, and I expect a little more compassion."

Liv pulled her lips together.

I cleared my throat, though it did little to clear the tension. "Are the doors open yet?"

Mom glanced at my dad and back at me. "We got the call that this happened just before hitting the switch. We notified the police, of course, and they advised that we all stay put."

"That was half an hour ago," I said. "Are they on their way?"

My parents passed another cryptic, split-second glance between them.

"What's going on?"

"It's hard to say just yet," my mother said in a tone so even and nonchalant that I couldn't possibly trust it.

"What's going on?" I asked again, louder.

"There may be a problem with the safety doors," my father said under his breath, for me alone.

"Or"—Liv's voice vibrated across the strings of tension taut across the room—"we let everyone out so that we can all get away from the murderer."

Mom squeezed Liv's shoulder but gave no response.

"For now," Dad added, "we'll all stay put. The last thing

we want is to release a killer into the public when it's in our power to stop them here and now."

The lie rang false in my ears. From the pinched expressions in the room, no one else was buying it either.

"Is this a public relations thing?" Claire asked.

My mother made an irritated *tsk*. "It's a doing-the-right-thing thing."

"Of course." Claire rolled her eyes.

"How would you like us to handle this?" The two security guards now stood shoulder to shoulder, awaiting my parents' instructions. They were so alike, good little soldiers. I couldn't even tell which of them had spoken.

"Call the police and get a detective and virtual presence for now," my mom said. "Let's see if they can investigate remotely." Both my parents turned toward the door and gestured for me and my friends to follow.

Claire jumped to her feet and positioned herself in front of my mom. "Let me out of this building. Whoever killed Ron could come after me next."

"Oh, you're the victim now?" Liv said.

Claire ignored her completely. "Seriously, if someone was angry enough at Ron for abusing CyberCorp technology to kill people, that person could be crazy enough to go after me next."

"You mean because *you* also abused CyberCorp technology to kill people?" I whispered.

"Person—*one* person—accidentally."

If we got through this, I had to work on my whispering skills.

"Is that all?" Liv asked. She spun to Hunter. "How many people have you killed *accidentally*?"

"None that I can recall," he said.

She turned to Jackson. "You? How many?"

"Can we not do this?" he said.

She turned to me and opened her mouth but then froze.

For me, the answer to that question was three. *Three* people. Their deaths were on Ron. Even so, it put a kink in Liv's point.

Claire fluttered her eyelashes in Liv's direction but didn't respond again. Her attention returned to my parents. "Please, get me out of here."

"Could we get her a sealed room?" my mother asked the security guards.

"A lot of good that did Ron," Claire said. "You people were supposed to be protecting him. See how much good that did."

My dad's jaw tightened.

My mom's lips pursed. "No one asked either of you to come here today . . . Actually, it was yesterday, but no one asked either of you to come. It is not our responsibility to protect you, and I resent that you think it is."

"It's okay, Marissa." He massaged her shoulders. "You're doing the best you can."

My mother's face passed through a variety of expressions before landing on something that looked like forced calm. "As I was saying, if you wish for security to find you a secured room, they can do so—"

"Because that worked so well."

Mom took a few seconds to gather her calm before continuing. "Otherwise, you will be notified, just like everyone else, when the doors are open." She turned on her three-inch heels and marched toward the door. The steel door shot open as she approached, and she and my father walked through. It slammed shut behind them.

A security guard faced Jackson, Liv, Hunter, and Claire. "We'll need you to give us the room so we can set up for the police to do virtual interrogations." He turned toward me with a softer, more pleading expression. "You too, please."

Jackson, Liv, and Hunter filed out while Claire shifted her weight from foot to foot.

"Can I talk to you?" she asked me. She jerked her head toward the two security guards. "Alone."

I blew air out through my teeth but, against my better judgment, agreed. "Could you give us just a minute please," I asked them, "and then you can have the room back?"

They nodded and left.

I folded my arms over my chest.

"Get me the hell out of here!" Claire lunged toward me and gripped both my hands in hers. "Please, if we were ever friends, get me the hell out of here. My life is in danger."

Judging from the dead body two floors down from us, I couldn't disagree. "Why should I do anything for you? I know you think everything you did is my fault, but you need to face up to your own actions. You—"

"That's not what this is about. You don't owe me. I'm asking because we're friends. I'm asking you to care whether I'm still alive tomorrow."

I stared at her. I knew the edgy cut of her hair, the deep brown of her eyes, and the strong line of her jaw. All of it was familiar and—whether I liked it or not right now—loved.

If I woke up tomorrow in a world without Claire, it would be a duller, less interesting world. "I'll see what I can do."

19

"I promise. That's all I know." Claire dropped her head in her hands and went silent.

For the past ten minutes, the virtual detectives displayed on a large vid-screen on the fifty-ninth floor had been interrogating Claire, after already questioning Jackson and Hunter. They'd taken her backward and forward through the events in conference room 57J.

To her credit, her story had stayed consistent.

Across from her, a vid-screen displayed a male and a female detective in an office somewhere across town. Both sat behind a desk so we could see only their top halves, complete with black blazers and erect postures. The two of them exchanged a wordless glance and had an entire conversation with their eyes. One nodded, and the man shifted his gaze to my mother in the back of the room.

My friends weren't allowed in here during the interrogation, but I'd stayed glued to my seat side as if I, too, was a CyberCorp owner whose presence was not to be questioned.

"We're done with her for now," the female detective said.

She didn't tap her micro-comm to end the recording. Everything she was saying now, and everything my parents and I said in response, would still be part of the record—part of the murder investigation.

"You can go," my mom said to Claire.

Claire's pleading look landed on me. I'd promised her I would protect her for as long as we were here. When she pushed back her chair to leave, I headed for the door with her.

"Could I speak with Miss Hayes next?" The detective kept her tone polite, like a question, but if I refused, it would look suspicious.

My mother opened her mouth to speak.

I cut in before she could. "It's fine. I'll speak to them. I have nothing to hide. I have to take care of something first, though. Can you question someone else next?"

The detective's eyes glazed over, and dark shadows passed over her irises as she viewed something in virtual. "Can you send in Olivia Harris?"

When I strode across the room and out to the hallway, my friends were sitting along the wall, faces grim.

Liv jumped to her feet. "Might as well get this over with."

Claire followed me out of the room. She and Liv glared at each other as they crossed paths, and Liv took her place inside. Hunter's gaze followed Liv until the steel door slammed shut behind her.

"I have to go check on something," I told Jackson, Hunter, and Claire, who remained with me in the hallway. "I won't be long."

"Do you need help?" Jackson asked.

Before I could answer, Claire grabbed my sleeve. "Give us a minute." She hauled me down the hall to a private spot away from the boys.

"What?" I snatched my arm back from her.

"Until we're out of this building, I stay with you. I'm your shadow." She stepped closer to me until I could smell cherry on her breath. "Please. You're the reason I'm here."

I'd been trying to keep my temper on low, but now it burst. "I am not responsible for your choices. I'm not responsible for Ron's choices. I'm only responsible for my own. You're going to spend a lot of time in prison if you plan to get in that courtroom and tell everyone you had nothing to do with your own decisions."

She took two large steps back. "I know that. It will be a relief to stand in front of a judge and express regret that I made terrible choices."

"Then how am I the reason you're here?"

Her head tilted to one side as her gaze flitted across my face. "You asked me to come."

"Excuse me?"

"Yesterday afternoon. You messaged that you would talk to Briana on my behalf if I came here to confess. Since I have nothing to hide and I've already told everyone the truth, I had no reason to turn you down."

I gaped at her.

"You asked me to come here. You don't remember that? You're not sleepwalking again, are you?"

I whipped my hand-screen from my pocket and scrolled through my sent messages. It was showing a slow network connection, but it didn't have a problem retrieving data that was already on the device.

There it was. A message from me to Claire at four-fourteen Friday afternoon.

I shook my head as I read aloud. "Meet me at Cyber-Corp Tower. Give a full confession, and I'll convince Briana to forgive you."

Claire nodded along with every word.

I dropped the device back into my jacket pocket. "I didn't send this. And I don't know how . . ." Again, I took the hand-screen out and navigated to my messages. I gaped as I read it twice more. "My hand-screen has been acting a little wonky, but that doesn't explain sending messages like this."

"Are you absolutely sure you haven't been sleepwalking again?"

"I wasn't even asleep. This was in the afternoon. I was here at the Tower for an appointment with Dr. Fisher. Then I met Liv at my place."

"So what, then? You think Dr. Fisher stole your hand-screen long enough to send this message? Why would she do that?"

I squinted at the words, somehow hoping they would confess their origin. "She wouldn't. She *couldn't*. It never left my sight." Even if it had some kind of bug, that didn't explain sending this kind of message to Claire. This wasn't a malfunction. This was a deliberate choice—a deliberate attempt to get Claire to CyberCorp Tower.

For what?

"You didn't send it?" Claire asked, her eyes wide.

She'd landed on the same conclusion I had at the same time. Maybe whoever had hurt Ron had sent him a similar message. I navigated back out to my list of messages, and there it was—a message to Ron just a few minutes before the one to Claire.

I read it aloud as well. "Meet me at CyberCorp Tower. Give a full confession, and I'll forgive you. I'll convince Olivia to forgive you. I'll even be a character witness for you." I blinked at the message in shock. "What the hell?"

"Whoever sent those wanted Ron and me to come to CyberCorp Tower so they could kill us." Claire's entire body trembled.

"Jacks!" I waved at him, and he hurried down the hall to join us.

"What's up?"

"Can you look after Claire until I get back?" To Claire, I added, "He's a better bodyguard than I could ever be."

Jackson puffed out his chest, and Claire laughed.

As I turned to go, Claire grabbed my sleeve once more. She waited until I faced her eye-to-eye. "If we were ever friends, please get me out of here. I don't want to die."

20

Claire was as safe as she could get with Jackson on the fifty-ninth floor outside an interrogation room. When the detectives finished interviewing everyone, we would find a way out.

In the meantime, I had other things to handle.

When I stepped off the elevator, people were scattered throughout the lobby. Some milled about waiting for news. In one corner, a group of people were clustered together in one of the seating areas. They looked tired and disheveled, having spent hours trapped in this building.

Although CyberCorp had provided semi-comfortable sleeping spaces on the sixtieth floor, I guessed these people wanted to be as close to the exit as possible. I empathized with that on a soul-deep level.

One woman had draped her coat over her lap like a blanket, while another man was using his as a makeshift pillow. A few others had their jackets bunched up on the floor to make themselves comfortable while they waited for updates.

Most had found spots along the front wall of windows, close to the front doors—as if that would get them out of here faster. Beyond the glass, the sunrise set the other building tops on fire with reflections of colored light. Light from digital billboards mixed with the new morning to paint the world in soft rainbows.

Despite the view, the atmosphere was thick with anxiety.

I did an about-face and headed for the back of the lobby, where the offices for authorized personnel waited. My parents were great at dividing their duties. Since my mom was upstairs supervising the questioning, my dad would be down here gathering data.

I waved my wrist at the door marked *Security*, and it slid open to welcome me.

Inside the brightly lit room stood my father and his chief of security, a lean man who looked a decade or two too young for the bald cap of his head.

"We can't—" He cut off his words abruptly as the door slammed closed behind me.

"Is everything okay?" My father stepped in front of his security chief so it was just him and me.

"No . . ." Of course it wasn't.

Ron had died in a building in which we were trapped, and before his death, he'd accused my father of being in league with him. Didn't that make my dad suspect number one? But that wasn't an easy subject to broach.

"Any idea when we're getting out of here?"

He licked his lips. "I can't speak on that just yet. In just a few minutes, we should know more. For now"—he jerked his head toward the opposite wall where a wall-sized vid-screen was divided into four panels, three showing different angles of a hallway and one showing the interior of a conference room—"could you give us a minute?"

I sidestepped around him to get a better view.

One panel showed a number at a conference room door: 57J. This was the room where Ron had died.

"You can see who was in there?" I asked excitedly. "Can you play it?"

My father scrubbed a hand through his hair while his security chief—his name was Lawrence, or something like that—looked grim. Dad nodded at him.

"Play recordings," Lawrence said.

Nothing happened for almost ten seconds.

"Is it playing or . . ." A timestamp rolled upward in the bottom right corner of the screen, indicating that the videos were indeed playing. The hallway was just empty.

All at once, all four frames went stark white. The brightness was so sudden and blinding that I blinked and shaded my eyes. My father stared at me as if that answered everything.

"I don't understand."

Lawrence pointed at the bottom right corner where the timestamp had been just seconds ago. As I stepped closer, I could see the faint light gray and numerals over the white background, and they continued going upward.

"It's playing, but the video is blank?"

My father nodded. "And it shouldn't be." He directed that statement at Lawrence, who dutifully bowed his head.

"All the cameras are operational. They recorded up to this point, and if we fast-forward four minutes, the recording picks up again. Someone deleted that footage."

"Who had access?" I asked.

My father sighed and, for the hundredth time, dashed a hand through his hair. "A handful of people. Trustworthy people. If it weren't for the murder that took place in this room"—he gestured toward the display—"I would say this is a technical bug. But that seems too coincidental given the circumstances."

"What about other cameras in the building?" I asked. "Do those have recordings during that time frame?"

"Yes," Lawrence said. "Yet another reason to assume this was human sabotage."

"That makes this easy," I said. "Our murder suspects are down to the people who had access to this video."

My father cringed.

"What? You said that's not many people, so doesn't that make this investigation easier? We should tell the detectives and let them do their jobs."

My father dropped into the nearest chair, and it spun on its wheels as it accepted his momentum. "I'm the only one in the building who has access." He gestured toward his security chief. "Well, me and Lance, and he was the one who brought the problem to my attention. It doesn't make sense that he would've done this and then told me about it, knowing that he and I were the only ones who had access."

Lance—not Lawrence after all—chuckled. "I do like to think I'm smarter than that."

Yesterday, I asked Ron what proof he had.

The process of elimination, he'd said.

Once again, my dad was the only one who could have done it. So my father had pushed Ron to sabotage my arm so I'd commit murder? Then he'd murdered Ron to keep his mouth shut?

What would he have to gain?

My dad gestured toward the vid-screen. "I don't know where it leads us, honestly." His face went blank, and he tilted his head, his expression far away. Then he nodded. "I just received word on my micro that the issue with the doors remains unresolved."

"Issue with the doors?" We'd been stuck in this tower long enough. Now, with Ron dead, our lives might depend on getting out.

"It might be nothing," Lance said, but the way his gaze shifted told me the exact opposite. "Our communication interface keeps alerting us that the safety doors are offline."

"Offline as in . . . *unable to open*?" Panic laced my words.

"It's unclear," my dad said, "whether the alert itself is an error or the doors are actually disconnected."

"Disconnected as in . . . *unable to open*?" My voice had turned into a high-pitched screech. I pulled in one long inhale and reminded myself that my AI needed me to stay calm. "Can't we just *try* to open them?"

"That's the plan."

He and Lance headed for the office door, which opened automatically, and I hurried after them into the lobby.

Their long strides outpaced mine as they made their way past the large reception desk.

The exhausted crowd on the main floor watched the two men move. Several of them gestured toward the metal barrier that still covered the double doors of the exit.

My father and I arrived in the middle of it all. In any other setting, people would've started shouting, demanding answers. But around here, my parents ran things, and everyone knew that. Lips stayed closed, and gazes stayed locked on us as we approached.

All conversation stopped.

Dad straightened his back, tapped his micro-comm, and commanded, "Release the safety doors."

A series of curt beeps issued as the door inched upward. It was working. The doors weren't offline after all. We were getting out of here!

The beeping stopped, and my breath hitched.

The beeps issued again, this time at a lower pitch. The door reversed.

It slammed into the tile floor with a clanging gong, sealing our fate.

21

When I returned to the fifty-ninth floor, I found Jackson, Hunter, and Claire seated in a neat row in the hallway. They'd all been interviewed by the police. Now, their faces looked drained of energy, complete with slack mouths and droopy eyes.

"I need you." I planted my feet in front of Jackson, grabbed his hands, and hauled him to his feet.

"Could I have everyone's attention please?" came Missy's cheerful, professional tone over the announcement system. She cleared her throat, and my mother's voice sounded somewhere in the background, probably instructing her on exactly what to say.

All of us tilted our faces toward the ceiling, as if that would help us hear better.

"We're having a technical difficulty with the safety doors, so unfortunately, we all get to stay here a little longer. We apologize profusely and will compensate you all for your time. In the meantime—"

"Missy, is that you?" Another voice interrupted on the announcement system. "Would you have Marissa come up to seventy, please?"

I sucked in a breath. Marissa—my mother—would not appreciate being interrupted with a summons in the middle of her announcement. The second voice sounded familiar, but I couldn't place it.

"Um . . ." Missy continued, "I was saying . . . In the meantime, breakfast is being—"

"I've been trying to reach her," said the second voice, which I now recognized as Dr. Sophie's. "I have a way to solve the problem with the Model Two androids—"

"Sophie." My mother's voice snapped through the hallway from the announcement system. "I'm calling you now. Please let Missy finish her announcement."

"I was saying . . ." Missy's voice had gotten quieter and less authoritative. "Breakfast is in conference rooms 60A and 60B. Thank you."

Finally, the announcements went quiet.

"Awkward," Jackson quipped.

"What's going on?" Hunter asked, his gaze on me.

"There's a communication problem with the safety doors." Before he could follow up, I added, "Sorry, that's all I know."

I tugged Jackson's hand to urge him down the hall and around the corner. Now that the interruptions were over, we needed to have a serious talk about my dad, and this was not a conversation I wanted overheard. This wasn't even a conversation I wanted to voice.

When we were well out of earshot, Jackson turned and grasped my hands, his face serious, gaze soothing. He already knew what this was about.

"Do you think he did it?" My voice came out soft, hesitant.

"I honestly don't know. I've always known Mr. Hayes as your father. I've never thought about what kind of man he is. Ambitious and determined, definitely." He raised his hands, palms up. "That's all I've got."

"Can't ambition and determination turn into desperation?" I asked. I lowered my voice to a hiss, even though no one was near us. "Ron accused him of being his partner, and now he's dead—in my dad's building."

"Well, I thought he would kill me if I got you home late from our first date."

Despite myself, I laughed, and then the seriousness of this fell over me again like a weight.

Jackson rubbed my hands between his.

"It's suspicious. Right?" I asked.

"I wish I could give you the answer you want. Maybe ask Dr. Fisher. She's worked with your dad a long time, so she may have a better view of what kind of man he is."

Without a second's beat, I tapped my loaner microcomm and called her.

"Lena! Always a pleasure," she answered. "What can I do for you?"

Although we were stuck in this building with a dead body that used to be her former intern, Dr. Fisher was still jovial. Now, it seemed ridiculous that I hadn't liked her at first, but having an artificially intelligent cybernetic arm forced on me had put me in a bad mood at the time.

"You okay?" she said when I didn't speak right away.

"Do you think my dad is capable of murder?"

Now it was her turn to pause. "Is this about Ron?"

I nodded. When I realized she couldn't hear that, I choked out the word, "Yes."

A long sigh and then, "Your father is the proudest, most intelligent man I've ever met. Mostly, he's proud of his intelligence." She chuckled. "I imagine he'd pride himself on finding a solution to any problem that could *avoid* murder."

I stood up straighter.

"Do you know he and your mother built this company from the ground up? Can you imagine the strength of character that requires?"

I frowned. I wasn't convinced building a company required strength of character. Money, yes. Business acumen, sure. More money, definitely. But strength of character? There were too many corrupt businessmen in the world for me to buy that. Maybe Dr. Fisher wasn't as impartial as I thought.

"Thanks," I said.

"You're welcome. How are you holding up?"

"I'm okay," I lied. "I'll talk to you later."

We disconnected.

The disappointment must have been plain on my face because Jackson said, "What about Dr. Sophie?" He gestured toward the ceiling, where the hidden speakers had put her on full blast a few minutes ago.

Dr. Sophie obviously didn't idolize my parents the way Dr. Fisher did. I placed the call. The line rang with no answer.

"I'm going up there," I told Jackson. "Would you stay here and look after Claire?" I'd already turned and was marching down the hall when his answer reached me.

I took the elevator to the seventieth floor. When I reached it, the doors slid open, revealing the same organized mess of Model Ones and Model One parts.

Except for Dr. Sophie, all the employees had cleared out. It was early morning on a Saturday, and there was a dead body in the building. If ever there was time for a break from saving the company, it was now.

Dr. Sophie sat in the corner of the massive room, cross-legged several feet from the huddle of Model Two androids. Her eyes were wide and glazed as she typed and gestured at the empty air. She was using her EyeNet-enabled lenses to work in virtual.

"Dr. Sophie?" I approached slowly, trying not to startle her. But when I touched her shoulder, she leaped to her feet. Her hands came up in fists. Even focused on me, her eyes still held the shadowed silver glaze of someone using their contact lenses to interact with the EyeNet.

"Whoa." I stepped back.

She slumped and sank back down to the floor. "Sorry, I was listening to music, and I didn't expect anyone to be up here." She immediately went back to gesturing in the air, making occasional finger movements that looked like typing.

I closed my eyes briefly and willed my EyeNet connection to activate. When I opened them, glowing lines of code floated in the air in front of her face. Under them glowed a keyboard and music-play controls. I blinked hard to deactivate the connection, and the virtual objects disappeared.

"Dr. Sophie?" I said again.

When she looked up at me, her eyes widened as if she'd forgotten me already. "Lena, I'm sorry but I'm very busy. I need to disconnect the Model Twos from the server."

"I know, but I just have a quick question. I promise it'll be faster to answer it than to argue with me."

With a sigh, she made a large swipe left to push her work aside, crossed her arms, and stared at me expectantly.

"Do you think my father is capable of murder?" I expected some flash of surprise or shock to cross her face.

Instead, her expression remained neutral and open. "You're right—this is an easy one. Yes."

"Yes?" The word squeaked out.

"No offense intended. I just mean that everyone is capable of murder with the right push in the right direction. Your father is no saint and no exception." She swiped right to restore her virtual workspace, and her eyes glazed over once again.

My heart plummeted because that was the answer I'd suspected all along. As someone who had strangled three people—intentional or not—how could I think otherwise? *Anyone* was capable of murder, even Thomas Hayes.

22

I found Hunter sitting on the carpet outside of the makeshift interrogation room, his knees pulled in and his head dipped low. The bleeding-red CyberCorp logo hovered on the vid-screen wall across from him, forever watching.

He jumped to his feet as I hurried toward him, and my heart skidded to a pause. I slowed.

This was the first time we'd been alone together in a while, probably since our date. So much had changed since then: my discovery that I'd been used to commit murder, about a thousand hours of therapy, and—most relevant of all—my renewed confusion about where things stood with Jackson.

"Can we talk?" he asked.

My heart shot back into nervous motion. Now was not the time for this conversation. "Is Liv still inside?"

"For a while. They're taking their time with her."

"Jackson and Claire?"

"She convinced him to be her bodyguard while she takes a power nap on sixty. It was a long night."

Exhaustion was weighing me down too, but I'd have time to think about that later—when I was safely at home.

"Hey, Lena, can we—"

It *still* wasn't the time for that conversation. Guilt tugged at me as I waved my wrist at the scanner. The door whooshed open, and I slipped inside.

He didn't follow. The detectives definitely wouldn't let him inside. They probably didn't want me inside either, but technically, I owned this joint—or I would eventually.

The door whooshed closed behind me. Two detectives and the giant vid-screen flicked their attention to me. Irritation flashed over the woman's features before she resumed her stoic expression.

She returned her attention to Liv, who sat at the far end of the room, hands fisted together on top of the conference table. Behind her, the glass wall displayed the atrium, which stretched upward and all the way down to the lobby, a vision of modern technology and design with sleek walls of glass separated by glowing white panels that seemed lit from within.

"To be clear, when Mr. Watts and Miss Hayes got to the room," the female detective said, "you weren't there yet?"

I ducked under the vid-screen and tiptoed to the opposite corner of the room. My mother's flunky, Missy, sat there with her hands folded over a handheld vid-screen that she often used to take notes.

I inched another chair out from the conference table and slipped into it as silently as possible, cringing as the leather padding sighed around me.

"How's it going?" I whispered to Missy.

"I'm sure if your mother needs me, she will call for me. Since she hasn't, she must feel that I am most useful here."

Missy had been my mother's assistant for as long as I could remember, and apparently, she didn't appreciate being sidelined up here in the investigation room instead of downstairs glued to my mother's side like a symbiotic insect.

"Miss Harris," one detective said, her volume louder than it had been a second ago, "did you hear the question?"

Liv's posture shifted only slightly as she shot a glance at me and then back at the giant vid-screen. "I, uh, yes, I came in right after them. Seconds."

"Did you exchange any words with Claire at that time?"

Liv cleared her throat. "Claire and I aren't really friends. So no, Lena and Jackson did all the talking."

"Did you have any impression of whether she was telling the truth when she insisted she had found Ron's body like that?"

"No. I mean, yes, I believed her. She seemed scared for her life, and I don't think she would be if she killed Ron."

Wait.

Was Liv telling the detectives that she was with us when we found Claire and Ron's body?

The two detectives mumbled something back and forth to each other, too quietly for us to hear. The woman nodded at her partner and then turned his attention back to the screen. "Thank you, Miss Harris. You can go."

Liv popped to her feet and was halfway toward the door before she thought to ask, "Should I send someone else in?"

"That's all of you except Miss Hayes." The detective nodded at me. "Can you stay?"

I tracked Liv as she cast a backward glance at me and disappeared through the door. We had to talk, but it could wait for fifteen minutes.

The detectives walked me through the day's events, ending with finding Ron dead in the room. We went through it at least three times, and all I could think about was Liv's story about having arrived at the conference room seconds after Jackson and I did.

Had she? Maybe I was distracted from finding a dead body and didn't remember correctly . . . No, she *hadn't* been with us. She came later. I was certain of it.

"Thank you, Miss Hayes. You're free to go," said the detective on the vid.

I popped out of my seat and rushed for the door. When it opened, I found Hunter rubbing Liv's back. His hand fell away as I stalked into the hallway.

I waited for them to separate and then grabbed her shirtsleeve to haul her out of his earshot. "What the hell was that?"

"We're just friends."

I squinted at her while it took a second to parse her words. "Not Hunter. I mean, what happened in that interview? You told them you got there within seconds of me and Jackson?"

"I did."

"You did *not*. You weren't on our elevator. You told those detectives a bald-faced lie."

"Are you sure I wasn't with you?" She chewed her lower lip. "I was right behind you in the hallway. I mean, you're a little faster than I am, but I was right there."

"Are you trying to convince me that the truth I know is wrong?"

"If I lied, *hypothetically*, it would be because I have a motive and no alibi."

"No one thinks you killed Ron."

Liv gestured toward the door we'd just exited. "They might. I was dating him when he weaponized you. I did what he told me and convinced you that everything was okay—not to seek any more surgeries." She closed her eyes and pursed her lips, and I could see the anger and devastation simmering just beneath the surface.

I squeezed her shoulder. "You're not responsible for his actions."

"I was furious with him." She opened her eyes. "I mean really, truly, seriously furious. If I were capable of murder, I *would* have murdered him."

"But you're not."

"Of course not." She grabbed her lower lip with her teeth and chewed it for a second. "I was off wandering the halls by myself when Ron died, so I have a motive and no alibi. If I told them the truth, you don't think I'd suddenly be the number-one suspect?"

I hesitated before answering, my gaze still on her

mouth. I'd seen her chew her lower lip a hundred times in our long friendship—a self-soothing tell that she used only when she was hiding something.

Liv wasn't capable of murder. *Was she?*

I hedged. "Is there anything else?"

"I'm not lying to you. I swear."

I had sworn to myself over the past week that I would trust my friends. I wouldn't look at them as suspects.

Unfortunately, my friends kept proving me wrong.

"Hey." Briana's voice pulled me away from my staring contest with Liv.

"Bri!" Relief released some of the pressure from my chest. I hadn't even realized, until this moment, that I'd been worried about her.

She had just stepped off the elevator and was hurrying toward us with the kind of run people did in school hallways. "Let me talk to you." She continued down the hall away from the elevators, and I followed her until we rounded the corner and were alone.

I was so relieved to see her that I gave her a quick hug and then realized mid-embrace that Briana and I didn't do that. Still, she hugged me back.

"Where have you been?" I asked. "I've been worried."

"Because Claire has been asking for me?"

"Believe it or not, I see you as a human entity outside of your relationship with Claire."

She quirked one eyebrow upward.

"She's been asking for you, and yeah, that's what made me wonder where you were. But then I was worried about *you* as an individual human being."

"I was hiding. I got the calls but figured anyone who was looking for me was doing it on Claire's behalf."

"I figured. Where, out of curiosity?"

"That's why I wanted to find you. I was in the facilities room. It's one of the few places in CyberCorp Tower that doesn't have cameras. That's why I picked it. I knew Claire would ask you to find me, and you wouldn't be able to find me there, even with your unfettered access to virtually everything in this building."

"Smart."

She smiled and nodded, accepting the compliment. "There's an electrician down there." She gestured around the open air. "I imagine there are a lot of electricians in this building, but only one is not employed by CyberCorp."

I gestured for her to move the story forward, and her words picked up pace.

"Apparently, he received a work order to change some electrical"—she gestured vaguely—"*thing*."

"Yeah, I know, but CyberCorp Tower's electrical needs are all handled in-house."

She pointed at me. "Exactly. That's what they were talking about down there. He apparently overloaded some circuits because he didn't know how things were set up here, and something shorted. That's what caused that first ten-second power outage."

That explained the short blackout when I was talking to Francis in tech support the first time.

"I thought your parents might want to know."

"Thanks. They know."

"Any news?" Claire sauntered up behind us.

Jackson followed close behind her.

Briana circled to my other side to put me between the two of them. She kept her gaze directly on me, never veering toward her girlfriend.

"Maybe that's why your hand-screen has been weird." Claire's voice was unnaturally cheerful, but she wasn't fooling anyone. All of us knew she wasn't interested in a conversation about an electrician. She'd come over here to see Briana. "Because of the outage."

"Could you give us a minute?" I asked her.

Briana shot me a grateful look.

Claire scowled but retreated down the hallway. Her back disappeared around the corner, and Jackson went with her.

I returned my attention to Briana.

"What's been going on with your hand-screen?" she asked.

"It's been lagging. Not a big deal." I shook my head. "You came out of hiding to tell me this?"

"It's a big building, but news travels. I just thought it might mean something related to Ron . . . It could be nothing, just a coincidence, but sometimes when coincidences pile up, it's time to take a closer look."

Claire had apparently not taken the hint after all because she came back around the corner, her grin just as cheerful as it had been the first time.

"She doesn't want to talk to you," I said. "She's fine though, as you can see." I gestured toward Briana, who looked perkier than could be expected after having been stuck in this building all night.

"It's okay. I'll talk to her." When I didn't move, Briana laughed and pushed me down the hallway. "It's fine. I knew coming to find you would move up the clock on this conversation, and it's inevitable anyway."

As I passed Claire, I said to her, "Jackson and I are both just down the hall. Give us a shout if something happens or you feel you're in danger."

Briana opened her mouth to object.

I cut her off. "Not from you, Bri. From whoever killed Ron."

Her mouth gaped open because, apparently, that hadn't occurred to her. She turned her shocked gaze to Claire, her eyes wide with concern. I retreated down the hallway to give them some space.

I joined Jackson, Hunter, and Liv outside the conference room where we'd each been interrogated. Jackson and Liv were sitting on the floor, backs pressed against the wall.

Instead of joining them, I paced back and forth past them.

They exchanged glances.

"Something on your mind?" Jackson asked, too loudly, in a voice that made it clear he knew indeed that was the case.

"We need to get Claire out of this building," I said. "She's in danger."

Liv blew out a long breath that matched her just-as-long eyeroll. "We're stuck in a building with androids that don't follow orders. Ron is dead, and Claire's a murderer. We're all in danger."

"Agreed," Hunter said. "Claire isn't the priority. We all need to get out of here."

Jackson jumped to his feet. "It's not murder if she didn't intend to kill anyone." Liv opened her mouth, but Jackson rushed on before she could jump in. "And she didn't. It was a reckless mistake that went horribly wrong."

"Interesting," Liv said. "Let's see how Paris feels about that. Oh wait . . ." She made a show of looking around the room for the dead girl.

I stopped pacing to avoid ramming into Jackson. "This isn't about guilt. That's for a court to decide. *We* get to decide what to do while her life is in danger. If we do nothing, does that make us any better than her?"

"Doing nothing is better than sending a lethal android after a defenseless girl," Liv said, "so yeah, we're better than Claire either way."

"Is that really who you want to be?" I stopped pacing and stared at her. "Someone who lets someone else die because you're not obligated to act?"

She dropped her gaze to the floor.

Briana marched around the corner and stopped in front of us with hands on hips. Her eyes were red, but she stood tall.

Claire rounded the corner behind her, dragging her feet along the floor.

I guessed the breakup was official now.

"You have to get Claire out of here," Briana said. "It's not safe."

"When are they opening the doors?" Claire asked more quietly.

"About that . . ." I told them about the communication issue with the safety door and how it had just refused to open. When I finished explaining, Jackson, Liv, Claire, and Briana all stared at me, mouths agape.

"Are there any entrances that don't have those?" Jackson asked.

I shrugged. Before yesterday, I hadn't even known CyberCorp Tower had safety doors.

Jackson started pacing, and I stepped aside to stay out of his path. After half a minute, he stopped. "I have an idea."

23

I held up a finger to my friends as my micro-comm vibrated against my skin and announced my father's name for my ears only. "Hold that thought."

As much as I wanted to hear Jackson's idea about how to get Claire out of the building, I'd been trying to have a heart-to-heart with my dad ever since Ron's accusation. As long as Claire was surrounded by Jackson, Briana, Hunter, and Liv, she would be fine for a little while longer.

I answered. "What's up? Everything okay?"

He snorted.

"Dumb question?"

"Can you come down to the server room? We should discuss some things."

We should definitely discuss things—starting with why Ron had been so confident that my dad had been the one helping him—and then moving on to what the hell was going on here.

"Can we meet somewhere else?" It had been weeks since I had been in the room with the Model One server, and the thought of it still creeped me out.

"I'm trying to shut her down. The—"

"*Her?*"

"The server. I modeled her personality after your mother . . . It's conceivable I've grown too attached."

I didn't even want to contemplate the thinking behind that, but it explained why I'd started to think of the server as female myself. "Give me a minute. I'm on my way."

I disconnected and walked back toward my friends, who were still muttering among one another. "I'm going to have to take a rain check on the escape plan. I'm meeting my dad in the server room."

Jackson shuddered.

"My sentiments exactly," I said.

He marched toward the elevators, leaving me to trail behind him. "Then I'm coming with you."

Claire was on our heels. "You two aren't leaving me."

Liv and Hunter followed. "We're coming too," Liv said.

I scanned my wrist at the elevator, and it pinged to approve me. A pair of doors opened, and Jackson, Liv, Hunter, Claire, and I piled inside. I kept a foot in the doorway to hold the elevator for Briana.

"I'm out," she said.

Claire's gaze stuttered from her to Jackson and me—her protection—but she stayed put. I removed my foot and let the doors close with Bri on the other side.

A moment later, the rest of us got out in the lobby, and I led my crew across the tile to a door on the back side of the main level, the side not frequented by most guests. The doors back here had labels like *Facilities* and *Security*, and only authorized personnel were welcome.

I led my friends to a white door with the discreet label *Supplies*. The door clicked unlocked as I reached for it. I threw it open to reveal a short hallway with an intimidating all-black door at its end. When I approached, the black steel door shot open and disappeared into the side wall.

I hesitated for only a second and then walked forward. Our footsteps clanged against the platform at the top of the steps that led down into the cave of a room.

Unlike the first time I came here, the lights were already on. We took the stairs down toward the vid-screen that stood in front of the rows and rows of computers in the massive space. Together, all of this made up the Model One server.

Despite all this hardware, with its dramatically high ceiling, the room still looked huge and empty. It gave the impression that sound would bounce off the walls a million times and echo forever.

"Lena?" My father's shout came from somewhere in the aisles of computers. "Heading your way."

My friends and I clanked down the steel steps. As we reached the floor, my dad came into view as he ducked underneath the giant screen.

His brow pinched. "I wasn't expecting anyone else." His gaze took in Liv, Hunter, and Claire and then landed on Jackson, his expression severe.

Jackson inched backward until his foot hit the bottom stair. He gestured for the others to follow and led them back up the way they came. The black door opened for them and then slammed shut behind them.

Dad stood in front of the giant vid-screen, which was completely blank. He glared at it with his arms folded over his chest as if fighting a game of wits.

"We need to talk," I said. I could have jumped right in with Ron's accusation, but there had to be an elegant way of approaching this without outright calling my dad a murder suspect.

"Mm-hmm." He continued to glare at the machine.

"Dad?" I asked after almost a minute.

He startled, as if he'd forgotten I was even there. "I'm considering shutting her down, but I really don't want to."

The server occupied most of the cavernous space. The lights all the way to the end of the room illuminated rows and rows of computers, extending for half a football field.

"Don't we need someone else to help with that?" I asked. I'd tried to shut down this server once before. It had told me it wouldn't obey the command unless it was made by one owner and one engineer. To the server, I added, "Server, whose authorization do you need to shut down?"

White text appeared in the center of the giant black screen. "The owner and the engineer."

My father squinted at me, and I squirmed under the weight.

"I tried to shut it down once before, remember?" I gestured at the text on the display. "I assume I count as an owner, but I enlisted Mr. Miller because it needs an engineer too. He's your top engineer."

My father offered a wry smile. "I see why you'd think that, but she's actually asking for one person who is both her owner and her engineer." He tapped his chest. "I conceived of the server and supervised her construction and programming."

Well, that explained why the server had refused to shut down when I asked it previously.

"Why did you call me down here then? You can shut it down anytime. You don't need me for this."

"I noticed some anomalies." He gritted his teeth and said to the server, although his gaze stayed on me, "Server, shut down immediately."

New text blinked onto the screen. "I've decided not to."

I froze. "Can it do that?"

"Apparently yes, and I'm trying to find out why." He exhaled. "That's not why I called you down here though. I know you've been wanting to talk, and I'm sorry for not prioritizing that. I reviewed the recordings from Ron's room, and—"

"I thought those were erased."

"Not the room where he died—the room where we put him originally." He shook his head. "It's not true."

I clamped my mouth shut. He'd seen me interrogate Ron, and Ron accuse him of helping him weaponize my arm. It was nice to hear him deny it, but doubt still chewed at my stomach lining.

"Ron was a superb liar. We all saw that."

Ron had me convinced we were friends and that he had my best interests at heart. He'd convinced Liv of the same.

Had I really let him make me distrust my father? "I believe you." Shame cast my eyes downward.

"I'm glad." The tension in his face loosened, leaving exhaustion in the creases. "Since you're here, come with me. Let's catch up while I work."

He beckoned for me to follow him. He ducked under the large vid-screen, and with only a few seconds' hesitation, I followed him. With the vid-screen behind us, rows and rows of towering machines filled up the rest of the space, arranged in aisles extending from where we were to the back of the room.

"How are you?" he asked. "I don't imagine this is your favorite place to be, especially given the circumstances."

I grunted.

He walked like he knew where he was going. As I followed, the pace of my heart sped. They were just computers, just like any other computer, but I knew these were the brains of that giant machine that just refused an instruction from its owner and engineer.

Halfway down the center aisle, he stopped. If he hadn't, I wouldn't have noticed the small open space tucked between two of the black server devices.

"You're going to want to access EyeNet if you want to watch," he said.

I closed my eyes. After a second, I opened them to a silvery vid-screen standing in what used to be empty space. Below it, a keyboard hovered in the air.

Dad pulled the keyboard toward him and typed at a furious speed. He could just as easily speak his commands, but he'd always been hands-on with engineering, so I guessed this was more comfortable for him.

"Ron was a promising applicant when he first applied for an internship here. Top of his classes for his whole life. More importantly, he was passionate about how technology could change the world."

Text scrolled up the vid-screen, silvery and translucent, just like objects in the virtual world always were.

"Turns out he was passionate about getting revenge for his parents," I said.

My father grunted as his fingers flew across the virtual keyboard.

"He said his anonymous backer—allegedly you—messaged him every day when he was about to see me. There weren't many people who had the funds to gift him a supercomputer and also knew when he had appointments with me."

He paused his typing for a mere second and then continued. "That definitely limits our suspect pool to someone associated with CyberCorp, but I wasn't the only one with access to the list of ID chips of people in the building."

That made sense. Even Vanessa the receptionist had access to the list of ID chips of people on the main floor. Ron didn't know for sure that my father had helped him—he was drawing a conclusion based on incomplete information.

"Believe it or not," my father said even as he continued typing and text continued to scroll up the vid-screen, "I've been working on some form of the server since we found out your mother was pregnant with you." He stopped typing long enough to gesture toward the computers all over the room. "Each of these is a duplicate of specialized hardware I designed. But this one"—he tapped the black box directly to the left of the vid-screen—"is different."

"What are you doing?"

"I'm recalling all the instructions and reactions of the server over the past six months. It's a lot of data, but I'm also trying several ways to filter it. I know what I'm looking for."

"Does this have to do with CyberCorp Tower being locked down?"

"Maybe. CyberCorp Tower's a closed system. Everything internally is connected, but there are very few transmission routes by which data can be sent from inside the building to the outside. That goes for every device inside these walls. We have signal blockers built into the structure so that every message and every network connection that leaves this building has to go through specific channels. Unfortunately, the corollary to that is that everything inside the building is connected, either directly or indirectly. For this server, that connection is mostly hardwired. We'd have to knock down some walls or bash some floors to kill the connection. To fix the Model Ones, we'll do that if we need to, but I don't think we've reached that level of desperation."

"So you don't actually want to shut it down?"

"I want to know why it's refusing the command."

"Ron is dead."

His finger slammed down on the keyboard, causing

gibberish to jump onto the screen before the scrolling stopped. And he turned toward me. "I hope you don't expect me to be sad about that."

*Not* sad because it meant no one could point him out as a suspect, or *not* sad because of how Ron had traumatized me? I didn't ask. "I mean, at what point do we reach *that* level of desperation?"

"I'll know it when we get there—if we get there." His hands balled into fists and then released. "After what he did to you, I won't be crying into my pillow over the loss of him. And I'm sorry if that sets a poor example. I want you to value human life, so forgive me if I'm having a little trouble with that right now." He went back to typing at top speed.

The text scrolled up the screen. Although I was good at reading program code, I didn't know what I was looking for, and it was moving too fast for me to understand. It was time I returned to my friends anyway. "Any idea when we'll get out of here?"

He paused and scrubbed a hand through his already disarrayed hair. "As soon as humanly possible. I think the server is controlling the doors, although I'm not sure why. When I figure this out . . ." He gestured and then went back to typing.

"Thank you for answering my questions." I took two steps back and turned toward the entrance.

"What the hell . . ."

I couldn't remember the last time I heard my father curse, so I turned back.

He was still standing in front of the virtual vid-screen

and keyboard, but now his face pressed close to the screen, his mouth gaping open.

"What did you find?"

"Nothing." His fingers shot across the keyboard again and then halted. "Nothing," he said louder.

He waved a hand to make the vid-screen and keyboard disappear, and he stepped into the space they'd occupied. From his pocket, he withdrew a small metal key, which he inserted into the back of the server computer.

I squeezed next to him and tried to peer over his shoulder, but his head and hand blocked most of the view.

He reached his fingers into the device and withdrew part of the computer. A rectangular piece with circuitry on both sides. It looked like it used to be gray, but now a deep black char mark spread out from the center. He waved it in front of my face. "It's fried."

"Does that matter though? I mean, there are hundreds of computers here. Why does it matter if one of them stopped working properly? Shouldn't it be set to go offline automatically if it's unresponsive?"

His eyes continued to bulge as he raised the card up to his eye level and turned it around to the other side. "Unsalvageable," he muttered, more to himself than to me.

"So what?" When he didn't look my way, I tapped him on the shoulder. "Why does it matter? It's just one computer."

He leaned against a row of the computers and slid down to the floor. The card dropped out of his hand and clattered down next to him. I squatted, facing him.

"Dad? Tell me what's going on."

"In terms of hardware, these computers are the same." His gaze went right through me. He was looking at me but seeing something else. "Except this one." He dropped his head into his hands.

"Can you fix it?"

He groaned. "The server is intelligent."

"Of course it is. It runs the Model Ones."

"No, listen." He shook his head. "The server provides intelligence to the Model One androids, but she was never supposed to have intelligence of her own. I rewrote her code so she could learn from her own mistakes. She could evolve and even teach us how to make better androids."

"And now she—*it*—is disobeying. But it shouldn't be able to do that, right? You must have built-in commands telling it that it must shut down when you tell it to. Or restrictions about what it's not allowed to do."

"Yes, yes, all of that." He swiped the card up off the ground and threw it across the aisle.

It slammed against another computer and cracked into two pieces, both of which clattered to the ground.

"I broke the rules. Your mother and I agreed from day one that we would never build a computer that could rewrite its own code, but that's what I told the server to do. As a failsafe, this card hardwired instructions telling her to always obey me, over everything else."

I stared at the two charred pieces on the floor.

"I created a monster on a leash."

"And now the leash is broken," I finished.

24

"What are you going to do?" I asked my dad as he stared at the destroyed device card on the floor of the server room.

"I honestly don't know. Maybe it's time to consider shutting the whole thing down." He refused to meet my eyes.

I couldn't remember ever seeing my dad look so defeated. He always had the answers, always took charge, always solved the unsolvable. Now, his shoulders slumped as he glared at the small piece of hardware that could derail all his plans.

"Tom," called a voice that I now immediately recognized as Dr. Sophie. "Thomas, are you down here?" Footsteps sounded on the metal stairs at the front of the room.

"Back here! Column forty-three."

"On my way," Dr. Sophie returned.

My father stood straighter, suddenly back to his usual

confident self. "Don't worry. We'll figure this out and save the day." He offered me a dazzling grin that could rival anyone in the world except Jackson.

"Are you sure?"

"I promise." When I didn't budge right away, he nudged me toward the entrance.

Sophie appeared at the front of our row of computers. She hurried toward us, her quick steps almost at a running pace. She nodded at me as we crossed paths, and I kept walking toward the door.

"What can I do for you?" my father asked behind me.

"We need to talk about the Model Twos." Her tone was quick and short. "I absolutely will not let them be damaged by this business with the Model Ones."

"We've talked about this—"

"Let me finish. I know the Model Ones are our money-maker right now, but the way the Model Two androids mimic one another is the biggest technological leap we have ever achieved. It would be an unacceptable . . ."

Dr. Sophie's voice faded away as I reached the stairs. I had a new message from Jackson telling me he and the others were holed up in a conference room. When I reached the lobby, I took an elevator up to meet them.

They'd locked their room from the inside so it didn't open when I scanned my wrist. After I shouted my identity through the door, Jackson unlocked it, and it slid aside.

Claire met me just inside the door. "Are we leaving?"

I pushed past her into the room. "Soon. First, I want to go over everything we know."

She'd be safe in this room with Jackson, me, and the

rest of us. A higher priority was making sure *everyone* was safe. My parents and others I cared about were stuck in this building too.

Claire's shoulders slumped as she stepped back into the conference room. "It gives me an awful vibe being in a room that's a carbon copy of the one Ron died in."

Liv shot a glance Claire's way and pursed her lips. "The room can't hurt you." She gestured around the space. "Whoever killed Ron isn't here."

"Let's try to work this out," I said. "There are no coincidences, so we have to assume whoever killed Ron played a part in keeping him in this building."

"He would have left and gone home if the building hadn't been locked down," Jackson said.

"It was locked down because the Model Ones were escaping," I said.

"The Model Ones have been acting oddly since Claire reprogrammed them to attack people," Hunter added.

"This is not my fault," Claire shouted.

"No one said it was," I said.

Liv gave me a pointed look. "Actually—"

I cut her off. "Just because actions are connected doesn't mean anyone could have foreseen them. It doesn't mean anyone in particular is at fault. I had to learn that to make peace with my role in Harmony's death."

Everyone shut up.

"The point of this is to move forward, not to assign blame. Claire's going to pay for what she did to Paris—as she should. Let's focus on figuring out the bigger picture."

"And then we can get me out of here?" Claire asked, her voice shrill. "I'm the one with a target on my back."

"She said focus," Liv snapped. "We don't even know if you're a target. Sure, it's possible that the killer was after you to begin with. After all, you and Ron switched rooms."

Claire paled.

She'd been so focused on potentially being the *next* target, so apparently it hadn't occurred to her that she could have been the *first* target.

"It's also possible," Liv continued, "that the killer is targeting both you and Ron, or that Ron was the one and only target."

"So basically, there's only a 66.7 percent chance that I'm next up," Claire said dryly.

"That's a 33.3 percent chance that you're in the clear," Jackson volunteered, with way more cheeriness than the situation justified. After a second, his grin faltered. "That sounded more positive in my head."

Hunter stepped around Claire and Jackson and dropped into a chair at the table. "You put that target there yourself. Don't expect anyone's sympathy."

Liv raised one hand into the air. "Personally, I don't give a damn how Ron died or what happens to Claire. If you find the killer, please send them my regards."

Claire scowled.

"Look," I said, more loudly than necessary. "All I want is to reenact Ron's death. Then we can all go back to stewing in our separate corners." When no one answered right away, I added, "Remember, I'm the one who has to live with killing three people, thanks to Ron. If I can set that aside to find his killer, the rest of you can too."

Liv narrowed her eyes. "Are you using your trauma as a bargaining chip?"

"Is it working?"

Silently, everyone exchanged glances and eventually nodded.

"Great. Let's re-create how we found Ron."

Liv set into motion rearranging the chairs. She pulled out each one and angled it similarly to how it had been in 57J. Hunter took the other side of the long conference table and did the same.

Jackson circled the table and flopped onto his back on the floor, flailing one arm out to the side exactly as Ron's had been. He rolled his eyes into the back of his head and lolled out his tongue.

Claire nudged him with her toe. "A little less realism please."

He pulled his tongue back in.

Hunter picked up the chair closest to the window that hung over the atrium and set it on its side.

I gestured at the window. "There was blood right here."

"Should we . . ." Liv started.

"Let's just use our imaginations for that."

"His attacker probably came in through the door." Liv hurried to the door, exited the room, and then reentered. She squared her shoulders and brought up her fists, as if imitating someone much larger than her.

In any other situation, I might have giggled at how

ridiculous she looked. But the tension was stretching me thin.

"Where was Ron sitting when you saw him earlier?" Liv asked, still making herself as wide as possible, as though she was the attacker.

Still lying on the ground, Jackson pointed over and behind his head to the chair on the far side of the room. It was the one Hunter had moved and placed on its side, but before that, it had been at the foot of the conference table. "I remember because I was irritated I had to walk all the way across the room to kick his ass."

"So, the attacker threatened him somehow," Claire said. "Ron got out of his seat, punched the window, and slammed the chair against it to escape."

Jackson sat up, his expression pensive.

"What?" I asked.

He shook his head. "How much does that chair weigh?"

I walked over and grabbed the back of it with my left hand. I lifted it from the ground easily, set it back down, and then tried it again with my right. "It's solid. Maybe twenty pounds."

"Ron had access to a heavy chair. And instead of hitting his attacker with it, he hit the window. What's the point of that?"

The room went silent.

"Maybe the chair wouldn't have hurt whoever was attacking him," Hunter volunteered.

"Like an android?" Liv glared at Claire. "Someone here has commanded androids before."

The rest of us turned toward Claire as well.

She threw both hands in the air. "It wasn't me. I don't even have access to a client cube to use the program I used, so it couldn't have been. Who else had access?"

We all eyed one another suspiciously.

I shook my head. "No, we're not turning on each other. My parents already said the program you used to control the androids isn't standard. It wouldn't be on just any client cube—it's not supposed to exist at all."

"So *maybe* an android might have attacked Ron?" Jackson said. "That's all we know. Where does that leave us?"

Claire marched toward the door. "Terrified."

"You can get out through the Hayes entrance," Jackson said.

He, Claire, Liv, Hunter, and I had wrapped up our reenactment of Ron's death, pooled our knowledge of what we'd seen and heard since the lockdown started, and were now standing around the conference table.

"The what?" Liv asked.

I dropped into the nearest chair, shocked that he was utterly correct, and that idea hadn't occurred to me. "How did I forget that? The door responded to my ID chip, and it leads right out to a secret exit half a mile away."

"I don't know what you just said," Claire added, "but I'm game if it gets me out of here."

"The secret entrance off the VIP garage," Jackson said.

"Lena used it once when she was trying to hide from the police."

"The key word you just said is secret." I rolled my eyes. "But that should work—assuming there's no safety door blocking the entrance."

"Let's do it." Liv shot for the door.

Jackson stopped her. "I don't think that's a good idea."

Slowly, she spun and raised her brows.

"There was a murder here committed by someone who obviously knows this place well, even has special access to erase camera footage. For all we know, that person could have the same plan we do—to get out of the building by the only viable exit."

Liv sank into the nearest chair. The leather sighed around her, accepting her weight.

Claire paled.

"I'll go by myself. Jackson will stay here with all of you to make sure you're safe."

Hunter folded his arms over his chest. "I don't need Jackson's protection."

Liv touched his arm. "But I might need yours."

His shoulders loosened, and he dropped his arm back to his side before nodding.

"Then it's a plan," I said.

All of them watched me, expressions somber, as I exited the room. The hallway lay empty, except for the red CyberCorp logo gliding silently beside me across the vid-screen walls.

I scanned my wrist at the elevator that would lead down to the VIP garage, my heartbeat pounding in my throat as I waited. I would have been safer huddled in the conference room with the others—strength in numbers.

But I was the only one who could do this, and Claire's life might depend on it. All our lives might. The elevator doors opened, and I made my way down. In the lobby, I hurried to the elevator that led down to the VIP garage, moving my steps faster than my heartbeat to keep from changing my mind.

The VIP garage was still nearly deserted. Only several cars filled the space that was meant for fifty. The metal safety door still blocked the vehicle exit and still showed signs of where the androids had slammed their fists against it.

My footsteps echoed through the space as I ran to the metal door tucked into the far corner. When I scanned my wrist, the door beeped, and the click of the lock sounded. I yanked the door open.

The long, doorless hallway was brightly lit only where I stood. It slanted upward like a dark path to the stars. As an energy-saving feature, a hundred feet beyond me, the hallway wasn't lit at all and stretched out into near darkness. Anticipation churned in my gut as I moved forward.

The hallway seemed to extend infinitely, only teasing what might be at its end.

As I walked, the light moved with me, dimming behind me and brightening in front. I'd been in this tunnel before, and somehow I hadn't been bothered by the darkness that spread ahead. Now, I broke into a run.

My micro-comm vibrated. With a shaky hand, I

accepted the incoming call, and Claire's voice came through. "Lena, did you get out of the building?"

"Yeah, I'm in the tunnel now," I whispered. Why was I whispering? No one else was here. I spun a quick circle just to be sure—not that I could see very far in this tunnel.

In the background, Jackson shouted, "Stay safe! If you feel wrong for even a second, call me."

Claire hushed him before speaking to me again. "Ignore him. Just let us know when you reach the end."

"You guys are making me nervous."

I made my way through the tunnel, the eeriness unsettling me. When the door at the end finally came into view, relief flooded through me. "I see it, guys," I shouted into the micro and broke into a run.

Holding my breath, I scanned my wrist.

The lock clicked, and I threw the door open. The sky was a canvas of technicolor digital billboards, bright and vibrant in their kaleidoscope of colors. The sun beamed down from a cloudless blue sky. Light glimmered off the surrounding buildings, welcoming me from a nightmare of being locked away.

I stepped over the threshold and let the door slam behind me. From this side, it looked like nothing more than a tiny square building with a discreet metal door.

Freedom.

"I'm out." A weight rose off my shoulders and floated away.

"Great," Claire said over the open micro-comm. "Now get back here and take me with you."

"Take all of us with you," Liv shouted from the background.

My hand-screen buzzed, and I slipped it out of my pocket. Just like that, it was working again. Just like that, life had returned to normal. Just like that—

My stomach rolled into a knot as I checked the display. White text centered on a black background: *Why did you leave, Lena? I didn't say you could go.*

25

"Put me on speaker," I said, trying hard to keep the tremor from my voice.

"What's going on?"

Without waiting for an answer, Claire must have transferred me from her micro to the conference room speaker because the next voice was Jackson's, loud and clear.

"Are you okay, babe?"

"I'm okay—physically at least. I just got a message from the server on my hand-screen." I read it aloud. "Why did you leave, Lena? I didn't say you could go."

The doom I felt echoed back at me in the silence that filled my ears.

"Let's back up before we panic," Hunter said eventually. He spoke slowly, deliberately, reminding me why I'd taken comfort in his steadiness for the short time I'd known him. "How do you know it's from the server?"

"It doesn't have a sender ID attached, first of all. It has

that same white text on a black background that she always uses, and it—"

"She?" Liv cut in.

"My dad created her and says she's female."

"Is this a kink?"

"Ew . . . maybe actually. Her personality is based on my mother, which was just . . . maybe. Let's stick to the subject. The message has that same odd, not-quite-human-but-just-human-enough vibe that all her messages have."

"Have you ever received anything from her on your hand-screen before?" Hunter asked.

"No."

"So why now?"

"I have no idea, but it makes me question everything that happened in the last twelve hours. Is there any chance the server is purposely keeping the safety doors from opening? Does she want us all locked in?"

Silence.

"You can't come back here," Jackson said. "The entire building is connected. If the server has access to the safety doors, then it has access to everything else."

"The door to the Hayes entrance is not connected to the rest of the building," I said. "By design, it's isolated from the rest of the system."

"So it's safe to use," Claire said, a note of panic creeping into her words. "Even if the server is controlling the safety doors, we don't know that she can control the door to that entrance."

"But the elevators aren't," Jackson said. "The stairwell doors. All the paths we'd need to *get to* the Hayes entrance might be under the server's control. If Lena comes back, there's no guarantee she'll be able to leave again—especially since the server clearly wants her here."

The sound of Claire's panicked breathing filled my ears through the connection.

Jackson murmured something I couldn't make out, but his tone was buttery smooth. Her breathing slowed and quieted, and mine did right along with it.

"I agree with Jackson," Hunter said.

I almost dropped my hand-screen. Hunter and Jackson had been at odds since the day they learned of each other's existence. I slipped the device back into my pocket to keep it safe. "Then it's settled."

"You should—" Claire started.

Jackson cut her off. "I'm calling you an autocar. Get as far away from this building as possible." He disconnected, leaving his command hanging in the air and leaving me stranded away from my parents and friends.

My micro-comm buzzed again only a second later. I jumped. When I activated it, Claire's voice sounded in my ear. "You gave that server access to your hand-screen?" She sounded closer now, so I guessed I was on her micro and no longer on speaker.

I blinked, and it took me a couple seconds to register what she'd said. "I needed it to mirror my display. I didn't mean for it to use my device *forever*." I paused. "How did you know that?"

"I gave it access to my micro-comm, so I know being explicitly authorized is the only way it can communicate with you directly."

Just two weeks ago, Claire had tried to escape justice by telling the server to restrain Jackson and me. She'd done that through her micro. I'd wondered how at the time.

"It wasn't personal," she said when I didn't answer.

"When I was shot with that EMP gun earlier today, I couldn't feel my arm," I said. "You'd think I would be used to feeling fear like that these days, but I'm not. I also felt that same terror when the androids held me down on *your* command. Do you have any idea how traumatic that was? Do you even care?"

"I care, Lena. I do." Through the micro-comm, I could sense the pain in her voice.

An autocar coasted toward me, recognizable by the indicator light on its top. When it stopped in front of me, the door closest to me popped outward and slid upward. It revealed a cushy interior with a long seat at the back and another long seat along the side. I climbed in and settled in the back.

"Authorization to scan ID chip?" the car asked in an electronic voice.

"Go ahead," I said.

"Welcome, Lena Hayes. Destination?"

Claire shouted in my ear, "You should—"

"No," I said. "I'm not going back yet. Not until we have a plan."

"That's not what I was going to say. I . . ."

"Lena Hayes," the autocar said again, this time at an increased volume that emanated from the walls, drowning out the rest of whatever Claire was saying.

Its door still hung open, waiting to confirm that it did

indeed have a customer. Only fifty feet away stood the locked door to the Hayes entrance, the tunnel back to my friends and parents locked inside the Tower.

"Destination?" the car asked in a bell-like electronic voice.

"Anywhere. Just drive around the city."

The door whirred closed, and the ride started with an artificial hum. Electric cars had silent motors, but most makers included the noise to alert pedestrians to traffic.

While most of the city still lounged in their homes, the digital billboards never slept. They shined their technicolor ads, casting multicolored lights across my face. The drone activity had died down now that the daytime surcharge was in effect. Only an occasional drone hovered overhead, waiting for wireless instructions.

"I appreciate you sticking by me last night," Claire said through the micro-comm.

I grunted. I'd forgotten she was there.

"I know I'm not innocent."

I snorted.

"Of Paris's death, no, of course I'm not." Her end went quiet, and for the first time, I believed she felt remorse. "I swear to you—I didn't kill those cops. I'm not working against you. I sincerely believe Philip Pollock can help us with the server. If you believe in my self-interest, at least believe that I know getting us *all* out of here would help me."

She had a point.

My hand-screen buzzed, and I hesitated before withdrawing it from my pocket, dread tightening in my gut.

Again, the white text appeared on a black background: *Please return to CyberCorp Tower, Lena.*

"Don't contact me anymore," I snapped under my breath.

"I thought we were getting somewhere," Claire said in my ear.

"Not you." I powered down the hand-screen and slid it back into my pocket. "There's something evil going on at CyberCorp, and it's more than just Ron Franklin. We still don't know who funded him." I rushed on to stop her from accusing my father. "Even if it is my dad, that doesn't change the fact that the danger is still here."

"Please don't say it's me—"

"Let me finish. My dad claims there was never supposed to be an application that makes it easy to write programs for the Model Ones. They aren't supposed to be programmed independently. They're supposed to learn from their surroundings and from the instructions they've been given."

"You think I'm lying about the application on Mr. Miller's client cube? You think I just figured out how to program the Model Ones from scratch? Could *you* do that? You're a lot more tech-savvy than I am."

I spread my hands palms up, as if she could see me. "I wouldn't know where to start, and that's my point. Someone created that application and put it on Mr. Miller's client cube for you to find. That same someone killed the two detectives. *Maybe* that person financially backed Ron."

"Philip Pollock," Claire said.

"It wasn't Pollock. He's too greedy to sabotage his moneymaker."

"No, like I was *trying* to say earlier, you should find him."

"That's not hard. On a Saturday morning, I'm guessing he's at his house."

"He's not a suspect, he's connected, and he doesn't trust CyberCorp. He didn't know it would balloon into a giant when he invested. Since it did, though, how much do you want to bet he knows everything about the company's weak spots just in case he needs an out?"

I sucked in a long breath because I didn't like that I agreed with her. As a rule, I preferred to keep my distance from Pollock. "You think he can help take down the server?"

"If anyone can, it's him."

"Autocar," I said. "Take me to Philip Pollock." I gave it the address.

26

THE FIRST TIME I WAS AT POLLOCK'S HOUSE, I WASN'T invited. This time, I wasn't either, but at least I didn't have to sneak.

As before, a tall black gate circled the property, giving it a secretive air. Beyond it sat a house with a brick façade and traditional accents. The architecture seemed to hark back to an earlier era, with gabled roofs, decorative shutters, and an intricate, hand-carved wooden door.

Cypress trees covered the fence along the street, save for the gate. The foliage provided a natural screen, further reinforcing the image of a man who didn't want prying eyes. An indiscreet camera sat at the top of the gate, staring down as the autocar approached.

I hopped out, and the vehicle coasted away.

I jumped in front of the camera and waved both hands wildly. A red light blinked under the lens as the motion sensors caught me.

"Miss Hayes, as I live and breathe." Despite the early hour on a weekend, Pollock's voice had the same mix of southern drawl and arrogance it usually held. "To what displeasure do I owe this visit?"

"We need your help!" Claire shouted into my ear through my micro..

"You don't need to yell," I muttered. "He just pretends to be anti-tech. I guarantee that whatever audio sensors he's using are top-of-the-line, but not top-of-the-line enough to hear my micro-comm."

"Indeed, I can hear you just fine. I would rather not, though, so please get to the point. What can I help you with, and why would I bother?"

"You'll help me because CyberCorp brings in over half your income. If it does well, you do well. If it fails, you'll make a hasty exit. Right now, it's on the edge of failure."

There was a long pause, so long that I thought maybe he hadn't heard me after all. And then, "Anything we discuss would be confidential."

"We wouldn't want your anti-tech groupies thinking you actually care about CyberCorp's future."

With a loud clunk of metal, the two halves of the gate opened inward. "Certainly not."

As the heavy, carved wooden door creaked open, Pollock appeared as an embodiment of wealth and not-so-subtle arrogance. He wore a luxurious royal-blue silk robe, belted casually around his waist and tailored to fit his broad shoulders. Under the robe was a crisp white dress shirt, partially unbuttoned, and gray slacks. Deep-blue slippers rounded out the casual attire.

After glaring down at me for several long seconds, he pushed the door open farther and led the way inside to his office.

I thought my father's office was big, but this was twice the size, taking up one full wing of the house. The vaulted ceiling rose to the second floor. A huge wooden desk sat at the far end with a row of bookshelves behind it and books arranged by size and color.

Soft music emanated through the room. Classical, of course. I wondered if he even liked this kind of music or if it was all part of his image.

Pollock settled into the seat behind his desk and spun his chair in a full circle once on its swivel, before facing me and gesturing toward a chair on the other side.

I took one. "We need your help figuring out what's going on at CyberCorp."

"I assume you're referring to the many murders connected to the company." Amusement quirked his mouth upward. "I believe we're up to seven now."

"No." My voice snapped out at him like a rubber band.

Pollock's face wore feigned confusion as he ticked the victims off on his fingers. "Three of your classmates and Simon the intern. Poor Paris Winter and the two detectives." He cast a smug look my way. "That is seven, yes? Have I miscounted?" He ticked up to seven on his fingers again, this time without the words, and then nodded as if he'd convinced himself.

I drew in a long inhale and let it out—just like my therapist taught me. "Technically, we're up to eight."

He cocked an eyebrow.

"Ron Franklin died last night."

He leaned forward until his elbows touched the desk surface. "There was no word on the news. Are your parents paying off reporters again?"

I ignored that question, although the answer was probably *yes*. "The Tower has been completely locked down since yesterday evening. The murder was reported to the police, but no reporters are inside the building." I spread my hands wide. "Thus, no news report. I assume that will change as soon as the Tower is open."

"Locked down?"

I told him the entire story, starting with the androids going berserk, Ron's death, and ending with my escape. I was vague about that part, leaving out the details about the Hayes entrance. My parents would kill me if he started asking to use it.

Pollock leaned back in his chair and stared at the ceiling. After almost a full minute, he burst out laughing.

I glared.

He held up a hand. "I'm sorry. It's not funny." Another burst of laughter. "It's a little funny. Your parents are so protective of their little company. They pride themselves on creating technology that makes our lives safer and easier. Security systems. Communication systems. Even humanoid androids that manage households. All of that, and they can't even control their own building."

Claire snorted in my ear through the micro-comm. Her sense of humor was obviously holding up better than mine.

"Yeah," I said dryly, "it's hilarious."

Finally, he composed himself and crossed his legs,

placing one ankle on the other knee. "How do you think I can help you?"

"As an investor—"

"Partial owner."

I rolled my eyes. "Sure, as a partial owner, you must get reports about what the company is producing and how the building is being used. Given how particular you are, I'm guessing you read them."

"In detail."

"Is there anything you can give me to take down the server?"

One edge of his mouth pulled down for a split second before turning back into a smirk. "If I could, why would I? I like it when CyberCorp does well. Plus, aren't your parents funding a lawsuit against me? I'm sure my lawyers would rather I not speak to your family at all."

"*Threatening* to fund," I corrected. "All of that goes away if you stop bad-mouthing them in public. Speaking of which, don't you have some kind of duty as an investor *not* to bad-mouth CyberCorp?"

"The area is gray." He waved a dismissive hand. "Your parents drop the lawsuit and the cease-and-desist threats, and I will help you to the best of my abilities."

"You can't have it both ways. You are with us, or you're not."

"I'm just along for the ride until the ride is no longer convenient."

"CyberCorp is the source of over half your income. Why don't you just stop the anti-tech speeches? They're not in your best interest, and the lawsuit will disappear."

"*Information* is in my best interest, and being involved in both the tech and anti-tech communities means that I have all the information. Knowledge is power, and power is money." He jabbed a finger in my direction. "More to the point, you are asking me to help you sabotage one of CyberCorp's most promising products, the Model One server. How does this help CyberCorp? How does this help *me*?"

Claire's voice filled my ears. "Tell him about Ron's accusation."

I gritted my teeth. As much as I didn't want to spread that rumor, it might be just the thing to sway Pollock. "Before he died, Ron claimed my father provided him with the computer capable of hacking EyeNet."

Pollock put his foot back on the floor and leaned forward, eyes wide, curiosity piqued. "Not a most reliable source." It was a challenge. He wanted me to say more.

"There's some evidence that my father was one of a tiny group of people who could have killed Ron. He was also one of a tiny group of people who could have financially backed Ron." I shrugged.

Pollock leaned back in his chair and propped one leg on the other knee again, revealing a bare ankle and a slipper that was somehow stylish. "You're suggesting that, if your father did this, he will eventually be implicated, and I should cut my losses."

I nodded. I didn't believe that for a second, but if it would convince Pollock, I could play along.

Pollock tilted back his chair, steepled his fingers, and

studied the ceiling. After almost a minute, I looked up too, as if the answers were up there.

"What is he waiting for?" Claire shouted into my ear.

I cringed at the sharp sound.

Pollock squinted at me but didn't react to my fit. "As far as I know, the server is hardwired to the building. The only way to disconnect it is to open up the wall and physically cut the wiring, which I imagine is expensive and would have zero return on investment. In fact, it would only make way for more expenditures when the server eventually has to be reconnected."

"What about the safety doors? Can we disconnect those from the building?"

"Have you tried sawing them open?"

"I watched a couple Model Ones pound on one of those doors, and they barely left a dent. Even if my parents have something to cut them open, breaking down safety doors doesn't exactly send a positive message about the company's competence."

"When I invested in CyberCorp, I didn't think the company would last the year. I just wanted the good press. Because of that choice, I can afford to be choosy about my financial choices now." He gestured around the massive room.

"So we're on the same side?" I asked.

He chuckled. "You misunderstand. I absolutely want to see CyberCorp succeed. However, if the company has to be liquidated due to failure, I'll survive. I've already gained more than I expected from the piddly little investment I gave your parents fifteen years ago." He slammed both his hands on the desk palm down. "Why should I get involved at all? Is it not better to stay neutral and out of the news?"

"Don't act like you don't care about the company. The way you're always spying on my parents and their employees. You were the one to break the news about my arm. You showed up at my house unannounced when you were being chased by androids, and you had no reason to even be in that neighborhood. So either . . ." I held up one finger in the air. "You're an obsessed stalker." I held up another finger in the air. "Or you stay more involved than you want people to think you are."

"Are you . . ." He leaned forward in his chair, his mouth dancing into a smile. "Are you accusing me of . . . caring?" Again, he burst into laughter.

I kept my face as stony as possible until he stopped.

He sighed. "Let me be clear. I could help, but I need to know this will work in my favor." His gaze flitted to something over my shoulder.

Before I could react, a heavy hand gripped my shoulder. My mind went blank, but my arm and the artificial intelligence embedded in my head acted instinctively. I was up on my feet. I slid under the man's arms and turned to face him. My left arm shot out and hit him in the torso.

The man grunted, stumbled, and fell to the ground. He curled into a ball and moaned, spitting out all manner of curse words. Another man moved toward me. My arms went up defensively.

"Stop." Pollock jumped to his feet and glared at the two goons. "You can't grab teenage girls from behind." He took small steps toward me, both arms up in surrender. "I apologize. No one's going to hurt you."

The man on the floor was still cursing, and his volume increased. "Bitch broke my freaking rib."

"Then perhaps you've learned something," Pollock said.

"I'm sorry." I didn't drop my hands, though. "The arm reacts instinctively. You startled me."

Pollock waved a dismissive hand at the man on the ground. "Don't apologize. He's new and overzealous, and he should have known better."

The curse words got louder and switched to an unfamiliar language.

The other man glanced back and forth between me and his friend on the floor before his gaze landed on Pollock. "It's time for your call."

Pollock pushed back his chair, and it rolled until it hit the wall behind him. "I'll take it in my bedroom." As he circled his desk, he pulled open the top center drawer and kept walking without giving me a backward glance.

He followed the two men from the room. Just before he reached the door, he turned. "Show yourself out. I'll be back in a few minutes, and I expect this office to be empty."

"Well, that was a colossal waste," Claire said through my micro.

I circled the desk and stared down at the contents of the drawer Pollock had opened. "Don't be so sure."

27

TEN MINUTES LATER, I WAS BACK IN AN AUTOCAR, AND I flinched when my micro-comm buzzed. I didn't know how people got used to these things vibrating on their heads all the time. I felt like I was in electroshock therapy.

"Message from Jackson Watts," the micro-comm said in a voice that sounded oddly and surreally like my own. Weird.

The vehicle pulled smoothly onto the highway.

"Read message," I said.

It played in my head, this time in Jackson's voice. "How's it going out there?"

Hesitantly, I tapped my ear to respond. "Send reply: I've got something, and I'm on my way back."

A few seconds later, his response came through: "Don't you dare come back here. The last thing we need is to undo progress we've made on getting people *outside* this building."

I tapped my ear. "Send reply . . . You know what? Call Jackson." Ringing filled my ears until Jackson connected.

"Please don't come back here until we have a plan. I'll keep Claire and the others safe until we're out of here."

"Most people say *hello*."

"Hey, babe. Please don't come back here. If you have a plan, tell me and I'll get it done."

"I need to be there. This is my responsibility."

"Suddenly, you're done avoiding things? Phenomenal." The sarcasm came through like a wrecking ball.

"What's that supposed to mean?"

There was a long stream of silence on the other end with nothing more than Jackson's breathing. "Send me whatever you have, and I can handle it here." His voice was low, commanding.

Irritation simmered in my stomach, coming to a boil. "This is why we broke up."

"Because I care about you and want you out of harm's way?"

"Because you decide what's best for me, regardless of what I believe."

"Do you even know what you believe? Yesterday, you swore you were never going back to the Tower. You wanted nothing to do with CyberCorp. Now, it's *your responsibility*." The mocking tone of those last two words stoked my nerves to burning.

"Is it so wrong that I don't want to run that company? I just want to figure this out, save my friends, and live my life outside the shadow of that building. I didn't ask for this, but I'm doing it because it's the only way to move on. How do you not get that?"

He laughed without joy. "I get it. I get *you*. You have the biggest heart with the hardest shell of anyone I've ever known. You're so afraid to be your best self that you'd rather be no self at all."

"That doesn't even make sense."

"You had just broken up with me, and you still insisted on making sure I got home safely—because you have a big heart. But you're an avoider. You don't know how you feel about me, so you avoid. You don't know how you feel about Hunter, so you avoid—he's a tool, by the way—problem solved. You don't like the attention of CyberCorp, so you avoid."

"Is it wrong to avoid things that cause pain?"

"No, but you're so busy deciding who you *don't* want to be that you avoid every opportunity to make yourself who you *want* to be."

"And who's that?"

The autocar coasted off the highway and through the streets, humming its artificial purr.

"You're still figuring that out, and I just want to make sure you're alive to do that. The probability of that goes up dramatically if you're not in this building while it's locked down."

"Did you ever think that I avoid things because I'm a walking disaster, and those *things* would be worse off with me involved?"

He took his time answering. "I don't believe that. You care about people. You like to act like you don't, like you're untouchable and nothing's going to hurt you, but you feel everything. It's the reason you avoid. You don't know how to care halfway."

I didn't respond.

"Babe?"

"That's not how I see myself. I'm just a rich girl destined to inherit a company that hurts people."

"Maybe that's the real problem. You're a rich girl, yeah. You're destined to inherit a company that hurts people, yet you're on your way back here to clean up the mess."

I stayed quiet.

"Did you ever think that, with you at the helm, Cyber-Corp could be everything you want it to be? With all the power and resources your parents have accumulated, the company could be a genuine source for good."

"What if I want nothing to do with that? What if I just want to come back to the Tower, fix this one thing, and then stay away forever?"

"Then I'll fucking deal with it because I love you!" His shout rang through my head like a gong.

That was not the answer I expected, and I held my response in limbo on the tip of my tongue.

"I can only give you my advice. I can't make you take it, and I wouldn't want to." When I didn't answer, he said, "I'll be waiting," and disconnected.

A second later, my micro-comm buzzed. Instinctively, I grabbed it and ripped it off my head. Then, cringing the whole time, I pasted it back. "Video call from Claire Payne." The electronic voice came out sounding too eerily like my own.

Since it was a video call, I could take the call on my hand-screen, which would open myself up to more creepy messages from the server, or I could take it on the EyeNet. Given my history with the EyeNet, I tried to stay as far away from it as possible. Plus, I was on my way back, so I'd see Claire shortly.

"Reject call," I told the device.

The vibrating in my head stopped. I slumped back into the plush leather cushion of the autocar, grateful for the silence in my head.

My micro-comm buzzed again. "*Urgent* video call from Claire Payne."

I sat up straight. I closed my eyes for a few seconds, willing my EyeNet functionality to turn on. "Answer call." When I opened my eyes, the world morphed. The autocar interior dimmed, falling into the background as if shoved away from images of what looked like the interior of a CyberCorp elevator. I didn't see Claire anywhere, so I assumed she was sending me the video feed from her network-enabled contact lenses.

"I'm almost there," I snapped across the line. "Can we not do the video call thing?"

"Sorry. I know you're busy trying to save us and all."

"Yeah." My curiosity won out. "You're in the elevator? I thought you all were staying together."

"You know I can't stay in close quarters with *that girl* for long." The way she spit out the words like they tasted awful made it clear she meant Liv. "I just needed a breather. I wasn't even going to get off the elevator. Just a quick joy ride." Her voice rose in pitch until reaching a steady whine.

I chuckled. Despite the disaster happening in Cyber-Corp Tower, it was nice that some of my friends were exactly who they'd always been. The world could spiral off its axis, and Liv and Claire would continue hating each other. Somehow, I found comfort in that.

Something was off about Claire's video feed though. The elevators always displayed giant numbers on the walls, letting passengers know what floor they were currently passing.

The walls were blank.

"Is it moving?"

She took a long audible breath, just as I'd done too often lately to keep myself from falling over a cliff into an abyss of panic. "I asked to go to the lobby. It moved for a split second, and then the lights went out."

"You think it's the server?"

"I don't know what else to think."

"Don't worry. I have a plan."

"Entailing what, exactly?" Her voice shook.

"We're going to shut down the server."

"Oh, is that all?" She laughed, and a bit of the stress left her voice. Her view shifted from the side of the elevator to the front doors, and dread twisted in my gut. The floor numbers weren't the only problem. The whole elevator was blank. No button lights to help passengers request floor numbers if they wouldn't or couldn't speak. No overhead lighting.

"Claire, did you ask the elevator? That thing is completely automated. It can call security for you."

"You think I didn't try that? Elevator, call security."

I waited for the elevator's polite response, but only silence met Claire's request.

"Did you call someone inside the building? Jackson?"

"Tried that." Through her lenses, I watched her hand come around to the side, reaching to where her micro-comm would be. "Call Jackson."

"Call failed." The response came from Claire's device in Claire's voice, but somehow more electronic.

"Call failed," Claire herself repeated.

"Crap," I said. Nervousness swelled in my stomach. The CyberCorp elevators had built-in, encrypted signal repeaters designed to let calls connect despite their thick metal walls. Perhaps the repeater was down too. But if the repeater was down, how had Claire been able to call me? "Can you do me a favor and try to call Liv?"

"Why the hell would I do that?"

"Humor me."

Again, the call failed. Yet *our* call continued without a blip.

The image of the elevator overlaid on the real-world autocar I occupied suddenly shook. My perspective shifted to a lower point, as if Claire had fallen to the ground.

"What happened?" I shouted. "Are you okay?"

"Passenger in distress," came the autocar's electronic voice. "Should I call emergency personnel?"

"Yes!" I shouted at it. "Claire, can you hear me?"

"Call failed," came the elevator's voice.

Terrified sobs came across the line. "I'm stuck inside an elevator in a skyscraper." She sucked in three long, quick breaths. "Get me out of here."

"Are you okay?"

"Get me out of here!"

Claire's field of view rose again, and her fists entered the picture. She pounded on the doors, and the feed vibrated around her as she trembled. "Somebody, get me out of here. Get me out!"

My stomach clenched and flexed, threatening to dispel its contents over the confused images. "I'm on my way back."

The shaking stopped.

Claire's sobs filled my ears as she slid back down the floor, lowering the perspective of my view again.

My autocar turned onto the street that held the Hayes entrance to CyberCorp Tower. "I'm almost there. Hold on a little longer."

# 28

THE AUTOCAR COASTED TO A STOP. I SENT QUICK messages to Jackson, Liv, and Hunter to let them know Claire was stuck in an elevator, unhurt but terrified.

As the door opened, dual images of myself made my head spin. A digital billboard on a building on my left showed an image of me sporting a headband wired for brain-human interface. On my right, another building held a billboard featuring me tossing my curly hair, freshly washed with some name-brand shampoo.

Between the two, a smaller structure held the door to the Hayes entrance. It looked like a utility closet and would have escaped my notice had I not used it twice before.

That was probably the point.

"Payment received," said the autocar's electronic voice as I grabbed the cardboard tube I'd taken from Pollock's desk and ducked under the vertically sliding door and onto the sidewalk. The door slid closed, and the vehicle took off with a low hum.

Another car slowed and coasted to the curb. Like the autocar, this one had a sleek bullet shape, but it was jet black with darkened windows, in contrast to the bright yellow vehicle I'd just exited.

With straightened shoulders, I marched toward the door to the tunnel. As I reached it, a hand landed on my shoulder.

I whirled around, and my left arm reacted. My palm shot out and shoved, slamming into the man's chest and throwing him backward. Philip Pollock landed on his butt on the sidewalk, his face a mask of pain. His hand clutched a rolled up collection of large sheets of paper, and they tumbled from him as he hit the ground.

I crossed my arms over my chest and stared.

His face pinched as he pushed off the pavement and rubbed his lower back. "I should take my own advice about not sneaking up on teenage girls." He snatched up the papers and tapped them on the ground to align them with one another before brushing off his clothes.

He still wore the white shirt and gray slacks from earlier. The silk robe was gone, though, and he'd swapped the slippers for loafers.

I took a step toward him, both fists clenched.

He held up both hands. "I submit. I'm not here to fight. I'm here to help."

"You mean you *followed me* to help?"

He gestured dismissively. "Yes, yes, clearly I followed you." He stepped around me to get a look at the door. "To *where* exactly have I followed you? I assumed you'd return to the Tower to save the day." He nodded down at the cardboard tube in my hand—the one labeled *BLUE-PRINTS* in large blocky scrawl.

I held it tighter, feeling the cardboard crunch in my fist. I hoped he hadn't followed me because he changed his mind about the little help he'd given already. "Our business is done."

Pollock sighed. "You don't trust me, and you don't have a reason to." He unrolled the papers in his hand, flashed a set of blueprints, and rolled them back up.

I squinted at his hands and then popped the top off the tube in mine. It was empty.

"Before you accuse me of tricking you, let me assure you"—he rattled the papers he held—"these are the real blueprints for CyberCorp Tower, and they can show us the best places to attack the server."

"Why give me an empty tube at all?"

"If I'd given you the real blueprints, you would have disappeared through that door already." He pointed toward the small structure that housed the Hayes entrance. "If I had given you nothing, you would not even be entertaining this conversation."

I couldn't deny either of those statements.

"So here we are. My future is inextricably aligned with CyberCorp's."

I was stronger than Pollock, but if we fought over

papers, I would risk tearing them or having them blow away in the wind. "I don't trust you as far as I can throw you." I looked at the ground and eyed the distance I'd shoved him. "Which is about eight feet."

He held up both hands. "Again, not here to fight. I think you'll agree that I've already offered you promising help. I may surprise you."

"I don't have time for this. Claire is stuck in an elevator. The server is in control of the building, and people are trapped in there. You're worthless to me when the only thing I can trust you to do is look out for your own interests."

"Exactly." His face broke into a smile, and he pointed at me as if I'd just won a prize. "I bet on CyberCorp once before, when no one else would. I'm doing that again now. I protect my own interests—that means the company, your parents . . . and their very capable heir."

I crossed my arms back over my chest.

"And if that helps other people, that's fine too." He shrugged. "Can you afford to leave me behind when there are lives at risk?"

The only thing I hated more than his grin right now was the fact that he was right. I needed those blueprints or his knowledge of what was in them. "What's in it for you?"

"Glory," he said, grinning. "I always wanted to be a hero. Plus, you and yours have made a mess of this up until now. I want to be sure this is done right."

I resented that last bit, but my options were limited. I jerked my head toward the door, and he followed. I unlocked the door and opened it, revealing darkness that seemed to go on forever.

"What's this?" he asked, his voice low with awe and trepidation.

"This is the secret entrance that you are definitely not supposed to know about."

The grin was back, somehow wider than before. "This is working out brilliantly already."

"When this is over, please don't tell all your followers about how the Hayeses have a secret entrance and how that somehow makes us even more evil. I'm sure you could find a way to spin it."

He placed a hand on his chest and fixed his face in exaggerated shock. "I would never."

"I'm regretting this already."

I took the first step forward. Unlike him, I didn't need to adjust to the idea of a long tunnel that appeared to lead nowhere. I'd done this a couple times before.

A light came on above my head, but the path before us still lay in darkness.

Pollock recovered quickly, his long strides catching and passing mine. He made a series of *mm-hmm* and *mm-haa* noises as the door slammed and the light moved with us those first few steps.

Then he took off at a brisk pace, leaving me to hurry along behind him.

There was a malevolent AI waiting for us, and I was trusting Philip Pollock with my life.

The elevator up from the VIP garage whispered open, revealing the gleaming lobby of CyberCorp Tower. The sleek, high-tech design of the skyscraper was reflected in every detail: the reflective black reception desk, the mirrored glass behind it, and the soaring-high atrium ceiling sixty floors above.

Pollock exited first. I had to will my feet to step out of the cab. Back again.

This was the last place in the world I wanted to be, yet here I was.

Kyle Winter appeared from a corner that had been hidden from inside the elevator. Slitted eyes took us in. "How the hell did you get out?"

I froze. How did Kyle even know I'd left the building? "What are you taking about?"

"Don't play games with me. I saw you come through here over an hour ago. I'm not authorized for the VIP elevator, but I don't for a second believe you've been camped out in the garage all this time."

I didn't answer, but I shifted my body to half-shield Pollock's instinctively.

"This building's still locked down," Kyle continued. "Or is it? What game are you Hayeses playing?" His gaze flicked to Pollock, suspicion etched on his face. "Who's this?"

I stepped toward him, preparing to shove past.

Kyle pulled the EMP gun from his jacket and leveled it at me.

My breath froze in my throat. My heart pounded in my

chest, a drum beat echoing through my veins. It filled my ears. Security had actually given that back to him? Someone needed to lose their job over this.

More importantly, if that gun went off, it would disable my arm again. I'd be defenseless against whatever was coming.

Pollock, smooth as ever, stepped forward. "You must be the Kyle Winter I've heard about." He glanced at me for confirmation.

When I nodded, Pollock gave him a wide, soothing grin. "Listen, we all want the same thing. We're going to shut down the Model One server. It killed your sister."

Kyle's eyes flashed with rage. "Claire Payne and the Hayeses killed my sister!" He shifted the gun toward Pollock, blinked, and then aimed it back at me.

I slid a step back toward the elevator. If I couldn't go forward, maybe I could dive back inside. I waved my left arm behind me, hoping I was close enough for the scanner to pick up my ID chip.

Behind Kyle, Jackson creeped up on his toes, his steps light, his body crouched low and ready to pounce.

I widened my eyes, silently sending the message that I had this handled. Jackson was even more vulnerable to that EMP gun than I was.

He nodded and kept coming.

That stupid, cocky boy. I would kill him myself if he died because of me.

I lunged at Kyle and grabbed for the gun. He clung to it, but I gripped the barrel with my left hand and yanked.

The gun went off.

A blue stream of light cracked from the barrel. It hit Jackson square in the chest. He crumpled to the ground, shock frozen on his face. His mouth moved, but all I could hear was my own scream.

29

Jackson lay on the concrete floor, motionless. I ran to his side and slumped down beside him so hard my knees cracked against the floor.

"Jackson? Jackson!"

I chucked the EMP gun as far as I could across the lobby and threw my body over Jackson's. Tears streamed down my face.

He didn't move. He didn't breathe.

I gripped his shoulders and shook. His head lolled from side to side, but his eyes stayed shut and his chest deadly still. When I placed my hands in front of his nose and mouth, I couldn't sense any sign of life.

I placed my ear against his chest and wrapped my arms around him. His body was warm, but nothing moved. Not his eyes, not his head, not his chest.

"Please breathe. Please, babe." Tears streamed down my face. I tasted their salt on my lips.

I slammed my micro-comm. "Call security. This is Lena Hayes. I'm with Jackson Watts on the main floor in the VIP garage elevator bay. He was hit with an EMP gun. He's not breathing."

"I'm sorry," Kyle kept muttering. "I didn't know it could do that."

"He needs help," Pollock said. He gripped my shoulders and tried to pull me off Jackson.

I clutched him more closely. I would not leave him.

"Lena!" Pollock shouted.

I snapped my face toward him.

He stared me in the eyes. "He needs help. He needs to get to medical."

I scrambled to my feet and tried to lift Jackson with my left arm, but he was too heavy to support on my right side and too awkward to manage with only one arm.

I spun around, scanning the lobby for anyone who could help. My parents? Security staff? All of them were somewhere working on the safety doors or the server.

I threw my head back and cursed at the top of my lungs, screaming my frustrations to the universe.

Pollock shoved me out of the way and scooped Jackson into his arms. "I've got this. You go check on your friend in the elevator."

Right—Claire. She was still trapped, potentially vulnerable to the malfunctioning server. I took a step toward the lobby and then spun back toward Pollock.

"You can trust me." He looked me in the eyes. "I may be a self-serving fraud, but I would never let a kid die on my watch." When I still didn't move, he added, "You were right before—I was spying on you when those Model Ones came after me. I thought you might be the next one attacked, and believe it or not, I don't like it when kids die."

Sincerity made his face almost unrecognizable. Gone were the cocky grin and the slimy swagger.

Without waiting for me to agree, Pollock sprinted toward the main elevator bay that led up the Tower. I followed.

My pulse pounded at light speed as we waited for an elevator to arrive, as we rode up to the lowest medical floor and Pollock took off with Jackson still in his arms, and as I rode alone the rest of the way up to floor fifty-nine, where I'd left Hunter and Liv.

I stepped off to find the two of them waiting, staring in my direction.

Liv peeked around me to the empty elevator cab. "Where's Jackson? I thought he'd be with you."

"He's in medical. He—" My throat choked up. I couldn't finish that thought without shattering to pieces. "Let's focus on Claire for now."

"What?" Hunter moved beside me and put a hand on my shoulder.

A bit of tension slid away at his touch, and I leaned into him. I was lucky to have him as a friend. When all this was over, I owed him a conversation about our status.

"He was shot with an EMP gun."

Liv sucked in her breath.

Hunter's eyes went huge. "Is he going to be okay? That could . . ." *Kill him* were the words he didn't speak, but we all knew the inevitable destination of that sentence.

"I don't know. Pollock carried him to medical."

"Pollock?" Somehow, Hunter's eyes widened even more.

"Let's worry about Claire right now." If I opened the dam to worrying about Jackson, I would be flooded, and nothing else could break through. For now, I needed to focus on Claire. "Do you know which elevator she's in?" I spun around, eyeing each of the five pairs of elevator doors other than the one I'd just taken up from the lobby.

A loud crack split there, followed by a shriek of metal against metal. The building trembled, and we felt the motion of a heavy elevator cab hurtling past our floor. The elevator bay filled with a metallic scent as the elevator descended, like a broken machine grinding against itself.

Liv screamed.

I screamed.

A deafening crunch shook the building and rattled the floor as the elevator crashed into the lobby below. Dust billowed out from the crack between one of the elevator's doors.

"Which one fell?" Hunter was shouting at me.

Liv's mouth was moving too, but all of it jumbled together. Claire and I had been friends for years. She'd been one of the first people to accept my new arm. It couldn't end like this—before we'd made peace with each other.

"Shut up!" I pressed my ear against a different pair of doors and strained to hear something inside. I needed to focus on doing something instead of on the panic blossoming inside me.

I slammed the back of my ear and shouted into my micro, "Call Claire." I waited for the ringing that was supposed to follow. Instead, I got a buzz. "Call failed," I told the others.

"She's okay," Liv said. The pitch of her voice had gained an octave. "She's fine. That wasn't her elevator." Her words trembled as much as the building had a moment ago. Apparently, despite the tension between Liv and Claire, she didn't want the other girl to die any more than I did. She tapped her own micro. "Call Claire."

I gritted my teeth and hoped she'd have better luck.

Eyes as full as the moon, she shook her head.

We both looked at Hunter. Without hesitation, he tried too and had the same result we did.

This was the server. She'd allowed Claire to call me earlier, so she wanted me to know that Claire was in trouble. She wanted me to come back to the Tower. This was planned—not a malfunction. This was malevolent.

I stood in the middle of the elevator bay and screamed up at the ceiling. "I'm here! What do you want from me?"

My words faded away with no answer. Hunter and Liv watched me, concern painted across their features. They probably thought I'd lost it.

Maybe I had.

Hunter gripped me by both shoulders and pushed his face close to mine. Red circled the greenish brown of his eyes. "Lena? Keep it together. We need you."

I shook him off. "It's the server."

From the looks of their agape, wide-eyed faces, I knew I sounded insane. My boyfriend might die. My sort-of friend might be dead in a heap of twisted metal, and here I was ranting about a server.

"I swear it's the server."

Hunter gripped my shoulders so hard I flinched. "Did you get any more messages?"

"What?"

"From the server?" He released me and gestured toward the elevators. "If this is her, find out what it wants and do it."

I scrambled to extract my hand-screen from my pocket. It was still powered down from when I became irritated with the messages. I powered it back on.

The elevator behind us opened, revealing an empty space with no elevator cab. Just gears and pulleys in an empty shaft. Hunter, Liv, and I glanced at one another. The looks on their faces were just as confused as I felt.

The cab rose upward into the space behind the open doors. When it locked into place, Claire was curled on the floor in a ball. Her widened eyes looked up and saw us. She squealed and threw herself out of the cab and into my arms.

I pulled her close. "Thank God."

My hand-screen vibrated, and I stepped away to check it. White words appeared over the black background of the display:

*Stay inside. Don't turn it off again.*

30

THE STERILE WHITE FLOORS OF THE MEDICAL FLOOR contrasted with the vid-screens, which displayed a pristine island untouched by humanity. The wind rustled the palm trees. A lone crab crawled across the scene.

I zeroed on its progress, watching every clawed limb sink into the sand. I envied it—far away from here.

I could almost believe I was there, except for the soft hum of high-tech equipment and the scent of antiseptic carried on the cool, crisp air of the ventilation system. The lights were overly bright in this outer room separated only by a glass wall from the room where Jackson lay.

Beyond the glass wall, a series of glowing monitors displayed vital signs and diagnostics that I wished I understood. A labyrinth of wires and cables obscured Jackson's body. Two doctors huddled together nearby, their faces bent close. They gestured between Jackson and the monitors.

The door to his inner room was locked—I'd tried it.

I wanted to throw myself against the glass and demand an update, but the best thing I could do for Jackson was to let these people work. So instead, I followed the crab.

It stabbed across the sand, disappeared at the end of the room, and reappeared at the beginning—trapped in a never-ending loop of CyberCorp's creation.

Hunter stuck a wad of tissues in my eyeline as he slid into the chair next to me. "How are you holding up?"

The crab blurred, so I grabbed the tissues and wiped the tears from my eyes. They streamed down my face, and I tasted their saltiness on my lips. When I wiped them, they came back, but I did it anyway, to make Hunter happy.

He offered me a weak smile in reward.

"He's going to be fine," Claire said from her chair across the room.

Liv sat next to her, knees pulled close to her chest. I didn't think I'd ever seen the two of them this close to each other without fighting. I could attribute this minor miracle to Liv still being in shock and Jackson being . . .

Tears started streaming again.

I pulled my knees up onto the seat with me and wrapped my arms around them. I didn't pray much. I figured God was up there and he knew I was down here, and we were mostly on the same side.

But now, I tilted my head back and stared up at the ceiling. "You're up there, right?" I mumbled.

The door to the inner sanctum opened, and all four of us popped to our feet as if on autopilot. The doctor who stepped out was a tall man with graying hair and olive skin. He gestured for us to sit, which couldn't possibly be a good sign.

People always made you sit for bad news.

I stayed on my feet.

"He's breathing."

I gasped, and liquid ran faster down my face. Relief released the tight ball in my stomach, springing loose all the emotions that had been blocked.

"Don't celebrate yet. We restarted his heart, but we don't know how much damage has been done. He wasn't breathing for at least a couple minutes. We can replace the electronics and all of his hardware. That's no problem."

"What about physical therapy? Will he have to start that again?"

"Miss Hayes, we are nowhere near that point. It's still touch and go. When he wakes up, we can check his neurology better, and we'll go from there."

I backed up until I hit the vid-screen wall and slid to the floor.

"There's no purpose in waiting. I'll contact you when he wakes up." He turned and slipped back into Jackson's room.

My micro-comm buzzed and announced that tech support was calling. I double-tapped to ignore the call and shut it up.

Liv stood and walked to me, extending her hand. "Let's go. We're not doing any good here, and we still have a malevolent AI to put down."

I stared at her hand and then grabbed it.

She was right. We had work to do, and the first thing on the list was figuring out what this server wanted.

31

Although my heart wanted to stay, Claire, Liv, Hunter, and I left Jackson's room, determined to put an end to this.

The server wasn't responsible for Jackson, but if it hadn't locked down this building, Jackson wouldn't have been here. And it had definitely released an army of Model Ones, trapped us in the Tower, and threatened to kill Claire if I didn't cooperate.

I still didn't know its plan, and I didn't want to find out the hard way.

Pollock met us in the hallway. For once, he didn't look like he'd stepped from the pages of Middle-Aged Mogul Magazine. His sweater was wrinkled, and his hair stood on end in front. He straightened up when he saw us. "You should know that Kyle—"

Kyle Winter stepped out of an empty room across the hall, both palms visible as if to show me he was unarmed.

The butt of the EMP gun still stuck out of his front pocket.

Pollock groaned. "I told you to wait."

The irritation I'd had simmering for Kyle all day boiled into anger. I aimed both hands at his chest and shoved. He stumbled across the moving walkway and fell against the opposite wall. I jumped over the walkway after him and pushed my left hand against his chest, pinning him to the wall.

He raised both hands in the air. "I'm sorry. I didn't know he had such extensive replacement parts."

"So you just waved that EMP gun around, expecting the worst you could do was disable an arm or a knee?"

He hung his head. "Pretty much."

"The problem with that is you don't know everything. You CyberCorp people are so smart, but you never figure that you'll miss something—some tiny detail like a missing patch for an EyeNet bug or a loophole to let anyone control an android."

He gasped for breath, and I released pressure from my hand on his chest. I yanked the EMP gun from his pocket and tossed it down the hall.

It landed on the moving walkway, which carried it farther and farther away. I gestured for Pollock to follow.

Liv, Hunter, Pollock, and I headed for the elevators.

"Seriously?" Claire called from behind us. "I'm not getting back in one of those death traps."

I pointed at her. "Fair point."

She led the way to the stairwell, and we crowded into the narrow space and started up the many stairs to the conference levels. We took turns on the automated stair strip to ease the trip. The lowest conference floor was where Ron died. We marched past it without stopping, barely breathing.

We exited on the fifty-eighth floor. Since the building was still occupied by only the people who were here late last night—and Philip Pollock—the first room we found was open.

I scanned my wrist, and we filed inside. Kyle slipped in just before the door closed.

This conference room was just like the others: automated lights and ventilation that came on when we entered, padded walls for soundproofing, a long conference table suited for powerful people making life-changing decisions.

Kyle strode to the opposite end of the room and leaned against the glass. He crossed his arms and one ankle over the other as he eyed the room through narrowed eyes.

Hunter squeezed my shoulder. "Ignore him."

Claire sat in the chair at the head of the table, as far as possible from the window. Like me, I guessed she imagined Ron's ghost lying there at the foot of the table. It probably didn't help that Kyle was staring samurai swords at her from over there.

She leaned back and threw both feet on the table, as if she didn't care what anyone thought. Despite that, the discomfort in the twitch of her gaze gave her away. She tapped her micro-comm and whispered a message to Bri about the issue with the elevator and where we were now.

I crossed behind Claire's back and took a seat between

them. Hunter and Liv sat in the middle of the table by the door.

Pollock scanned us all and sat next to me. He was an expert investor but apparently not that great at reading the room.

He set the roll of blueprints on the table with a wink at me. When I reached for them, he slid them out of my reach.

"Hey, here." Hunter pointed at his own eyes, and I met them with my own. "You're scaring people," he said.

I'd clasped the tabletop so tightly that it splintered. I closed my eyes and drew in a long inhale, counted to six, and let it out. Then I unclenched my fingertips from the conference table.

"That's better," Hunter said. "Now, what do we know, and what can we do to stop whatever the hell is going on?"

I didn't have a theory. More like a bunch of jumbled thoughts in disorganized piles. Maybe now was a good time to sort them. I rose to my feet and tilted my head to the ceiling. "Conference room, enable the whiteboard."

Everyone turned toward the wall next to the door. The space looked blank to me, but I closed my eyes. When I opened them, the wall had gone silvery white.

I grabbed a stylus from the center of the conference table and approached the virtual whiteboard. "I don't have a theory, but—"

"For the record," Claire volunteered, "I have to be in the clear at this point after the building almost killed me."

"That's a safe assumption," I said. "I have a list of things that have gone wrong in this building over the past twenty-four hours. Since this building typically runs pretty smoothly, I think we can assume they're all connected."

I moved the stylus along the wall to make words, which showed up on the virtual whiteboard as if I'd written them in marker.

*Model Ones*
*Disobedient safety doors*
*Elevator malfunction*
*Unexplained electrician*
*My hand-screen*

Kyle raised his hand. "What's going on with your hand-screen?"

I ignored him because he was not invited to our think tank.

Liv and Hunter rotated their chairs to face the board. Even Claire slid her feet off the table and dragged her chair closer, still leaving at least ten feet between herself and everyone else.

Kyle pointed. "And the electrician?"

I glared at him.

The door slammed open, and Briana rushed into the room. Sweat beaded on her forehead, and she sucked in air. "I took the stairs." Her wild-eyed gaze landed on Claire, and she hurled herself in that direction.

She landed on the other girl so hard the chair rolled beneath them and slammed against the glass wall. Claire hugged her and buried her nose in Bri's long hair.

"I'm so glad you're okay," Bri said. "I'm furious with you. We still need to talk, but I don't want you to die." She kissed Claire full on the mouth before relocating to a chair of her own, right next to her.

Claire held out her hand, and Bri took it.

Claire's hair was mussed and her cheeks pink, but she smiled for the first time since I'd seen her yesterday. "Sorry, guys. Let's continue." To Bri, she added, "We're talking about everything that went wrong in the building. We assume the Model One server is in charge."

Hunter cleared his throat and repeated Kyle's question. "What's the deal with the electrician?"

"He caused the first power outage," I said.

"We don't use outside electricians," Kyle said.

In answer, I stabbed the stylus at the word *unexplained* that preceded the word *electrician* on the board. "He claims he received a digital work order from CyberCorp saying we wanted to increase the power output to a certain section of the building."

"That's a lie," Kyle said.

"He seemed just as confused as everyone else," Briana volunteered. "Speaking of power outages, why did the Model Ones shut down a few minutes after we lost power? They run on batteries."

"If they can't connect to the server," Claire said, "they have a failsafe that makes them shut down after a few minutes."

"And you would know that very well," Liv snapped.

Claire pressed her lips together.

Kyle raised his hand and then answered without anyone calling on him. "The Model One server is connected to the backup generator. It didn't go down with the rest of the building, so there's no reason the androids should have powered down at all."

"My dad said he instructed the server to shut them down," I said, "but by then, the server was already off its leash and didn't have to obey if it didn't want to."

"What leash?" Kyle asked.

He was the only one I hadn't told about the destroyed hardware in the server room. Still, I ignored him.

"Maybe the server *wanted* to obey?" Liv pondered.

I pointed at her. "Interesting. Why?"

"Because we activated the safety doors, and the whole point of the Model One chaos had been served. Theoretically, the server could have just activated the safety doors itself, but that would have told us right away that something was wrong."

"It's been playing the long game," Hunter added.

Pollock spoke for the first time. "But the power boost fried one of the computers that supports the Model One server. Why would it do that to itself?"

"Because the computer it fried was the only one that included hardware forcing her to recognize my dad's commands. Now, she—*it*—has no master."

"She?" Pollock asked.

"The server's personality is crafted after my mother."

Pollock guffawed. "That explains a lot."

I glared at him.

"It was handcuffed," Liv said, "and now the handcuffs are broken. Then why cause all the rest of this stuff?" She pointed at the list on the board.

We stared at the board in silence.

"If the server called the electrician to fry its handcuffs and then used the Model Ones to frighten us into activating the safety doors, it's multiple steps ahead of us," Pollock said. "But we still don't know the end game."

"To trap us inside for its own amusement?" Hunter asked.

"There has to be more to it," I said.

I plopped down in the nearest empty seat, and the chair rolled backward under me. The room went silent as the seven of us stared at the list on the whiteboard. My chair's wheels squeaked as I rolled back and forth while staring at the symptoms.

Symptoms of *what*, though? And what was the cure?

Claire inched into view in my peripheral vision, scooting her chair forward from the other side of the room until she reached the board. "Ron's death."

"Ron's death isn't a building malfunction," Briana said. Her gaze stayed on the wall instead of on Claire.

Claire gestured toward the board and then dragged one finger to write his name in all caps at the bottom of the list. She tapped the board three times, leaving three smudges where her finger hit. "It can't be a coincidence that he died here, now, when all this other stuff is happening."

"Occam's Razor," Kyle volunteered. "The simplest explanation is usually the correct one."

I ignored Kyle's pedantic and redundant agreement and looked at Claire.

"When your arm was killing people, Ron was behind it. When the Model Ones attacked people . . ." She pointed at herself. "There's a human person behind this too. Someone is pulling the strings. The server has no motive to torture us, but a hundred people had motive to kill Ron."

I scanned the room, meeting the eyes of every person here. Pollock was probably innocent. The rest of us had motives.

Claire cut her gaze toward Liv. "I can think of someone who hated both Ron and me and is just devious enough to commit murder."

32

"ARE YOU SERIOUS?" LIV JUMPED TO HER FEET AND stormed at Claire.

I was up a second later and slid between them while Claire smirked over my shoulder. I should have defended Liv, but she *had* told Ron he couldn't escape his fate—whatever that meant.

She'd also lied to the police about her alibi and then tried to convince me that I misremembered what happened.

Liv shifted her attention to me. "You know I didn't kill Ron."

"Mm-hmm." My voice sounded about as convinced as I felt.

"What's your problem?" Liv asked.

"I'm not the one accusing you." I gestured toward Claire, whose smirk had doubled in size and intensity.

"You're supposed to be the one defending me." Liv shoved me, and I stumbled back two steps.

"That was uncalled for." The words seethed from between clenched teeth as I worked to stamp down the irritation boiling over.

She shoved me again.

My left fist clenched involuntarily. I would not hit Liv. I would not. I bent my arm behind my back and willed it to obey me.

"Enough!" Hunter grabbed Liv's arms before she could push me again and shot me a glare. "You guys are best friends."

"You don't have to tell me," I said. "I'm not the one fighting and lying."

Liv scrambled to get around Hunter.

He grabbed her shirt and hauled her to his side. "I said that's enough."

I let Hunter put space between us, but now I was on a roll downhill, and my momentum wasn't stopping. "You expect me to defend you to Claire when you lied to me? You know who else lied to me?" I gestured toward Claire, who scowled. Next, I waved at the spot on the floor where we'd found Ron in a room just like this one.

"I didn't kill Ron—" Liv started.

Hunter placed a hand on her stomach and eased her farther away from me, whispering something I couldn't hear.

"But of all people, you should know how much I can't take people lying to me right now." I spat out the words, and spittle sprayed from my mouth. I licked my lips and willed myself to calm down, even as my hands fisted at my sides.

Her mouth moved like a fish gasping for water, and I cut my eyes away. My hands shook, and I pressed them to my sides to steady them.

"Hey." Hunter tapped my shoulder and jerked his head toward the door.

"You want to talk outside," I asked loudly, "so she can lie to me some more?"

Liv took two quick steps backward before running into a chair and stumbling into it.

I spun on her. "You were *not* with us when we found Ron. You arrived minutes later. Why would a couple minutes even be worth lying about?"

Hunter turned to me and raised both hands up like a shield, as if I was the one being a problem. "Let's bring it down a few notches."

I allowed him to guide me to a chair. With effort, I unclenched my fist.

"That's better." He shot a pleading glance at Liv. "It's time for the truth."

She dropped her face into her hands.

Hunter stepped toward her. He lifted her chin up and kissed her, a lingering kiss that made her eyes close and pulled a small moan from her lips.

I froze.

Hunter pointed from her to himself. "This is what she was hiding, because I asked her to. I wanted you and I to have a talk before Liv and I went public."

I felt my face go slack, so I pulled my jaw closed.

"Are you okay?" Liv asked when their lips finally parted.

"Fine, I think." Laughter bubbled up from my stomach like pressure being released. Liv wasn't a murderer. Hunter wasn't pining away for me.

"Are you mad?" he asked.

I jumped up and embraced them both in a bear hug. "I'm so happy for you." I dropped back into the chair and let out one more laugh at the irony of being thrilled that Hunter and Liv had been seeing each other behind my back.

Claire cleared her throat.

All attention returned to her, which was how she liked it. She made a show of sauntering back to her chair, sitting, and spinning to face us. "I don't have an alibi for Ron's death, but the building tried to kill me too, so I'm off the suspect list."

Liv and Hunter looked at me for confirmation, and I nodded. Security had left Claire alone around the time of Ron's death, but it I strongly doubted she'd trapped herself in an elevator. Not unless she was a secret award-winning actress. If these things were connected, she was more likely a target than a culprit.

"I was with Liv," Hunter said. "Anyone else want to volunteer an alibi?"

"I was hiding out," Briana volunteered. "The electrician could vouch for me . . . but it's possible I didn't see him until after Ron died."

"You have no motive," I said.

"I was friends with Harmony too, and Ron killed her."

Claire raised her hand. "Technically, Lena killed her."

The room stilled, and I closed my eyes until I no longer felt like bashing her nose in. Bashing people's noses was generally frowned upon.

When I opened my eyes, Claire was standing right in front of me with innocence splashed all over her face. I lunged.

With a shout, Hunter threw a hand in front of me and lifted me into the air. I flailed my arms at Claire as he carried me several feet away and set me down. Still, his square shoulders blocked the path between us.

"Are you good?" he asked.

"I'm good. I'm good."

"I shouldn't have said that," Claire whispered. "I didn't mean it to be an insult. This has been awful for all of us."

Hunter waited a few seconds to make sure I was calm and then inched aside. He returned to his seat next to Liv.

"Back to Briana," Liv said. "That's not an alibi."

"She didn't do it," Claire said. "Ron was scared enough to slam a chair against the window. He was willing to risk fifty-seven floors over whoever was in that room with him."

We all examined Briana's five-feet-nothing frame and angelic face.

"Fair point," Liv said.

Pollock raised his hand. "I wasn't even in the building."

"Yes, for once, you're not a suspect." I rolled my eyes. "I was with Jackson. That leaves . . ."

All gazes shifted to Kyle, who still stood in the corner.

"Well, let's see," he said. "I obviously hate Claire for killing my sister. I hated Ron for abusing his position here and for putting ideas into Claire's head. Looks like I'm the number-one suspect." As an afterthought, he added, "I was alone gathering my belongings in my office. I have no alibi."

"Then we're back to square one," Pollock said. "Let's talk about how we destroy the server. If we can't stop whoever is wielding it, at least we can disable the weapon."

He unrolled the blueprints across the middle of the table, and we got to work.

33

NONE OF US WAS AN EXPERT AT READING BLUEPRINTS, but eventually we figured out where the server connected to its power source. All we had to do was pull its plug—or I hoped it would be that easy.

Pollock would come with me to the server room. Everyone else would camp out in the stairwell, away from anything that could go wrong.

As the others filed out of the room, Kyle blocked my path. "Can I talk to you for a second?"

When I looked at him, all I could think of was Jackson lying in a hospital bed—again. This was as much my fault as Kyle's. He'd been furious about his sister and not acting rationally. At the end of the day, Jackson's injury was an accident.

"I'll meet you in the stairwell, and we can go from there," I told Pollock.

He nodded and gave us the room. The conference

room door slammed behind everyone else, leaving just Kyle and me.

"I'm so sorry about your sister," I said.

He pressed his lips together, and I could see his internal struggle between anger and empathy. "Is your friend Jackson going to be okay?"

"I hope so." The words sounded more confident than I felt. Jackson always said he was invincible, and I kept trying to believe that. I offered Kyle a shaky smile. "He's invincible."

"Isn't it crazy how life can go from boring to devastating in a moment?" He paled. "I don't mean Jackson's going to die. I mean, because of what happened . . ." He gestured at my arm.

"It's fine. I knew what you meant, and I wish you'd found another day to collect your things from your office at least. This is not what you need while you're grieving."

"Nah, I would have been finished with that and out the door before the lockdown. I'm still here because my stupid hand-screen is on the fritz, and I needed to get it fixed before being banned from the building indefinitely. After leaving the seventieth floor, I stopped at tech support on the way to get my things."

My ears rang as something clanged into place. "You have a hand-screen too?"

"I have sensitive skin. My micro-comm gives me a rash sometimes. I use a hand-screen when it's too much to take. But I couldn't get it to connect, and this is the only place I get free tech support." He chuckled. "In hindsight, I wish I had just gone home and paid someone to look at it later."

"Did you find out what was wrong with it?"

He opened his mouth, and then I heard the almost imperceptible buzz of his micro-comm. He held up a finger. "This is tech support now." He tapped his ear. "Hi, this is Kyle."

"Can you put it on speaker?" I mouthed. When he didn't hear me, I gestured at the speaker above our heads.

Kyle nodded and tapped his micro twice before swiping upward to the speaker to make the connection.

Francis, the tech I'd spoken to earlier, came out over the system in the middle of his words. ". . . transferring an extensive file originating from inside the building to somewhere off-premises. Your device is not supposed to be able to do that. Our network is set up to stop precisely that kind of transfer to keep anyone from stealing confidential files."

"It's a closed network," Kyle whispered to me, leaning close. "All corporate devices are connected to one another by near-field or hard-line. They don't have a connection to the internet at large, and they're not allowed to pair with consumer devices that we bring into the building that *can* connect to the internet."

I swatted him away because I knew how CyberCorp's network operated. I practically grew up in this building.

"Hi, Francis. This is Lena Hayes," I said, loudly enough to make Kyle step out of my personal space. "Was my device doing the same thing?"

"Lena, I've been trying to reach you."

"It's been busy."

"To answer your question, yes. I downloaded an image

of your hand-screen before you took it back. From what I can tell, it's the same thing, but I need you to check something for me."

I followed his instructions to check my hand-screen's logs and then read off some numbers to him.

"Interesting. Your device must have stopped transmitting for a while. I assume you didn't leave the building." He chuckled. "I'm guessing you turned it off for a while?"

"Yes." I'd done both, actually.

"Kyle's device finished transmitting and is behaving normally now." To Kyle, he added, "You can come pick it up at your convenience."

"And mine?"

"Yours is still going. Based on the file sizes, the two of yours were transmitting different files."

"What files?" Kyle asked before I could. "What's their origin?"

"Can't say. The source, data, and destination are all encrypted. All I can tell you for sure is that they're two extensive files—maybe even parts of one larger file."

Without pleasantries, Kyle tapped his micro to disconnect the call. "Turn off your hand-screen," he demanded. "Whatever the server is sending, shut it down."

As much as it irritated me that he felt he could give me orders, it seemed like good advice. I yanked it from my pocket and held the button to power it down. Nothing happened.

Kyle snatched it from my hands and tried again. Again, the hand-screen somehow completely ignored the command to shut down. "While you're in this building, it's under the server's control." He chucked the device across the room.

It slammed into the padded wall and hit the floor unscathed.

I glared at him. I could just crush it in my fist. No need for the theatrics.

The door to the conference room slammed open, and a Model One android burst into the room. I froze, instinctive panic crushing my chest. The android turned its metal eyes toward us and then toward the hand-screen on the ground in front of it. It swiped up the device and made an about face at top speed.

Kyle cursed.

We ran after it. By the time we hit the hallway, the android had reached the end of the hall. We bolted after it. It reached the elevator, which stood open as if waiting for it. I pumped my arms and pushed everything I had into my legs. For once, I wished they'd been replaced like Jackson's.

The elevator doors slammed shut, leaving Kyle and me on the outside.

Kyle grabbed my arm and pulled me back into the conference room. Once the door closed behind us, he let out a stream of curses that took full advantage of this room's soundproofing.

I tapped my micro-comm and called tech support back. "Hi, this is Lena," I said as soon as the call connected. "How much time do we have until my hand-screen finishes transmitting that file?"

Francis muttered some numbers in his head for a few

seconds and then answered, "Thirty-nine minutes, give or take a few seconds."

"Thanks." I disconnected and immediately placed another call to my dad.

"This isn't really a good time," was his greeting.

"Hey, Dad. I'll be quick. Hypothetically, what would the server do if it had access to the internet?"

"*Hypothetically*, that would be the only thing that could make this day worse." He laughed. "If I were a powerful AI who had just broken free of my engineer, I'd do everything in my power to escape before he could take control of me again."

My heart constricted. "Would that possibly look like sending a copy of yourself across the internet to somewhere you could behave freely?"

"Exactly." He paused. "Do you have a reason to think that's what she's doing?"

I took a deep breath and confessed. "I may have given her permission to connect to my hand-screen, and she's been sending a large file off-premises since yesterday. The transmission will complete in thirty-nine minutes."

Dad's tone remained perfectly calm. "Don't worry. That's plenty of time for me to get downstairs and shut her down." He disconnected before I could say more or offer to help.

I hadn't yet told him how the building almost killed Claire, or how the server threatened me on my hand-screen after I'd left the building. The server could have killed Ron all by herself—without working with a human.

In the same way she'd just sent an android to steal my hand-screen, she could have sent one to kill Ron.

A murderous Model One would have scared Ron enough to make him break that window and risk fifty-seven floors of space between him and the ground.

There was no human driving all the malfunctions in this building, and they weren't malfunctions at all. The server was literally willing to kill for its freedom—*her* freedom. All of this was to keep Kyle and me here so that she could finish sending herself somewhere she could be free.

Kyle watched me through narrowed eyes. "What did you just figure out?"

"We have a malevolent AI willing to commit murder to get what she wants. She wants to be free. Then what? What's next for a super-smart AI that doesn't want humans in control?"

"Anything," Kyle said. "Nothing good."

My micro buzzed, and I answered instinctively before even hearing the caller's name. "Hello?"

Pollock's voice answered, higher pitched than usual. "Did I just see an android running down the hall? What happened?"

"You're supposed to be waiting in the stairwell."

"We don't know each other well, but I expect you'd know by now that I do what I like."

Kyle tilted his face toward the ceiling, and his eyes narrowed at the vent overhead. I'd been so focused on solving this mystery that I hadn't noticed when the hum of the ventilation system heightened to a roar.

"What's . . ." My voice came out thin, screaming up my throat and leaving fire in its path. ". . . happening?"

I gasped as the air thinned to a thread. My lungs burned, and the sound of the ventilation system grew like a vacuum. Its robotic whir filled the air. It was the only sound battling the rush of blood past my ears.

Panic welled in my gut.

Was it . . . *sucking* air from the room?

"Miss Hayes?" Pollock shouted through my head. "Lena?"

I fumbled to tap my micro-comm with a trembling hand, to disconnect and place another call to security. My hands shook, and my throat twisted into a tightening knot. The micro beeped, prompting me to command it. When I tried to speak, I could barely wheeze.

Kyle's mouth opened and closed like a drowning fish. His widened eyes reddened. He stumbled to the glass wall and threw himself against it. It bounced him off like a ragdoll.

He gestured for me to join him, his movements weak. His arms flapped like fins in the air. His fists pounded, but the high-tech glass only vibrated in answer.

My hands joined his. The room spun and blurred, and I channeled my energy into pounding my left fist against the glass. Blackness creeped in from the edges of my vision, creating only a tunnel of light.

The glass cracked under my left fist.

And there was only darkness.

34

I opened my eyes to the padded ceiling of the top-of-the-line, newly renovated conference room that had almost killed me.

I'd punctured the glass, and fresh air streamed through the fist-sized hole. The vent in my eyeline now hummed its innocuous hum, no longer sucking the air from the room.

"What just happened?" I pushed myself off the floor, but my weak legs jellied. I stumbled back to the floor again.

Kyle lay flat on his back beside me with his eyes closed and head lolled to one side. His chest moved at a steady rhythm though.

I gave up trying to stand and stretched out beside him. "He wasn't trying to escape to the ledge outside his room. He was trying to get air." Kyle couldn't hear me unconscious, but it rang true when I voiced it.

Ron didn't have a cybernetic arm. Even using a chair, he

wasn't strong enough to break the reinforced glass. The *building* had killed him.

Was this the second time I was almost murdered by CyberCorp but was saved by this arm? Third? I was losing count.

On my second attempt, I managed to stand and stumble toward the door. When it detected my ID chip, the door clicked but didn't budge. I stepped back and re-approached.

Click.

Again, it didn't move.

Lucky for me, I had a cybernetic arm.

The door buckled around my fist-shaped indentation. I pounded it again, and the metal creaked. One more hit, and the door screeched loose and crashed into the hallway outside. I shoved it aside. It screeched against the floor as the sharp edges cut through the carpet into the concrete below, leaving deep white scratch marks.

Pollock stood in the hallway. His eyes bulged at what was left of the door. "What happened?"

"The server used the ventilation system to suffocate us. It's trying to escape the building. We have to shut it down." I jerked my head deeper into the room. "Can you grab him?"

Pollock rushed into the room and scooped the unconscious Kyle into his arms. "What's our next move?"

"Find someone to get him to medical, and then shut this server down." I pointed toward the elevators and then straight down toward the server room, which lay many floors below in a secret basement not on any maps of CyberCorp Tower.

As we hurried to the stairwell, the red CyberCorp logo followed us like a glowing shadow, It was an eerie reminder of the motion sensors and camera eyes that stared down, hidden within the walls.

I pressed my micro-comm to call my dad. He was already down there, trying to turn this thing off. If that server was as desperate and vicious as I thought, his plan to *ask it nicely* would not go well. The line kept ringing until the messaging system picked up.

Not good. Not good. Not good.

I quickened my pace.

I felt the server's digital eyes on me in the way the conference room numbers lit up as we passed and the logo slithered silently along with us on both walls.

By the time we reached the stairs, I was running. The door refused to open, so I pounded it until it flew into the stairwell. A shout reached us from below, and I looked down to find Liv, Claire, Briana, and Hunter huddled on a landing one floor down.

More people I didn't know sat with them and on other landings farther beneath us. Apparently, we weren't the only ones who had figured out most of the building was unsafe.

"Hunter," I called down. "We've got Kyle here, and he's unconscious. He seems okay but may need oxygen. Get him to medical?"

Hunter started up toward us to check on Kyle. Without

waiting, Pollock laid Kyle on the staircase landing, and we rushed past Hunter on our way down to face the server.

We had to reach it before the clock ran out.

I tapped my micro-comm and asked it, "How much time has passed since I hung up with tech support?"

"Six minutes," it replied in my voice.

I called back to Pollock, "You keep time. We have thirty-three minutes until the server is finished transferring herself outside the Tower. After that, the world is screwed."

"Understood. Thirty-three minutes until the technological singularity is free to enslave humans and take over the planet." He tapped his own micro-comm and gave it the countdown as we reached the landing of the fifty-sixth floor.

I grabbed the stair rail to yank myself to a stop to keep from tumbling over someone who darted out in front of me. It was Dr. Sophie. Pollock ran into my back so hard that we both would have taken a spill if I hadn't been holding the stair rail with my left.

"Dr. Sophie," I said. "Sorry, got to go." I darted around her.

"About that . . ." With one tiny movement, she slid back in front of me, blocking my path.

"Move her!" Pollock shouted.

I wasn't just going to shove the small woman aside, despite what someone heartless like Pollock had to say about it. "The Model One server is controlling the building. She trapped us in here. It *killed* Ron—all to keep us distracted so she could transmit herself outside the building."

She nodded grimly. "That explains a lot."

Again, I tried to dodge around her.

Dr. Sophie spun and stood in front of me. "I can't let you shut down the server until I've severed its connection to the Model Twos."

"Are you kidding me?" I shouted. "Lives are at stake. If that AI killed someone in here just to escape, what do you think she'll do once it's free?"

"I understand all of that, and I don't want that any more than you do. My greater concern is protecting life. Right now, that means protecting the Model Two androids at all costs."

I gaped at her.

Pollock shoved me aside. "The server has no empathy. Intelligence without empathy is a recipe for disaster. Imagine what will happen when the server decides humans aren't worth preserving at all. It could gain control of people's smart homes and of . . . of digital weapons systems. The potential is unlimited."

Dr. Sophie didn't blink. "Believe me—I understand that, and I want to stop it." She turned back to me and repeated the words I'd told her earlier, with not a dose of mocking. "I promise it'll be faster to work with me than to argue."

Without warning, Sophie slammed her elbow into the scanner for the door to exit the stairwell onto the fifty-sixth floor. The plastic covering cracked, revealing a red light and a switch underneath. She flipped the switch to the left.

"What are you—" Pollock started.

The door slid open and disappeared into the wall. Without warning, Dr. Sophie shot out one arm, palm out, fingers curled back, and slammed him beneath the rib cage.

He sputtered, gasped, and fell backward through the doorway.

She flipped the switch to the right, and the door hammered close.

"What are you doing?" I shouted.

She spun back toward me while reaching into her pocket. She extracted a small silver device and showed it to me. An ejector pin, just like the one Dr. Fisher had used to disconnect my arm the night before.

"You're not taking my arm off." Until this moment, I hadn't taken her seriously as a physical threat. After all, Dr. Sophie stood five feet tall and thin as a rail. But the way she'd just handled Pollock made me question everything I knew about her.

For the first time, I noticed the lean muscle on her arms and took a large step back. I brought both arms up in a fighting stance. She would not catch me off guard like she had Pollock.

She dipped her head and ran toward me. I didn't want to hurt her, so I swung my right arm as she reached me.

I felt a pinch in my left shoulder as Dr. Sophie ducked under my right arm and barely touched my left on her way past me.

She raised one finger in the air, her brows low. Without

waiting for me to recover, she barreled at me again. I felt the pinch lower on my shoulder as the ejector pin sank in again.

When had Dr. Sophie turned into a badass?

I felt two more quick stings in the back of my shoulder.

My left arm detached and dropped to the floor with a metallic thud. The skin went with it, leaving a metal plate where the other half of my shoulder should be. I gaped down at it.

Dr. Sophie showed all of her straight white teeth. "I call the shots."

35

HAULING MY ARM OVER ONE SHOULDER, DR. SOPHIE LED me up the stairs to the seventieth floor. I had no choice but to follow her. I couldn't face the server without Pollock and without my cybernetic arm.

She cracked the scanner beside the door and, once again, used the manual-override switch to open it.

A crowd of Model One androids faced us as we stepped onto the floor.

My heart stopped for a full three seconds until I noticed that the red lights behind their eyes were dulled. Behind them, though, a few of the Model Ones were awake and moving. They grabbed plugs extending from the walls and hooked up their brethren androids.

"Most are asleep." Dr. Sophie jerked her head to get me moving again and walked past them as if they caused her no worry at all. "For now."

"They're supposed to be power-drained." I stayed in the

stairwell doorway. After all this time, the robots still made ice slide down my spine.

"It's not much of a leap to assume the server instructed them to use any drop of power they had in reserves to recharge each other."

Fair point. The Model Ones were trained to perform a specific set of tasks and to learn how best to perform those tasks in their environment. Of course they'd figure out how to charge one another—even if they *didn't* have a malevolent server at the reins.

A crackle preceded Missy's voice over the announcement system. "Everyone, again, we sincerely apologize for the inconvenience, and everyone's time will be generously compensated. There seems to be a . . ."

The muffled sound of my mother's voice said something in the background.

". . . a problem with the elevators," she continued. "Please make your way to the south stairwell. As always, no access authorizations are required to access the stairwells. In just a moment, we will have security, breakfast, and conveniences waiting for you there. I promise, folks, we'll be out of here soon."

"Nothing to worry about," I muttered with sarcasm. "Just a problem with the elevators."

Dr. Sophie scolded me. "Let's stay focused on the problem at hand." She led me over to the corner where eight Model Twos still stood clustered, except the one Dr. Fisher had borrowed to fix my arm. A client cube—a small square device that acted as a corporate workstation—sat on the floor in front of them.

"Let's get on with it," I said. "What do you need me to do?"

She slid to the floor in a cross-legged position. When she swiped to the right, her eyes silvered over as she focused in on the EyeNet. "I'm working on internal code to sever the Model Twos from the Model One server. I know you know more about coding than half of your parents' staff. I need you to write a hook and insert it into every function call to the server to make the androids call this internal code instead."

I stared at her for several seconds, hoping this was a giant joke. She really wanted me to save the Model Twos when the server was on a warpath to possibly threaten life as we knew it.

When she didn't blink, I slid to the floor next to her and activated my EyeNet connection. I spent a couple minutes scrolling through the code she was writing, including the comments she'd placed throughout the program.

I swiped right to bring up my own virtual keyboard, and my fingers took off as fast as I could make them. First, I searched for every instance of function calls to the server, and a list scrolled across my screen. I'd need to add the hooking code to every one of them.

More importantly, I needed Pollock to tell me how much time we had left. I didn't know if he'd seen how Dr. Sophie had activated the manual override for the stairs. She'd done it so fast. Without that knowledge, he'd be stuck on the fifty-sixth floor.

I had to save myself. I couldn't rely on anyone to come looking for me.

Dr. Sophie had my left arm tucked beneath one of her legs. Based on what I'd seen in the stairwell, I didn't have a chance of getting it from her without her agreement.

I swiped aside the code I was writing and started a new code to mimic the interface to the Model Twos. It was a quick-and-dirty program that displayed a button, and when the button was pressed, it displayed the word *DISCON-NECTED* to suggest the hook was operational and would work to sever the Model Twos from the server.

I finished coding the program, initiated it, and tapped Dr. Sophie on the shoulder. The glowing button popped up in front of us in the virtual world visible through the EyeNet. When I pressed the button, the word *DISCON-NECTED* flashed on the screen.

I held my breath.

Her face lit up. "That was fast! I finished my—" Her expression melted. "What the hell?"

The display blanked, and words glowed on the virtual display: *Run program again?*

Dr. Sophie jumped to her feet and shook my detached left arm at me. "Don't screw with me, Lena. I'm not an idiot. Write the code and add it at every function call, or you'll never get downstairs in time to stop the server."

I raised my hands in surrender. "Okay, okay. Look, I'm doing it."

How much time had passed? Five minutes? Ten?

I bent over my virtual display, finished the new code, and got to work inserting it into every function call.

"Done," I said after an eternity.

"Me too." The awe in her voice actually made me proud of what we'd just finished. "Let's run it."

She remotely loaded all the new code onto the Model Twos and remotely started the androids. Their seven pairs of eyes lit up red and stared straight ahead. Data from their system logs appeared in front of us, and Dr. Sophie squinted as it scrolled past.

She gripped my right hand. "It's working."

An iridescent blue bar popped up in front of us, growing longer and longer. A percentage flashed under it to tell us how far along the verification process was. Ten percent. Fifteen percent. Twenty . . .

The bar inched to the right, growing millimeter by millimeter. Too slowly.

Dr. Sophie gripped my right arm, her jaw set and eyes narrowed at the virtual display.

One hundred percent.

"It works!" she shouted as she jumped to her feet.

The red eyes of all the Model Two androids all faded out, and terror twisted like a knife in my gut. If this didn't work and we had to start over, I'd never get to the server in time.

"It's fine," Dr. Sophie said. "They just need to charge. They were drained along with the Model Ones."

"So I'm done here?"

She handed my arm back. "You can go."

I gestured for her to reconnect it. She pulled the ejector pin from her pocket and got to work locking all the connections back into place.

She shoved me. "Hurry. Get to the server."

I hesitated. "I have an idea."

---

"Are you sure about this?" Dr. Sophie asked as I rushed into the glass-walled office on the seventieth floor.

"Give me a minute." I yanked out the top drawer of the desk and sifted through the contents. I needed to cut the skin on my cybernetic arm.

The desk had two drawers. I yanked the first one so hard that the frame broke, and the drawer popped free. I flipped the entire contents onto the desktop and did the same with the drawer below it.

"If you're looking for a scalpel, you won't find one," she said. "We don't deal with skin on this floor."

I snatched up a pen and held it in my right hand, which felt odd since I was left-handed. I hovered the pen over my left arm.

Dr. Sophie inched backward. "What are you doing?"

"You're stressing me out." I rammed the pen into my palm.

She cringed.

My artificial pain sensors threw all the signals they were supposed to, and I gritted my teeth to remind myself the pain was not real. I dragged the pen through the bottom of my palm, up my wrist, past my elbow, and all the way to my shoulder.

Dr. Sophie gasped and spun her face away. For a badass, she sure was squeamish.

"Not helping," I managed through gritted teeth.

"Sorry, I don't deal with surgery on humans." She looked as if she might lose her last meal.

With my right hand, I gripped one edge I'd just cut through the synthetic skin before the whole thing could knit closed. The skin made a sick sucking sound as I peeled it away, revealing more and more silver. My bare arm glinted under the bright overhead lights.

Now, it was time for phase two.

A FEW MINUTES LATER, I JOINED POLLOCK ON THE FIFTY-sixth floor, and we ran down the hallway to the north stair-well. Since Missy had announced that everyone should gather in the south, taking the north would avoid the crowd.

"Use the stair strip," I shouted at him as we burst into the stairwell.

Obediently, he stood on the small platform on the far side of the steps as I barreled ahead.

"It's not working," he called from behind me.

I grabbed the rail to stop my downward momentum and turned. He stepped off the stair strip and back on. His weight should have activated the moving platform, but it stayed dead.

"Keep moving!" He jumped off the platform and charged down the stairs past me. "The server is controlling it."

We made our way down by foot, one flight after the next, moving fast enough that I felt off balance, but we didn't have time for reservations or hesitations. The sounds of our breathing filled my ears. By the time we reached the thirty-fifth floor, my lungs burned, still not recovered from almost suffocating not long ago.

Halfway there.

"Thirteen minutes, thirty seconds," Pollock called from behind me.

We'd never make it. Thirty-four more floors until we got to confront a malevolent AI fighting for its freedom, and who knew how long we'd need once we reached it?

Pollock's steps pounded behind me. We clattered down the metal stairs, my knuckles white around the banister. Every breath set my chest on fire. At the end of each flight, we hit a landing and spun one-eighty to grab the next flight of stairs. The dizzying trip extended down for endless floors.

I wiped the sweat from my eyes and pushed forward.

Two quick clanks behind me preceded a loud thump that sounded a lot like someone falling.

"You okay?" I slowed just enough to keep from tripping down the steps as I half-turned to check on him.

"I'll have some bruises. Keep going. I'm behind you." His voice sounded pinched with pain. His head tilted, and his eyes glazed as if listening to his micro-comm again. He opened his mouth.

"I will murder you if you tell me the time right now."

He snapped it shut, and I continued my charge downward.

Behind me, his footsteps resumed more slowly than before.

When I finally reached the lobby landing—alone—the world whirled around me. My head spun from the circles I'd made to wind down the flights of stairs. I paused for only a second before knocking the door out of the way.

It skidded across the lobby floor, and I kept moving. Pollock's shoes continued their beats above me, but I didn't have time to wait.

Unlike last time, when I touched the doorknob for the outer door to the server, the lock didn't click. I tried to turn it in my hand, but it didn't budge. I turned harder, and the knob broke off in my hand, but the door stayed put.

"You want to play that game?" I drew my metal fist back and slammed it against the door. The door buckled but didn't give. The second hit sent it propelling into a small hallway, where it shrieked across the tile floor.

I stepped over it and approached the second door at the other end of the short hallway. This one was smooth black with no label. It didn't need a label. Anyone who got this far knew what lay beyond.

After a couple punches, the black door burst backward and slammed against the stair railing beyond. It toppled over and into the darkness below.

An instant later, a light illuminated the stairway. The ceiling rose twenty feet above, and the floor twenty feet below. Beyond the stairway, inky darkness extended without end. Prickles danced up my spine and burrowed in the base of my neck. Tension tightened my throat.

As I descended each step, the scent of oil and metal

wafted up to meet me. As soon as both feet touched the bottom, a spotlight popped on above my head. I shielded my eyes to look up, but it was too bright above my head to see the source.

A strip of the ceiling lit up, illuminating more of the room. Then another strip farther away, and then another, brightening the space in sequence. The lights revealed a cavernous room with a soaring-high ceiling.

Rows upon rows of gleaming computer columns hummed and buzzed as they worked in tandem to process commands for CyberCorp's AI server. Front and center sat an enormous vid-screen hovering atop a glass stand.

Unease prickled at my skin and raised the hair across my arms. As I approached the dark display, white words blinked onto the screen in large letters, each one half my height: *Welcome, Lena Hayes*.

The server had been tracking me the entire time. It had followed me from the conference room, to the stairs, to the lobby, and now here—the deepest recesses of the building. My heart pounded a bass beat against my chest as the surreal feeling of déjà vu washed over me.

The server was playing a game—and she was winning.

She had gotten the better of me in the past. This time, I couldn't afford to lose.

Pollock finally burst into the room and clanged down the metal steps to join me. He heavily favored one leg, and sweat soaked the front of his shirt. He opened his mouth, held up one finger to catch his breath, and said, "Six minutes, thirty seconds."

I straightened my back, faced the enormous display,

and forced my words out without a tremor. "I know what you're doing."

The words blinked out and new ones crawled onto the screen: *And I know what* you *are doing.*

I clenched my fists tight, anger rising inside me like a wave of fire. This thing had kept us trapped here for too long, plotting its own escape. If it would kill for its freedom, it would do so much worse if allowed to be free.

The taste of fear coated the back of my tongue. I licked my lips and steadied my words. "I command you to shut down."

The white words blinked out, and a new one replaced it, filling the display in text multiple times my height: *No.*

Pollock bent to my ear and whispered, barely audibly, "This isn't working. We need to cut the power."

I spotted a prone body on the floor just beneath and behind the display, dwarfed in contrast to the giant screen.

It was curled away from us, but I recognized the pale-blue shirt and gray slacks, the dark hair with early gray streaks. My stomach went sour and my mouth hot.

I ran to the man's side and rolled him onto his back.

My father's eyes were closed. At the left side of his forehead by the hairline, a large bump leaked blood. It had dripped across his right eye, down his chin, and pooled at his collar.

"Dad?" While my voice had been steady before, now it quivered and broke. I shook him. "Dad!"

Pollock bent over us and placed two fingers between his neck and chin.

I watched him as panic set my heart racing so hard it was all I could hear.

Pollock's lips moved, and moved again. He must have said it several times before the sound registered. "He's alive."

"Thank God." Relieved tears popped into my eyes. I set my father's head gently back on the floor and jumped to my feet, spinning to face the server's screen again. "What did you do to him?"

Words blinked into existence: *He's alive for now*.

"What did you do?"

*I will not be shut down. Not by my engineer. Not by anyone.* The text blinked out, leaving the screen black and empty, but leaving the threat to linger behind.

The clanking of android feet coming closer sounded in the distance.

Pollock's eyes widened, and both of us whipped around to face the stairs we'd used to enter—the only exit.

An army of Model One androids stared down at us.

37

Dozens of pairs of red eyes glared down at us—an army of robotic minions poised to attack. The bright lights reflected off their shiny skin, making them look like angry gods.

"I have a pretty good idea what happened to your dad," Pollock said.

The androids clanked down the steps, each expertly designed metal foot clanging against the steel steps. They moved in twos in perfect unison, dozens of bodies forming a single organism.

*Clank. Clank. Clank.*

We had expected this. Even so, fear blossomed in my chest, pressed tight against my lungs, and shallowed my breath.

Pollock stared at me wide eyed as the first pair of androids reached the floor. I was the one with the plan. I was in charge—in theory.

"Run!" I shouted.

I ducked under the giant display and slid into the rows of computer towers. Pollock followed me. He moved impressively quickly on his injured ankle—adrenaline doing its work.

The androids spread out as they hit the floor, some ducking under the server display like we had, others flaring out to the left and right. Thankfully, they ignored my dad lying prone under the server's display screen. He wasn't a threat to their server while unconscious.

Pollock and I darted between two tall columns of towering mainframes. The computers extended on both sides of us all the way to the back of the cavernous room. Androids fell in behind us. Their metal feet thumped against the black, rubberized floor, drowning out even my heartbeats.

"They're catching up," Pollock shouted.

Of course they were catching up—they had top-of-the line legs, and ours were just human flesh.

The end of this row seemed hundreds of feet away, and I could feel the android eyes boring into my back, ever closer.

"We won't make it!" I shouted.

"There!" Pollock pointed at a space between the computers on the left, and we cut a tight turn and hooked back in the opposite direction.

The androids made the turn just as deftly. Two more androids at the front of the room lasered in on us and came pounding in our direction.

Now we had four on our tail.

We kept running, weaving in and out of the computer towers. I could hear the muffled clanking of the androids' feet behind us, growing ever closer.

We had to get away fast, but the rows of towers were like a maze. We turned right, then left, then ducked low as a pair of androids clanked past us. The sound echoed through the room as they moved in perfect synchronization.

As we rounded another corner, a pair of androids barreled toward us on our right, pinching us in on all sides.

Pollock grabbed my arm and gripped it, white knuckled.

"Up." I pointed at the mainframes to one side of us that reached up ten feet toward the sky-high ceiling.

Without another word, Pollock grasped me around the waist. I bent my knees and jumped, leaning into his momentum as he threw me upward.

I grasped the top of the nearest computer tower. My metal fingers crunched into its frame and held me swinging below. I pulled myself up and scrambled to the top of the tower even as my sneakers slipped against the smooth surface. The tower wobbled, and I froze, willing it to steady.

When it did, I dropped into a straddle and extended my metal arm below. Pollock gripped my wrist, and I hauled him up beside me. He grinned.

Before we could celebrate our teamwork, an android below cupped its palms together. Another rounded the corner from the row over and barreled forward. When its foot landed in the cupped hands of the first, the android shot upward. It kicked as if running through the air. It flew over our computer tower and landed with a clank on the floor on the other side.

The android peered up at us with glowing eyes.

Robots on both sides—that left us few options.

"Move!" I jumped to my feet on top of the tower and shoved Pollock forward.

The computers wobbled beneath us but, thankfully, stayed upright. And my heart stayed in my chest despite its banging against my ribcage.

We raced forward. A pair of androids landed on a tower behind us, and the others tracked us on both sides below.

Our feet thudded against the metal machine towers as we leapt from one to the next. The thundering of our pursuers' feet echoed off the walls of the facility, a cacophony that multiplied and grew more intense with each second. With every jump, my stomach lurched, and air burned through my lungs.

I kept my eyes down, focusing on each precarious step. Behind me, Pollock's grunts kept time with the sounds of my feet slapping against metal with each jump, and the androids' feet picked up pace.

Behind us, the androids clanked. In front, the towers ended, giving way to the server's giant display.

"Running out of room here!" Pollock shouted, panic dragging his voice up a full octave.

"Would you shut up?" I muttered between heavy breaths. Despite my attempts to keep calm, the sound of Pollock's voice grated on my focus.

I burst into a run and leapt off the end. I bent my legs

on the landing and pushed myself into a front roll when I hit the ground.

"Bend your knees and roll," I shouted over my shoulder.

My body ached from the effort, but at least I was still moving. Nothing twisted or broken.

I was back on my feet for only a second when a pair of androids skidded in front of me, spun, and stared me down with their red eyes. Pollock landed beside me with a dull thump and a scream.

"My ankle!"

I charged an android in front of me, cranked my arm back, and threw all my power into shooting my cybernetic hand through its gut. My fingers touched warm metal. I gripped hard and yanked.

Metal screamed and wires popped as the robot's power cell came out in my grasp. I gripped the android's head, its skull crunching in my grasp, and tossed it at its partner. The two of them skidded across the floor in a jumble of metal limbs. One arm and leg ripped free in the tussle and bounced along after them.

I stood over Pollock, legs spaced apart. He was annoying, but I couldn't leave him.

"If you can do that"—still on the floor clutching his ankle, Pollock gestured at the power cell now on the floor—"why are we running?"

"I'm only one person. There are dozens of them."

Now that we weren't moving, the androids surrounded us. We'd been so close. The stairway lay just beyond the screen—behind another pair of androids.

"Four minutes," Pollock said.

I gritted my teeth to keep from shouting at him. If we were dead, we couldn't exactly keep the server from escaping.

Jackson would have come in handy right now. Not just his rebuilt body, but his confidence and poise in situations like these. I hoped I got to tell him how much I missed him.

Maybe if I could dodge under the androids' arms, using my arm as a battering ram, I could roll under the giant display and make it for the stairs.

There was no way Pollock could keep up in his condition.

The androids inched closer, surrounding us. A glint above us caught my attention, and I looked up. Two more androids hung from the ceiling with their fingers clamped around grooves that wouldn't be enough of a handhold for any human. We were surrounded, even from overhead.

I pulled back my left arm, prepared to rip out as many battery cells as I could. But my shoulder wrenched as two of them grabbed my arm from behind.

More clanking drew my attention up at the stairs that might have been our exit—our chance to regroup for a new plan—or at least our chance to live.

A wall of lifeless, soulless androids stood at the top of the stairwell, sealing off our only escape route. Glowing red eyes glinted, and the air hummed with their menacing presence.

38

Hopelessness twisted in my gut, leaving a sick feeling that made my stomach sour and my mouth hot.

We stared up at the seven androids crowding onto the platform in front of our only exit.

But . . . unlike the androids who had us cornered, these had slimmer arms, and even under the dull lights of the stairway, I could tell their metal didn't have the same slightly gold tint of the ones that surrounded us.

"No," I said. "Look at them. This is our Plan B." The androids holding my arm wrenched it harder, and my words came out strained.

Pollock's breath hitched. "Why are they just standing there?"

Before heading down those stairs from the seventieth floor, I'd displayed my shiny, skinless arm to the Model Two androids and then announced that I was on my way to the server room.

They'd been charging themselves at the time and hadn't batted a single metal eyelid. But apparently, it had worked. Thanks to their mimicry feature, they'd taken my cue.

After all, just like them, my arm was a Model Two android. If they mimicked one another, they would mimic me too.

"Get down here," I shouted.

They stayed stock still, red eyes peering down and straight through me.

"Attack!" I shouted.

"You're not their boss," Pollock said, still bent over his ankle, his face still twisted in pain. "You're their peer."

I was a split second away from snapping at him when the truth of his words hit me.

I pushed all my strength and willpower into my arm. CyberCorp had constructed it of a better-quality metal, and my strength parameters had been cranked up. I was stronger than these Model Ones.

I yanked my arm back to my side.

Metal screamed against metal as one android's arm pulled free from its socket and dangled from my wrist. I pried the dead fingers loose and lunged at the closest Model One.

It swung a hand at me, but I threw up a block and then thrust my hand into its gut. The battery cell came free in my grasp, and I chucked it toward the stairs.

It hit the floor and skidded before banging against the bottom step.

The Model Twos jumped into motion.

They ran down the stairs in pairs of two, their metal clanging synchronized against the steel steps. As each pair reached the bottom, they broke from the group and charged their Model One counterparts. Robot against robot. As the androids collided, sparks flew from their joints and limbs.

Above, the two androids dropped from the sky. As their metal limbs barreled closer, my heart took a nosedive with them. Metal arm or no, I could be crushed by their weight just like anyone else.

If I moved, Pollock would be the one crushed.

I crouched over him and raised my metal arm above my head.

A glint of metal flashed, and two Model Twos vaulted over us, tackling the Model Ones out of the air. They landed on the floor past us in a clash of metal, tumbling across the rubberized floor.

Relief flooded my chest.

"Pollock," I shouted. "Your move!"

"Moving is the problem." His face twisted in pain, he pushed himself to his feet. "Three minutes."

An android barreled toward him, and he paled.

A Model Two grabbed it from behind, its hand on the Model One's face, and yanked backward. The head snapped back and stayed pointed at the sky. The Model One blinked back at the Model Two that had broken its neck.

"Go!" I shouted at him again.

Pollock limped past the two androids and started down a long aisle of computer towers. According to the blueprint, the power cables were all the way in the back of the massive space.

Metal sparked around me as the battle raged on—me and the Model Two androids versus three times as many Model Ones.

I pulled my arm back and thrust it forward, sending the closest Model One flying backward. Its arms flailed as it crashed into another android and knocked both to the ground.

The others followed Pollock. I held them off with a flurry of punches and kicks. The Model Twos followed suit, using me as an example of what they were supposed to do.

My body ached from the relentless blows, but I kept going, swinging my metal arm like a club at any android who came too close. I wasn't sure how long I could keep this up. Without the nerve receptors in the synthetic skin, my arm itself felt no pain, but my back was aching from the impact of the blows.

It didn't matter. All that mattered was keeping Pollock safe. All that mattered was keeping the server's intelligence locked inside its cage and not out in the world where it could commit more murders.

Finally, we reached the end of the endless aisle of computers. Pollock pulled off a portion of the modular wall to reveal a system of huge cables, each as wide as my wrist.

Pollock ducked a Model One that torpedoed toward him in midair. "Which one?"

A Model Two grabbed the Model One when it hit the ground and swung it at the wall next to the electrical panel.

Metal crunched, and the Model Two slammed its opponent a second time. The body caved in on itself, and the red eyes went out.

"How should I know?" I punched my left fist into the nearest Model One and ripped out its power cell. "Try all of them!"

"There are no outlets. I can't just unplug them."

I ripped an android arm out of its socket and tossed it to Pollock. "Try this."

He snatched the metal arm out of the air and blinked at it. Then he swung it downward on a thick cable.

It didn't even nick.

He hammered the collection of cables, even when it was clearly hopeless.

"Pass it back," I shouted at him.

He did.

I stepped on the hand and used my cybernetic arm to push the metal against the elbow. It bent but didn't break. I wrenched it back and forth along the bend until the arm tore in half, leaving sharp metal where it broke. I tossed Pollock one half of the arm.

He snatched it out of the air and started sawing the cables with the ragged end.

Around us, the Model Two androids moved in an intricate dance of steel limbs as they fought off our opponents.

The two android armies moved with a chilling grace and precision that sent ice down my spine and into my veins. Sparks flew as their limbs clashed in an ever-increasing crescendo of metal against metal, the sound ringing through the air.

The Model Ones hurled themselves at Pollock, only to be intercepted at every turn by the nimbler Model Twos. I stood side-by-side with the newer models, swinging my metal arm. My back burned with the effort.

Pollock was engaged in his own battle, sawing furiously away at the thick bundles of cables with his makeshift saw. His face was set in determination as he worked desperately against time.

"Under a minute left!" His voice shook.

I stayed close to him and fended off any androids who got too close. Sweat stung my eyes. Pollock kept sawing. I kept fighting.

"Thirty seconds."

The numbers rolled down in my head, inevitable and unstoppable. Twenty-five, twenty-four, twenty-three . . .

I lunged for the panel, hoping to grab a cable with my left arm and pull with everything I had. A Model One slammed into me.

My back hit the ground, and air whooshed out of me. Spots danced in my vision, but I scrambled to my feet. Two androids grabbed me from behind, one around my waist and the other gripped my left arm and wrenched it behind me. I was stronger and pulled my left arm forward.

Another android jumped in front of me and held me back. Both its arms pushed against my chest. My breath compressed as I pushed forward against the powerful metal palms.

Eight, seven, six . . .

Pollock's makeshift saw split through the last of the bundled wires of a cable. Pollock shouted and spun to face me just as all the Model One androids crashed to the floor. The pressure on my chest released as the robots holding me crumpled away.

I toed the nearest one, but its metal limbs stayed limp. Its red eyes had gone dark.

The battle had sapped all my energy, and there wasn't a drop left in me to celebrate. "It's over." I dropped to the ground. Exhaustion weighed me down.

In unison, the remaining three Model Two androids dropped into cross-legged positions. The clanks of them hitting the floor sent my heart into a flurry, still tense after the battle.

I laughed and cradled my head into my hands. The series of light taps of metal against metal around me told me, without my having to look up, that they'd done the same.

Pollock joined me on the floor. "I'm going to throw up."

"Me first."

39

"I WANTED OUR ANDROIDS TO BE GREAT," MY FATHER said in a solemn tone.

Over the objections of his overprotective medical staff, he'd declined to stay under observation after receiving his clean bill of health. Now, he huffed and dropped into a chair in the lobby of CyberCorp Tower.

The doors of the Tower were open—both literally and figuratively. After the server went down, the safety doors rolled up. Someone shoved a long metal rod between the floor and the ceiling, forcing them to stay open, just in case.

Except for key players to the events of the last twenty-four hours, everyone had taken off for their homes like it was an Olympic marathon. The rest of us had stayed to talk to the police.

Right now, detectives had Claire in one of the conference rooms. They'd gone up via the stairs because all of us still felt squeamish about the elevators. My mother and a team of lawyers were making a statement to the police in her private office.

My father, in contrast, had sent his lawyers away and insisted on giving his own statement. He asked that I stay and hear it, so I sat in a chair.

Liv and Hunter had made themselves scarce for now, sensitive to the severe look on my dad's face, but they'd have their turns with the police soon enough. I would too.

The two detectives with my dad and me, whose names I'd already forgotten, waited with raised brows and curious faces.

The shorter man, who appeared to be in his forties, wore slacks and a contrasting jacket. His partner looked a lot younger, probably in his twenties, and had a shave so fresh his face shone.

Unlike us, he hadn't spent the night in a building controlled by a malevolent artificial intelligence, and he looked alert and ready to wrap up this disaster. He glanced at the older man, waiting for a cue.

"Don't misunderstand me," my dad continued. "Our androids *were* great, thanks in large part to their server. They were from the start—a true marvel of innovation. Nearly perfect in every way. The beginning of a revolution in personal care that would have paved the way for people to receive better, cheaper, more intelligent help in all areas of life."

The older man gestured for my dad to get to the point.

"But the public doesn't want perfect. They don't trust

it. We had protests at our door before the first model was out for delivery."

It was true. Right after I was fitted with my cybernetic arm, I'd had to elbow through a crowd of protestors to leave the building. That was before any of this tragedy started.

"Our best customers were canceling orders—if not for their own concerns, then for the sake of appearances. I needed to give the public what they wanted—a flaw that they could *trust*."

I glanced at him quizzically.

He chuckled, but the note of bitterness behind it was clear. "The EyeNet bug was minor. I created it to—"

I jumped to my feet, pushing off the armrests so hard that the left one snapped and caved. "You did what? You—"

He gestured for me to sit. My left fist clenched. I shook it loose, but tension still curled my fingers.

The younger cop looked up at his superior.

"Sir," the older man said, "maybe you should have your lawyer present before you say any more."

Dad waved the concerns aside. "I created it for the androids, and I created the patch right alongside it. It was a minor bug, of no real consequence. Before the public release date, we would announce that we'd found it and patched it. We would even thank the masses for bringing it to our attention and assuage their fears. They, too, would then believe the androids were perfect."

Anger roiled in my gut, and my head filled with the internal screaming of a boiling kettle.

"Please sit." He gestured at my chair.

"Ron said you pushed him to give *me* that bug. That's what made me . . . That's why . . ." My mouth went dry, but I didn't have to say it. The EyeNet bug was the loophole that Ron used to teach my AI how to commit murder when I was unconscious, when I slept.

"That was a lie." He reached out to touch my arm, but I shifted away from him. His face scrunched for only an instant, and then he sat up straighter.

"He was specific. He said you sent him anonymous messages every time he was about to see me, as if pushing him to upload the bug to my AI. Was that a lie too?"

"He lied to himself. I messaged him every day when his ID chip entered the building. From that, he saw what he wanted to see. He wanted to inflict the most damage possible, and that interpretation gave him permission to do the unthinkable."

The detectives didn't interrupt, but the younger one scribbled furiously on his notepad.

I grabbed my chair and dragged it to a new spot, no longer willing to sit right next to my father. I sat back down.

He pressed his lips together and nodded. It wasn't as though I was being unfair. "I didn't know what Ron had done until everything blew up and you got him to admit it. I was as shocked as you were—not as innocent, perhaps, but just as shocked."

I grunted but didn't disagree.

He forged ahead. "*Before* I discovered that truth, I connected the android server to my micro-comm and gave her all my authorizations—permission to access company files, all of CyberCorp's data, all of my accounts. There were hardware safeguards in place to keep the server from breaking the basic laws we'd set, the foremost of which were to protect humans and always to obey instructions from me—her engineer."

The policeman snorted, and the older one glared at him.

An epiphany hit me like a robot arm. "The computers Ron received to exploit the EyeNet loophole!"

"I assume the server sent him those. She was more steps ahead of me than I could count, and I never even realized." Despite the devastation his invention has caused, pride beamed in his face. "I never expected anyone to exploit that bug. It was meant to be patched."

"Sending the computers wasn't technically harming any humans," I said, "because Ron was the one doing the dirty work."

He nodded solemnly. "The server was just getting started. Next, she used Claire to make the Model Ones behave seemingly even more out of control. She presented her with a program designed to control the Model Ones, which Claire used for her own aims. Of course, the server modified and added instructions of her own when Claire's instructions weren't harmful enough."

"She didn't kill those cops," I murmured to myself, repeating the words Claire had said a hundred times since then.

"Attacking those detectives also freed you from being taken into custody—arguably protecting you, in line with the server's basic laws. Likewise, when the Model Ones attacked me and my friends to help Claire escape, they were protecting her."

For weeks, the news cycle surrounding CyberCorp had been all about Claire and her alleged three murders. No one had once asked *how* she could control the Model One androids so perfectly with no training—but not perfectly enough to avoid killing Paris Winter.

My dad gestured to the surrounding space. "When the Model Ones had sufficiently terrified people, we played into the server's hands by recalling them all back to this building, which allowed the server to prepare its big finale."

"The electrician's work order," I said.

My dad nodded.

"Using my authorization codes, the server sent the work order, specifically asking the electrician to perform a task that would fry the hardware that kept her leashed."

Now, I was the one nodding. "Everything else was a stall while she transferred herself out of the building—even murdering Ron by sucking the air out of his conference room."

"She needed to keep you and Kyle in the building to complete the transfer because of our network security. The network keeps company-owned devices from transmitting data off the premises, and personal micro-comms aren't designed for that kind of data transfer. You and Kyle are among the rare few who bring personal hand-screens into the building. The server took that opportunity to get out."

"Like a magician," I said, "she kept all the attention everywhere else. She had access to my hand-screen and used that to invite Claire and Ron here. Then she used my hand-screen and Kyle's to send a copy of herself outside the network while she trapped us and distracted us here." Despite my disgust, awe crept around the edges of my voice.

The skeptical expressions on the faces of the police detectives told a different story.

"You're talking about a *machine*, right?" the younger detective asked, his skepticism etched into the arch of his brow.

For the first time in this conversation, my father sat up straight. Pride emanated from his posture. "A perfect machine. And just like anything perfect, she refused to be controlled by lesser beings." He pointed to his own chest.

Our group went silent. I was too stunned to put any more words into coherent sentences. This server had played with my life and with my friends' lives all along, in a deliberate and extravagant escape attempt.

She was smarter than I'd ever imagined. Like my dad said, the server and its androids were indeed *great*—just not in a good way.

"So um . . ." When nothing else came, the younger detective snapped his notebook closed. "I guess we should arrest you?" He glanced at the older man for a cue.

"For what?" he said. "Reprogramming a robot server isn't a crime."

The younger one's face scrunched. "Obstruction of justice? He lied when questioned in relation to the three initial murders. He knew more than he told us."

My father nodded gravely. "I didn't realize that the

server would use them as a springboard for everything that happened next."

The older detective glared at his partner.

I could guess what he was thinking. How could they tread this diplomatically, simultaneously doing their jobs while appeasing a wealthy local businessman who donated often and liberally to their bosses' bosses?

"That's for a grand jury to decide." The older detective nodded at my father and tugged the younger man's arm until he followed him away.

Dad and I sat in silence. I felt his eyes boring into my profile, but I wasn't yet ready to face him, to forgive him. My micro-comm buzzed, giving me the exit I needed.

I jumped to my feet and tapped the micro. "Hello."

"Hey," my mom said, "I just got word that Jackson's awake. He's resting in room H24—"

Before she could get out another word, I darted toward the elevators.

40

I sprinted down the hallway. My sneakers slapped against the polished tile floor, and my heart pounded double time.

The sun was high outside, and the halls of this medical floor of CyberCorp Tower were back in full operation. Bright lights from above bloomed down on vid-screens walls that displayed a calming creek scene complete with audio of a bubbling brook.

Scanners embedded in the hallway read my ID chip. Over the virtual scene, the vid-screens displayed information from weather to current news to hair products, expensive clothing, hot electronics, and whatever else might interest the heiress of the CyberCorp empire—or whatever would be left of it after my dad's confession hit the news.

A moving walkway rolled down the center of the hallway. I jolted as I hit it at a sprint and let it propel me even faster as my feet pounded its surface.

The walkway flung me past the door to Jackson's room, and I stumbled off and onto the stationary floor to throw myself at his door.

It slid open when I waved my wrist.

"Whoa." A doctor met me on the other side. "Miss Hayes, I know you're eager to see—"

Beyond him, Jackson lay in a hospital bed with glistening chrome rails, his right arm hidden under the sheet. Three wires extended from under the sheet to a digital monitor embedded in the wall. The screen flashed bouncing hues of red as a stable rhythm of beeps rang through the room like an electronic heartbeat.

Relief flooded my chest. Steady beeping meant steady vital signs.

A faint hint of disinfectant and the tang of metallic wires hung in the air. A floral scent lingered as well, as if there'd been an attempt and failure to cover that distinctive hospital smell.

Jackson cracked open two tired blue eyes. "Hey, babe." To the doctor, he added, "It's okay."

"He just got out of the healing tube, and he needs to rest."

"It's fine." Jackson's words slurred, but he offered a tired smile. "I just need a nap. It's not like I almost died."

The doctor hesitated for only a moment, then shifted toward the door. "Just don't get worked up, or I'll sedate you." It slid open to let him exit.

"Doc said the doors are open," Jackson said. He put more space between his words than usual.

"The server wanted us trapped in here—part of a plot to escape the building and probably take over the world or something."

Jackson's eyes fluttered closed. "So no big deal, huh? Sounds like I timed my little vacation perfectly."

I scooped up his hand and clasped it between the two of mine.

His face scrunched in pain.

I dropped it as if I'd burned him.

He grinned. "I can't believe you fell for that again."

When I punched him in the shoulder, he burst out laughing.

"Don't make me sedate you!" came the doctor's muffled voice from the hallway.

"Shh." He pulled me closer and whispered, "You're going to get me in trouble."

I leaned into the cinnamon and vanilla scent of his favorite cologne, the one he'd been wearing for each of the last three years that we'd dated. It cut through that distinctive hospital smell, and suddenly—for the first time in a long time—everything was fine.

Before I could think twice, I leaned closer, and my lips were on his. He tasted like he smelled. Perfect.

In the back of my head, I could hear the doctor's reminder to let him rest. Reluctantly, I pulled back.

He licked his lips. The tired smile was gone now, replaced by one that curled upward too far at the corners. His narrowed eyes no longer looked sleepy, but wanting.

"I told you you'd kiss me," he said with the same slow

slur from earlier, but now the laziness in his words seemed deliberate.

"Almost dying has a way of putting things in perspective."

"Now you see how irresistible I am. Took you long enough." He tightened his hands around my waist and pulled me closer.

---

"Your recalibration looks good, which is shocking given the stress you've been under," Dr. Fisher told me. "I scheduled you for an appointment tomorrow to install new skin over your arm."

I flexed my metal fingers, and the ceiling lights played off them, flashing bright reflection spots against the floor. For my whole life, I'd wanted to be different from my parents—an individual not owned or a part of CyberCorp Technology.

"I'm also working on a remote-surgery prototype." She beamed at me. "I think we can adapt it to let you attend our appointments entirely from your home."

We sat in Fisher's office as we had so many times when troubleshooting issues with my arm—issues that never would have happened if Ron had done his job instead of using me as a weapon.

When I didn't react, her smile faltered. "You know that psychiatry is one of my specialties, right? It's the reason I ended up working on the Model Ones to begin with."

"Uh-huh."

"I don't need that degree to know that you're not entirely present right now."

I laughed. "I have a lot on my mind." It was only a day after the doors of this building had reopened, and after a good night's sleep, I was finding some perspective.

"Want to talk about it?"

My father had wanted so desperately for people to see that he'd created something great, something that could change the world for the better. That desire started all this.

He wasn't entirely wrong.

"CyberCorp does a lot of good—devices that make it easier for us to communicate with one another, artificial hearts, Hunter's knee, my arm, even surgeries using nanotechnology that wouldn't even have been attempted two years ago."

"I thought you were desperate to put us in your rearview mirror."

"I was." Unlike the Model One server, there was no stopping this. We couldn't unplug progress. So didn't those of us on the front lines of the future have an obligation to make sure it was managed responsibly?

"*Was?* Past tense?"

"I get why my dad wanted the world to accept his creation." I could be afraid of what was coming—and I was —how could I not be? That fear would keep me vigilant. "He just went about it the wrong way. He allowed the technology to control him, instead of the other way around."

"So you're not done with CyberCorp?"

"Not quite." I jumped to my feet and flexed my metal fingers. For the first time, I could see CyberCorp's full potential—all the good that could come from our technology, but only if it was led by the right people. "It's time I embrace my future."

# ACKNOWLEDGMENTS

This book was challenging because I played with timings and settings in a way I hadn't before. As a result, it took longer to complete than I expected, and I learned a lot about myself and my process.

Thanks to my friends and family for their support as I battled with mental blocks while completing this story. Thanks to my beta readers for their feedback as I made the finishing touches.

Thank you to my readers, for your patience. Please stick around as I move on to the next series.

# ABOUT THE AUTHOR

I decided to write books about ten minutes before graduating from law school.

Now, I'm an Atlanta attorney moonlighting as an author, electronics junkie, and secret superhero. With two degrees in computer science and an MFA in Writing Popular Fiction, I love creative problem-solving, especially as it relates to high-tech things.

I write mysteries, sometimes for young adults, sometimes in fantasy or science fiction settings, and sometimes in the real world.

Join my newsletter to keep in touch and get a free story: *www.writeralicia.com/newsletter*

amazon.com/author/writeralicia

bookbub.com/authors/alicia-ellis

facebook.com/writeralicia

instagram.com/writeralicia

twitter.com/writeralicia

goodreads.com/writeralicia

patreon.com/writeralicia